D0293438

After twenty years writing everything from local news to celebrity profiles to book, film, food and bar reviews, Melinda Houston scored her own dream job—TV critic— in 2006. These days she contributes to most Fairfax newspapers and to radio 3AW and 2UE. She lives in Melbourne. *Kat Jumps the Shark* is her first novel.

KAT JUMPS THE SHARK

MELINDA HOUSTON

TEXT PUBLISHING MELBOURNE AUSTRALIA

textpublishing.com.au

The Text Publishing Company
Swann House
22 William Street
Melbourne Victoria 3000
Australia

First published in 2014 by The Text Publishing Company

Cover and page design by Imogen Stubbs
Typeset by J&M Typesetting

Printed and bound in Australia by Griffin Press, an Accredited ISO AS/NZS 14001:2004 Environmental Management System printer

National Library of Australia Cataloguing-in-Publication entry:
Author: Houston, Melinda
Title: Kat jumps the shark / by Melinda Houston.
ISBN: 9781922147813 (paperback)
ISBN: 9781922148803 (ebook)
Subjects: Reality television programs—Fiction.
Dewey Number: A823.3

This book is printed on paper certified against the Forest Stewardship Council® Standards. Griffin Press holds FSC chain-of-custody certification SGS-COC-005088. FSC promotes environmentally responsible, socially beneficial and economically viable management of the world's forests.

This project has been assisted by the Commonwealth Government through the Australia Council, its arts funding and advisory body.

To jump the shark:

A term to describe the moment when something that was once great begins to decline in quality, generally through a bizarre or unlikely development. The phrase comes from the *Happy Days* episode where, in an attempt to boost ratings, the Fonz jumped a shark on waterskis.

1

'Excellent,' murmured Kat, crouching. A used syringe. Slipping her headset back on, she buzzed Ted, raising one hand to hail him and pointing to the ground with the other. The grizzled cameraman ambled over, dropping his cigarette end underfoot. (*Steve Bisley? Or perhaps Chris Haywood?* After all these years Kat still couldn't quite decide.)

'One of yours, mate?' he asked, peering at it.

'Not at this stage of the shoot,' said Kat cheerfully. 'Ask me again in six weeks.'

Ted gave a half nod accompanied by a half smile—the warmth of his response a testament to their long and fruitful acquaintance—and walked unhurriedly back to alert his crew.

Kat dialled down the volume on her headset, letting the buzz and chatter wash over her. Barring some disaster—and, of course, disaster was never far away—most of her work here was done. She'd even managed perfect weather: windless, rain-free, and not nearly as cold as it might have been. On screen it would look miserable, but out here in the street it was almost pleasant.

No need for set dressing, either. The footpaths were already littered with the perfect quantity of cigarette butts and chewing gum, takeaway wrappers, empty bottles, and yellowing pages from discarded freesheets. Even a used syringe.

But no vomit. No used condoms. Perfect.

And the street itself... People didn't realise how hard it was to find a street like this. Especially in the CBD. Kat tilted her head back and took in the view: dirty high-rise windows uncleaned in thirty years, sills crusted with bird shit; crumbling low-rise Victorians sandwiched between the worst of 1970s low-budget Brutalist and 1990s post-recession utilitarian, all smudged against a flat sky. The occasional broken window was patched with cardboard. A tattered flag flew from one building; outside another a shattered neon sign blinked wanly.

And as your eyes—or the camera—panned across and down you met the shopfronts, every third with a *For Lease* sign, others spruiking karaoke, dodgy fast food (and worse coffee), sweatshop fashion, and the kinds of doomed small businesses that made you feel a little bit tired just contemplating them. Perfect, thought Kat with satisfaction. Perfect.

The problem with Melbourne, she mused, digging her hands a little deeper into her coat pockets, was it was just too damned prosperous. And far too pleased with itself. Some days it seemed there was no corner of the CBD that wasn't being remade, tarted up or pulled down and completely reinvented. Ornate Victorians were sand-blasted and tuck-pointed. Architecturally adventurous apartment buildings with office-retail lower floors and ubiquitous licensed cafés were erupting from old parking lots. Even the laneways had taken on a festive air thanks to street artists, hospitality mavens, and edgy design firms.

Finding something truly grubby that wasn't in the immediate vicinity of a building site, hot new bar, or residence of a local councillor had been a Herculean quest. But she'd done it. And here they were. Under budget. And on time!

At least, they *had* been on time.

Across the street Kat noticed their Assistant Director, Harry, had disappeared and First Unit were slouching disconsolately, texting their mates, wondering whether to brave another coffee from the Gourmet Takeaway. She saw GC, one of the producers, striding towards her under full sail, and braced herself.

'Darling.'

'Morning boss,' Kat said.

'Remind me how long we have this morning?'

'Until 11.30. Problem?'

'Not yet.' GC glanced around at the decaying shop-fronts. 'We're just waiting on some extras. For some reason only half of them have turned up. It shouldn't take long once we get going, but we can't have the contestants outnumbering our "crowd" two to one.'

Kat gazed towards the end of the block where the crowd-control guys were having difficulty living up to their name. 'If all you need are people walking up and down the street...'

GC met Kat's eyes with a doubtful expression. 'Real people?'

'It *is* supposed to be reality television.'

'Factual,' GC corrected automatically. Then: '*Real* real people?'

'I know. But we're running out of time.'

GC sighed, ran a hand through her hair, then reflexively ruffled it back from 'messy' to 'tousled'. Rebecca Gibney, thought Kat, in her 1980s shag-perm period. 'Okay. Let's offer them a free lunch and their face on the telly. See what happens.'

'Worth asking,' said Kat. 'Worth getting Harry to ask.'

The women exchanged looks. GC was charming, but Harry was in another class. 'I'll get Harry,' GC said, and began striding back the way she had come, talking into her radio.

Between them, Kat was confident Harry and GC would have a dozen citizens happily participating in a scene for public broadcast—without payment and without having any idea what the finished product would be—within fifteen minutes.

It must be nice, she thought, to have such social skills. It must make life much easier. Part of the reason you end up the boss, Kat supposed. Although God knows their other producer, BC, didn't have them.

Which was why, of course, he was BC. Barry Cohen, the Bad Cop. To Genevieve Clarke's Good Cop. But he did have energy. Force of personality. Kat suspected that combination was the secret to Cohen Clarke's success.

And me? Kat thought, strolling up the street to catch Harry at his persuasive best. Lacking either well-developed social skills or force of personality, I have what? A second-tier job. She smiled to herself again.

4

Because we can't all be chiefs. The world needed Indians too. The world needed cogs, specialist cogs, who could find you Paris, New York, New Jersey, London, Brisbane, Rome, all in the one town. Who could find you the disreputable corners of the nicest city in the world. Who knew about a place outside Geelong that looked just like Utah, and a paddock in the Cranbourne vicinity full of giant cacti, should you happen to need a slice of Mexico. Besides, Kat had never wanted to be the boss. It seemed like a quite unnecessary—and unrewarding—expenditure of energy.

Harry was trotting up the other footpath, stopping to have a word with the crew on the way. They disposed of coffee cups and butted cigarettes in his wake while the female techies buoyed him along on a wave of admiring glances.

Everybody loved Harry. Even Kat loved Harry, and she was naturally suspicious of anyone in possession of that much easy charm. It was an interesting quality, she thought. Charm. Charisma. Different from being good-looking, or confident, or courteous.

In her line of business she had met plenty of people—often actors—who were both supernaturally good-looking and supremely confident. And hadn't warmed to them at all. Strangely—or perhaps not so strangely—the really attractive people, the charming ones, tended to be behind, not in front of, the camera.

Now one of them—her mate, her protégé—took a megaphone from a crowd-control guy, ran a hand over his close-cropped head (a young Marcus Graham, Kat had decided. The *Good Guys, Bad Guys* era) and called the mob to order.

Who fancied being on telly? Who wanted to help get this shoot over and get the street open again? All you had to do was walk down the street, then back again. Maybe two or three times. Just walk. Pretend to talk on your mobile, if you like. Talk to each other. Walk to the end of the block, come back, do it again. Maybe three or four times. Keep close together, don't look at the cameras, don't look at our people—they'll be in among you. Just look like you're in a hurry to get somewhere. To the end of the street then back. Maybe four or five times.

Lowering the megaphone, keeping up an easy banter with the crowd, Harry recruited half-a-dozen teenage girls first. Then a handful of older women. Then, in answer to a specific appeal, a small cohort of businessmen. Some tourists, already capturing the action on their phones, were more than willing. A couple of young blokes, who looked like they might take advantage of a press of people to conduct a little business of their own, were finally ringed in. They had twenty, maybe thirty people now. Combined with the extras and shot nice and tight, they had a bustling throng. Kat glanced at her watch and felt her first little spasm of stress.

As Harry and GC corralled the extras, crowd control dropped their signs and released the pressure on the rest of the mob waiting to use the street. Once they'd sluiced through, they repositioned themselves to block entry and suddenly things came alive.

Emerging from a doorway, the director looked less than impressed when he realised a third of his extras were mug punters. He had a word with the stars—a dozen equally inexperienced real people who had happened to sign up for the opportunity of a lifetime—got them into position, then hunched in front of the monitor. In her headset Kat could hear him instructing the camera crew as Harry, arms wide, herded his milling crowd into something resembling a tight-packed one. At a sign from the director he raised the megaphone again, shouted 'Go!', and stood back.

Surrounded by the 'crowd' the contestants, in an elongated S-shape, began walking down the street. The paid extras kept in tight around them, but half the punters were either striding ahead or dawdling in an embarrassed fashion at the back. One of the teenage girls made some kind of gangsta gesture at the camera, while a puddle of businessmen and middle-aged women hovered on the corner, still not sure what they were supposed to do.

The director raised his hand tiredly. 'Cut!' yelled Harry, and GC sailed in to help regroup the masses. Under their combined offensive everyone embarked on a second take, and this time the whole mob moved as one. But just as they reached the halfway point, a narrow gentleman in an inexpensive suit pushed through the cordon and walked straight through shot towards Kat.

'It's after 11.30,' he said, as the three senior members of the crew yelled in unison, 'Cut!'

'I know, I know. I'm so sorry,' Kat said, trying desperately to channel GC. 'We've had a few hitches, but we're almost done. Literally minutes away from finishing up.'

'We've already lost significant parking revenue.' Though his tone was mild, Kat knew this bloke could bring the whole shoot to a grinding halt. Finding great locations was hard, but dealing with middle-level Council officers was undoubtedly the most diabolical part of her job—and dealing with those responsible for parking inspectors the worst of the lot.

She laid a hand lightly on his upper arm and lowered her voice, forcing him to lean down to hear her. As she assured him of her sympathy, their shared exasperation, and the fact that the delays were absolutely unavoidable, she began walking, out of shot and back towards the cordon.

'QUIET!' the director yelled.

'Roll cameras!' called Harry.

'We really are trying to wrap this up as quickly as possible,' Kat murmured, gazing up earnestly.

Someone's phone rang. Loudly. *La Cucaracha*.

'CUT!'

Kat winced.

'I don't know why you had to choose this street in the first place,' the revenue manager said crossly. 'It's not the image we want to project of the city.'

Kat continued to guide him away from the action, saying soothingly, 'Storytelling is all about contrasts, about conflict and resolution.' She was almost whispering now. He leaned in closer. 'We want to contrast the hard face of the city with the kindness of its citizens. This is a positive story about the city. And I know you'll be happy when you see the final product.'

He glanced at his watch without disengaging her hand from his arm. 'It's almost 12pm.'

'I know. All I can do is apologise. I promise it won't happen again. And,' she added rashly, 'we're more than happy to compensate you for the loss of parking revenue.'

Well, she had saved on set dressing.

'Ten more minutes?'

'Ten minutes. And just send us an invoice. You know where we are.'

'You know the City of Melbourne wants to facilitate the work of film and television crews,' he said. 'We're a very film-friendly city. But there are rules. And we did have an agreement.'

'We did, I know. And we take full responsibility for this.' She gave him one more beseeching look. 'I hope this won't affect our working relationship going forward.'

'Of course not,' he said, flushing. 'These things happen.'

Suddenly her headset buzzed urgently.

'Kat!' Harry hissed. 'We need you!'

She removed her hand from her companion's arm. 'I'm sorry, I have to go. Send us an invoice. And again— so sorry!'

Having safely walked her visitor beyond the cordon, Kat abandoned him to dash back down the street. Contestants, extras and increasingly bored punters were gathered at one end of the street under the stewardship of GC. In the middle of the road a sallow man exuding a powerful scent of stale fat was banging two saucepans together. Catching sight of Kat he dropped his arms and said accusingly, 'You said 11.30!'

'I know, I know, we're almost done,' Kat said breathlessly, trotting up to him. 'I'm so sorry.'

'You're sending me broke! Know how many coffees your lot have bought this morning? Five. Five fucken coffees. And the street's still closed!'

'I know, I know,' repeated Kat. 'I really am terribly sorry.' Throwing Harry a desperate *Hurry up*! look over her shoulder, she shepherded Mr Gourmet Takeaway back into his premises and closed the door firmly behind her. 'This almost never happens. It's just been one of those days.'

'Five fucken coffees!'

Holding one hand palm out in an effort to hush him, with the other Kat reached into her bag, took out her purse, opened it, took out two fifty-dollar notes, and thrust them towards him.

His face softened. 'Ah love. Your own money? You don't have to do that.'

'We really have to wrap this up. We have to get these shots today. I'm sorry for the inconvenience but...we just *have* to get this finished.'

He hesitated, then took the money. 'I suppose you'll get it back from the company,' he said comfortably.

'Expenses!' Kat said brightly, thinking: *In my dreams.* Then: 'Let's watch this last little bit. I'm sure this'll be the last take.'

'Like a coffee?'

'Love one!'

With the weak, bitter beverage in her hand she stood to the side of the window, watching the contestants and a now rather threadbare crowd make their way towards her.

Suddenly a dark blur dropped through her line of vision, followed by a thump clearly audible through the glass. She saw first the faces of the extras. Then Peru, the prettiest of the contestants, fixed in horror and disbelief. There was a high, thin, sustained scream. Finally Kat shifted her gaze to the street, where a body lay, all angles, in an extravagant splatter of blood.

'Oh dear,' said Kat. Then started, helplessly, laughing.

2

'Long day?'

Kat walked into Miles' arms, and held on tight. After a moment's surprise he adjusted his perfunctory hug accordingly, gave her a squeeze, then started rubbing her back.

'Had a few drinks?'

She nodded.

'That bad?'

More nodding.

'Drive home?'

She shook her head, released her grip, stepped away and ran a hand through her hair. 'No, left it at Unit.' Realising just how wobbly she was, Kat lowered herself onto one of the kitchen chairs and propped her head in her hand.

'Told you you should never have said yes to a reality show,' said Miles, sitting down opposite her.

She met his eyes. 'Someone *killed* themselves today.'

'Jesus.'

There was a silence, a long one. It was conversation-killer sort of news. Finally Kat said, 'Could you make me a coffee?'

Miles stood, went to the sink, began to rinse the coffee things. Kat laid her head on her arms. After a moment he asked: 'Who killed themselves?'

Kat inhaled deeply, exhaled. 'I don't know. Just some guy. We were almost finished the morning's shoot, about to wrap and suddenly—*blat!* This guy drops out of the sky into the middle of the street.'

'No one you knew?'

'No. Just some guy. I think he might have worked in one of the buildings. He looked kind of business-y. Not that I really looked.' She took another deep breath. 'But no. Just a guy suddenly deciding to top himself. Around lunchtime on a Tuesday. In the middle of a shoot.' Kat rubbed her face, shook her head, felt herself begin to smile in spite of herself. 'You should have seen GC.'

Miles turned, wearing his concerned face, and Kat quickly stopped smiling. 'Poor Gen,' he said, pouring coffee.

'And poor Harry,' she said, taking the cup in both hands. 'The contestants were hysterical. We had almost thirty extras, all flipping out. Cops and paramedics all over the place. Harry and GC had to organise trauma counselling. For *everyone*. The network is going to go spare over the cost. And—God—*The Mail* was there for a set visit.'

'Ruby?'

'No, Darren. So at least he didn't have a fit. But I'm not looking forward to the story tomorrow.'

'Assuming they run it. You know how the papers are

with suicides. There was nothing on TV tonight.'

'No, thank Christ. It was all cleared away pretty quickly. But *The Mail*? And a new reality show? I don't think they're going to be able to resist. BC is going to go absolutely mental.'

Miles clasped her hand. 'You okay?'

She smiled. 'I'm okay. Tired. Pissed! Me and Harry and some of the crew—the ones who didn't need counselling—had a bit of a debrief.'

She decided against telling Miles how riotous that debrief had been. Somehow it had all seemed much funnier over a number of pots drunk in rapid succession. But that was okay, wasn't it? Laughing in the face of death? And it wasn't like it was someone they knew. Or did that make it even more heartless? Making terrible jokes about some stranger who'd decided life wasn't worth living. Maybe that should have made it more tragic, not less.

What *was* the proper way to feel about these things? A kind of mid-level gravity with a side serve of moderate sadness? A profound distress and anger at the heartlessness of the modern world? Even an aching sorrow at one man's loneliness and desperation? But not, perhaps, a profound sense of the absurdity of it, or plain old irritation at the disruption to their schedule.

'Why do you think he did it?' she asked, turning her hand to grasp Miles' fingers.

'God, I don't know. Maybe he had cancer.'

'Cancer?'

'I don't know, Kat. People do these things. There's not always an explanation.'

'Isn't there?' She frowned. 'There must have been a reason. You don't kill yourself for no reason.'

13

'Well, no. I suppose not. I'm just saying...'

'Kat?'

They both turned to see Bonnie silhouetted in the doorway, hair electric, her drooping pyjama bottoms exposing a half-moon of belly.

'Hello darling,' said Kat, reaching out one arm.

Bonnie shuffled forward. 'You didn't come in and see me,' she said.

'Sorry petal. I worked late, then just wanted to have a cup of coffee and a chat with your dad first.'

The little girl hauled herself onto Kat's lap, dislodging her pants even further, then wrapped her arms around Kat's neck. She grimaced.

'You smell.'

Kat gave a spurt of laughter, causing an even more pronounced look of disgust before Bonnie slid back to the floor.

'Yucky.'

Kat felt that hysterical amusement rising again, but managed to say calmly, 'Why don't I clean my teeth, then come in and give you a kiss?'

'And wash your face.'

'Clean my teeth, wash my face, then come in and give you a kiss.'

Bonnie nodded, rubbed the side of her face resignedly, and shuffled back down the hallway. Kat met Miles' eyes, unable to read his expression. She was never quite sure whether he was pleased or miffed that she and Bonnie had taken to each other so readily, or the extent to which he approved of her style of child wrangling. Now he simply said, 'It's time we were all in bed,' and began to clear the table.

Kat watched his back for a moment, feeling a rare, visceral surge of affection: for the handsome cut of his shoulders and the tidy shape of his arse; for his laborious, strangely courtly domesticity; even his wary relationship with emotion. She always imagined him approaching feelings, especially complex ones, as you might an echidna: intrigued, but cautious, and wearing thick gloves. Physically, she thought, a 1990s John Waters. Post-*Playschool*, pre-*All Saints*. Personality? She was still pondering that, these days with growing fatigue.

In the bathroom she glanced at herself in the mirror and shuddered. It had been a big day and she was past the age when dishabille was enchanting. She let her eyes rest for a moment on the smooth, off-white marble of the vanity, the gleam of the elegant taps, the high-end grooming products arranged neatly on either side of the basin. The floor was chill but refreshing under her stock-inged feet and the cold air was a faint, bracing mix of expensive soap, perfume, aftershave. Unlike her breath, which—according to the experts—reeked.

As she brushed her teeth, gargled, washed her face, slapped on moisturiser, combed her hair, she could hear Miles stack the dishwasher. In the room next door Bonnie would be curled in a tight ball under her Angelina Balle-rina doona, perhaps already asleep. Kat took a long drink of water then met her own eyes in the mirror again. Much better.

Some poor sod had decided today that life wasn't worth living, but for her, here, now? Things could be worse. She switched off the light and crossed to Bonnie's room, where the little girl was blinking in a desperate effort to stay awake. Propping gently on the edge of the bed

Kat bent and kissed her forehead, letting her lips linger. 'Better?' she murmured.

Bonnie turned and pressed her nose into Kat's cheek, inhaling theatrically. 'Much better.'

Kat stroked her hair for a moment. 'Sweet dreams, darling. See you in the morning.'

'See you in the morning,' sighed Bonnie, and let her eyes fall closed.

Back across the hall Kat undressed quickly and slipped into bed. Miles brushed his teeth, then wandered into the bedroom—now lit only by the streetlight filtering through the blinds—unbuttoning his shirt with unself-conscious concentration. Kat watched him disrobe in his usual orderly manner. There was a lot to be said, she thought, for routine.

When he stretched out beside her she cupped his cheek in her palm, kissed him, ran her hand lightly down his neck, across his chest, down over the soft line of hair that marked his flat belly. He placed his hand on hers before it could go any further and squeezed it gently, kissing the top of her head. 'We've both had a big day.'

Kat considered persevering with her half-hearted seduction. A joyful bedroom workout was just what she needed. On the other hand, a more forceful rejection was just what she *didn't* need. And she knew which outcome was more likely. So she simply returned the pressure of his fingers then moved her hand onto her own belly.

She lay there for a while, the other hand under the back of her head, watching the play of light on the wall of books and DVDs opposite the bed. Books were nice, she thought. Books. Routine. Four-year-old girls. These were all nice things. Clean bathrooms with handsome fittings and soft towels and taps that didn't drip. She wriggled her toes. Not having to worry about paying the bills. Security. Tranquillity. Spending all day driving around, with no one looking over your shoulder. Autonomy was nice. There were plenty of reasons to be cheerful.

She moved her hand on Miles' stomach again. 'Are you asleep?'

'Almost.'

'Would you do it?'

'Do what?'

'Kill yourself?'

'For God's sake.' She felt him tense under her hand, then he rolled on to his side, his back to her. 'Of course not,' he murmured in a gentler tone. 'Go to sleep.'

3

Harry gave Kat's shoulders a squeeze. 'Ready for this?'

'You bet.'

They took their seats at what constituted the board-room table, a series of old school desks jammed together running the length of the room. Cohen Clarke might have been one of the most successful production companies in the country and the Five Network continuing to post handsome profits, but on the coalface things remained rudimentary. Bottles of water and juice and plates of greying sandwiches were dotted along the table, and at one end a large-screen TV hummed in anticipation. GC smiled and lifted her fingers in greeting. Kat smiled and raised her hand in return. Most of the key people were there: the director, the editor, one of the senior guys from Five, the network that would broadcast the show. Digby, the series creator; Ted, the director of photography; and Bev Corser, the production designer.

Like Ted, Bev wasn't exactly a mate, but she and Kat had worked together often in the past and Kat liked her. She had a wonderful eye, an incredible work ethic, and a wicked sense of humour (a sort of Betty White, thirty years younger). Between the two of them they created the look of a show: Kat found the room, Bev put stuff in the room. Collaborating with her was always fun.

Today Bev grinned and raised her eyebrows at Kat, mouthed: *Here we go!*

Then BC burst in with his usual aggression and strode to the head of the table. Kat had never seen him walk like a normal person; he always seemed on the verge of either breaking into a sprint or tackling someone to the ground.

'Sorry people. We all set?' Taking a breath, he launched into his spiel. 'As you know, this is the first look at the first scene of the most adventurous factual series Cohen Clarke has ever made—and we've been pioneers in the field. I'd like to thank the Five Network for taking the leap and commissioning it, I know you're as excited as we are.' He nodded to the gent from Five, and took another breath. 'Of course, last week's shoot wasn't without its dramas. These things happen. I'd like to thank everyone who was there on the day for keeping their cool, and keeping a lid on it. Especially our First AD—' Harry gave a smart wave '—for keeping, as I understand it, thirty or forty screaming women under control. I believe he's had some experience with such things.' Now Harry coloured. 'Opening titles are pretty rough,' BC went on, 'and this is still a rough cut. But it'll give us all an idea of how we're looking so far, and what needs to happen next.'

He stalked to the other end of the table, opposite the screen, and signalled for the lights to go down.

The screen flickered, then faded into a sweeping shot of blue sky that panned down to a residential street in South Melbourne, a broad avenue of elm trees (caught, thank Christ, at the perfect moment before scenic autumn became blasted winter), low sun glinting off the spotless windows of impeccably renovated Victorian homes, the vista drawing the eye all the way to Beaconsfield Parade and, beyond it, the glittering bay.

'Good street,' whispered Harry. Kat nodded happily and hugged herself a little.

Melbourne, intoned the voice-over. *One of the world's most liveable cities.* A montage of city and suburban scenes followed: shops, bars and restaurants, AusKick, street markets, crowds in the foyer of the Arts Centre giving way to grainy CCTV footage of brawls in King Street, of dirty bedding piled under the Tennis Centre overpass, Russell Street drug dealers, blank-eyed skinny kids hunched on the benches outside St Paul's. *But for a growing number of ordinary people, living in Melbourne has become an hourly struggle for survival.* Quick shot of a body bag being zipped closed.

Kat shifted uncomfortably. So it was true. They were using it. The crew—they couldn't help themselves—had just kept filming. At least two of them were old news hands. When something like that happened the last thing you did was turn your camera off. Which is how Ted had returned to Unit with, apparently, appallingly graphic footage of the paramedics levering their Suicide Guy off the street and into the black plastic wrapping.

Once that had happened—well, BC was always going to consider it too good to waste. And in a way it was poetic: a series about how unliveable Melbourne could

20

be and a man who had found it all, literally, unliveable. It's not like you could see his face. Or even blood. Just gloved hands zipping the black bag closed. It was, Kat had to admit, incredibly powerful. Unethical, maybe. In bad taste, certainly. But powerful.

Momentarily distracted, Kat missed the next few seconds and refocused on the screen just in time to see the mock-up title card: *Survivor: CBD.* She raised her eyebrows at Harry; he replied in kind. *Survivor?* Really?

The voice-over stopped and there was silence. 'We'll put some sound in here,' BC said, his voice booming around the room. 'Just a little bit of wind noise, probably. Maybe some rustling paper or a rattling bottle.' Again, a long pan down, this time from last Tuesday's bleak grey sky, past those grubby windows and frowsy shopfronts to the empty street, the litter, the used syringe. Then feet walking down the street: just one pair to start with, then a growing crowd, then a slow pan up to bodies and faces—there was that twit who kept gesturing to the camera—until the zoom into close-up. The contestants.

Twelve ordinary people, of all ages, from all parts of the country and from all walks of life, have left their comfortable homes, their jobs, their families. They're about to experience how the other half lives, without food, shelter or any kind of security. They'll spend the next six weeks on Melbourne's mean streets, where they'll discover if they have what it takes to be... an Urban Survivor.

The screen went blank. GC started clapping enthusiastically, and the rest of the team joined in, some, like Kat, chiefly from relief. They wouldn't have to reshoot after all. As the applause faded BC said, 'Comments? Suggestions?'

21

Digby, the series creator, cleared his throat and said mildly, '*Survivor*?'

'It's a working title. As was your original.' He nodded to GC. 'We decided *Down and Out in Yada Yada* was too long...'

'It was a reference to Orwell...'

'We all know that, mate. But unless you want to call it *Animal Fucking Farm* we can probably do without the Orwell references, *Big Brother* already being taken. As I said, this is just a working title, but it's more in line with what we need. Something punchy. Something the audience is going to respond to. Something to give whatever we do next a bit more focus.'

Losing a little colour, Digby persevered. 'I thought we were pretty much decided what we do next?'

'We are. But you know the process, Dig. Things are tweaked as we go. Nothing's set in stone.'

Kat doodled determinedly on the notepad in front of her. Luckily, this was not her department. Her presence here was really a courtesy, to see how those first handful of locations scrubbed up. She, Bev and GC had already organised the nuts and bolts of the next few weeks' production, including the tortuous negotiations with Council and assorted suspicious shop owners, and she had a pretty good idea of how and where the final stages of the series would play out. Now came the really fun bit. The actual shoot. And while Miles—and a large part of the general population—might despise that broad category of television sneeringly described as 'reality', Kat had a bit of a soft spot for it.

This was her fourth reality project, and they'd all been fun. Despite their heavily manufactured and sometimes scripted nature, they all at some point delivered exactly what they promised: an unexpected and often revealing slice of *reality*. And this one was full of promise.

Kat liked these new contestants. They might be a little too excited at the idea of getting their heads on the box, and a little too well prepared for it, but that just came with the territory these days. She knew that, in the end, nothing could prepare them. At some point they would be obliged to stop performing and just live it. And the decision they'd all made—to test themselves, with diminishing resources, against a hostile city and citizenry—would eventually lay each of them bare.

So, she thought, as the conversation washed around her, bring it on. Let's stop the posturing and the repositioning and tweaking and get started. Above all, let's get out of this blessed meeting. Through the high, dirty windows she was aware of the sun shining. It wouldn't be exactly warm out there but a sparkling afternoon was wasting away. A rare chance for some vitamin D.

The car would be toasty. She could be cruising around the city, aimlessly scouting. Or maybe snatching Bonnie out of childcare, heading back into Fitzroy for a latte and a babyccino. The one problem with her grungy locations for this series was the execrable stuff served up in the nearby cafés. She hadn't had a decent coffee since the weekend.

'Happy, Kat?'

GC's voice brought her head up. She laid down her pen, smiled. 'Very happy.'

'All right. I think we're done!' GC pushed her chair out from the table.

'Craving caffeine?' murmured Harry.

'You read my mind.'

23

'Not exactly,' he said, nodding to her notepad where she'd sketched a foaming cup with steam rising from it.

'Oh. Yes. Well… Thank God for Wilson. My shout?'

'Love to, but I need to talk to these guys.' Harry nodded to the director, still making some crucial point to BC while Digby stood by disconsolately, studying the toes of his sneakers.

'No problem. See you tomorrow.' Gathering up her various bags and folders—she seemed incapable of going anywhere these days without half her body weight in luggage—she followed the stragglers from the office.

The sun was slanting low through the stairwell now— Kat glanced at her watch, four o'clock—and she stood for a moment and felt the rays on her face, before clattering down the rest of the stairs, out the front door, and into the café.

The joint still looked the same: white and bare, with cheap tables and chairs placed sparsely around the tiled floor and a meagre selection of chocolate bars dotted forlornly on the Laminex counter. The same pale winter sun was glinting on the shaved head of the bloke behind the counter and the fair stubble—possibly grey—on his chin. In a shapeless hoodie and a pair of unfashionably faded jeans, Wilson looked more like a brickie than a barrista.

When word had filtered upstairs—from GC? From one of the crew? Kat couldn't remember—that the café downstairs had reopened and was serving world-beating coffee, they'd all instantly formed their own idea of who was behind this revolution. These ideas generally fell into two camps. Some imagined a beanied hipster serving single-source Fair Trade; others were picturing some smooth young Italian behind a high-art Gaggia.

None of them had expected Wilson: a calm, good-humoured bloke in his late thirties, maybe early forties, who had absolutely no interest in creating a fashionable establishment but every interest in the quality of his craft. And while Wilson's café was strictly about the *caffè*, not the *cibo*—and there was certainly no menu—he'd make you an egg-and-bacon sandwich (crisp and buttery) and even, on a good day, a batch of muffins, the processing of which seemed to take place entirely in a blender but which emerged from the tiny benchtop cooker exquisitely puffed and golden.

At first it had seemed hilariously incongruous to watch this big bloke (Wilson was easily six-two, with the burly physique of a retired bouncer) carefully mixing eggs, flour, fruit, then pouring the mix into the muffin trays with the same placid concentration. It quickly, though, became a sight of great comfort, and no one minded the twenty-minute wait for them to come out of the oven, especially as he always seemed able to produce any number of excellent coffees and keep up a bit of laconic chat at the same time.

Today Wilson looked up and smiled when she came through the door. 'G'day Kat.'

'Hi. How are you?'

'Not too bad,' he said. 'Takeaway?'

She nodded. 'Please.'

Wilson had also rapidly managed to memorise the names and tastes in beverage of the fifty or so people who were in and out of the production office on a regular basis. Kat suspected it was a point of pride.

Now, while Wilson deftly constructed her coffee, she

flicked through a tattered copy of *The Mail*, hoping and dreading in equal parts further mention of Five's controversial new reality series. As she predicted, the chief media reporter had gone to town on the suicide last week—making the inclusion of the body bag in the opening credits even more risky—but having stirred up a vigorous online reaction (divided pretty evenly between readers excoriating him for making copy out of suicide, and excoriating Five for making reality television at all), he seemed content to let them be for the moment.

Except by the rather tenuous link of reality television being enough to make someone want to kill themselves, there was no way they could be held accountable for someone dropping off a rooftop into the middle of their shoot. And as Five had issued an appropriately sombre press release deploring the situation and extending heartfelt sympathy to the loved ones (assuming there were any), it seemed like the matter might be allowed to rest. Until, of course, the show went to air.

'One strong latte, no sugar.'

Absently, Kat fumbled some change from her purse, handed it over, picked up the cardboard cup, baulked.

'Problem?'

'A heart?' She looked in distaste at the artfully carved crema on her coffee.

'Isn't that the sort of things you ladies like?'

She looked at him, not sure if he was taking the piss, took a sip. It was bloody good coffee. 'Not this lady,' she said.

4

'I can't believe you're still driving this thing,' said Betsy.

'Of course I'm still driving it.'

'It can't be practical.'

'It's compact,' Kat said, glancing over at her friend and grinning.

Betsy's knees were pressed up in an uncomfortable V, her arms tucked in tight to her sides. Behind her, her son Leo was strapped into the booster seat, idly opening and closing the doors of a model vintage Alfa Romeo. It was his preferred toy when he knew Kat was coming to visit. He never ceased to wonder at the magic of holding in his hands the very car in which they were driving and was fond of explaining in detail, to anyone who'd listen, where the two matched and where they differed.

True, the vehicle was undoubtedly designed for a diminutive Italian stallion and his even more petite companion, not a woman built on Betsy's Amazonian scale. But Kat, generally uninterested in cars, had developed a deep affection for the idiosyncratic sedan.

It had been her mother's, bought new in the month of Kat's birth, in 1970. That would always make it special. And she still had faint memories of it being brought out occasionally for the family to simply 'go for a drive', for no other purpose than the pleasure of tooling around in it, her in the back (no child seats then), her father in the front, her mother behind the wheel. Kat loved most the smell, which the old girl still carried, of real wood and leather with a rich undertone of engine oil. There was something both luxurious and comforting about it.

Then there'd been the accident. That had been the end of family drives, the end of her father, and the end of her mother's interest in motoring. She bought a Volvo to replace the annihilated family car and used it to drive to the supermarket or, occasionally, drop Kat off at school. She took the tram to work, but could never quite bring herself to get rid of the Alfa. It sat in the garage for more than a decade until, six months before Kat's eighteenth birthday, she began surreptitiously—while Kat was out, or studying—bringing it back from the dead. And presented it to Kat on the day she got her driver's licence, along with the service history, a *Melways*, and the name of a good mechanic.

Kat's first thought had been to dispose of it discreetly at the first opportunity and get herself a proper car like her friends drove. A Corolla automatic, maybe, or a little Honda. Something that at least had FM radio. Her mum would understand. But within days the silky feel of the oversized wooden steering wheel, the chased chrome lid of the ashtray, the goggle-eyed dashboard displays and rich, red upholstery had won her over. That, and the delicious scent. She'd even fallen for the dour grey paint job and squat, unassuming styling. From the outside it was so plain it was almost invisible; on the inside, it was a treasure trove of quirks and extravagant finishes.

Within a fortnight she found she'd named it: The Box. (A twee habit she despised in others but was strangely unashamed of in herself.) She wasn't sure when she'd started talking to it, but now few trips commenced without her informing the car where they were going and why. ('Let's head north, Box, see what Bets and Leo are up to.') More than twenty years later she felt towards it as she might a beloved pet. Part of the family. Her only family, really, since her mother died (cancer, so unexpected and so rapid). That was more than a decade ago now, but sometimes Kat still liked to imagine Nancy riding shotgun.

Plus, it just worked. People made jokes about Alfas' reliability, but with regular servicing The Box ran like a dream. And even though it wasn't quite capacious enough for someone of Betsy's build, for Kat it was a perfect fit.

'Fine if you're the size of a mouse,' Betsy said, trying to shift into a more comfortable position and bumping her head against the roof.

'Almost there, mate,' Kat said, swinging into Nicholson Street. 'Coffee's my shout.'

'And carrot cake?' Leo asked from the back.

Kat glanced over her shoulder. 'I thought you were buying the cake. Didn't you bring your money?'

Leo looked stricken and Kat said quickly, 'All right. I'll buy the cake too. But you'll owe me.'

'Okay,' said Leo. 'Bets can pay you.'

Kat raised an eyebrow at her friend.

'He suddenly realised he's the only one who calls us Mum and Dad,' Bets murmured. 'The perils of the only child. I think he figured if everyone else calls us Bets and Jim, so can he.'

'How do you feel about that?'

'Cheated! If you're going to put up with all the pain of being Mummy, you at least want some recognition for it.'

Kat slid neatly into a park, glancing in the window of the café. Two months ago bohemian mamas and papas and their interesting offspring were queuing for a table here on a Sunday morning. For a latte, or a chai latte, and a piece of toast. Maybe some muesli.

Living in Coburg, Kat had longed for a decent café, a pleasant bar. Now, as Brunswick oozed steadily north and threatened to engulf her beloved Burg with its Crocs and off-road prams and facial hair and pedigreed coffee, she unwished it. Along with Merri Creek, women in headscarves, and kick-to-kick in the street, the thing she counted on about Coburg was its dagginess, its steadfast resistance to any kind of fashion.

Fitzroy was Fitzroy. You understood that vegan sourdough and ostentatiously seasonal menus were as much a part of the culture there now as multi-million dollar properties and designer retail. That's the price you paid for a decent bookshop, a decent wine shop, and being able to walk into the city. But Coburg?

'How much longer?' Kat murmured.

Understanding her, Betsy patted Kat's hand. 'We're safe for a bit yet,' she said.

Fortunately, mid week, St Simeon was only half full—as Kat was ruefully aware, with parties just like hers:

30

women of a certain age dressed in black or grey, towing mad-haired children with names like Leo. At least, she thought, we've arrived here in an unapologetically green-house-gas emitting imported car and not on our damn bicycles.

They sat in the window in the thin winter sun and ordered their friands and coffee—not skinny, not decaf, not soy, just coffee—and carrot cake for the boy.

'God, it's good to get out of the house. And away from the kinder committee!' said Betsy, stretching her legs luxuriously. 'Tell me about the shoot.'

'Oh Bets,' said Kat, feeling the inappropriate laughter bubbling up all over again. 'I wish you'd been there!'

'I'm pretty glad I wasn't!'

'Oh, yes. It was terrible, of course.'

'Yet strangely hilarious?' Bets grinned at her fondly.

'Uh huh.' Kat sipped her coffee. 'The day was just spiralling out of control. It felt almost inevitable. It was like either a derailed train was going to come steaming down Lonsdale Street, or someone was going to throw themselves off a building into the middle of the shoot.'

'And someone threw themselves off a building into the middle of the shoot.'

'Exactly. And—I know it's awful—but I just started laughing!'

'Awful. Yet not surprising, my friend.'

'I know, I know. But it wasn't just me. It seemed like the only thing you *could* do. It was just too, too bizarre. And it wasn't like it was someone we knew.' Kat nibbled the edge of her pastry, casting Betsy a glance. 'I'm not explaining this very well, am I?'

'I understand perfectly. Like that time our studio burnt down.'

'Exactly. Although, of course, no one actually died when your studio burnt down.'

'No. But you are much more ruthless and hard-hearted than me.'

'And cynical.'

'And cynical. You do work in television, after all.'

'Reality television.'

'Nuff said.' Betsy reached out and squeezed her hand. 'Seriously, are you okay? This breezy demeanour isn't concealing deeply repressed terror? No nightmares? No sudden fascination with tall buildings?'

'No,' Kat sighed. 'I almost wish it did. The only thing that bothers me is that I'm *not* more bothered.'

'Don't worry about that,' Bets said comfortably, gesturing for more coffee. 'You'll have plenty of real problems to bother you soon enough.'

Kat thought of the lurid *Survivor* title card that had appeared at the last screening and shivered a little. 'True enough,' she said. 'And how about you? Nightmares? Repressed terrors? Niggling concern over interest rates?'

'No, no, and not really,' Bets said. 'Although I also disgraced myself this week.'

'Yes?' said Kat, leaning forward in anticipation.

Betsy pinched her nose, smothered a giggle. 'One of those wish-you'd-been-there, glad-you-weren't moments.'

'Don't keep me in suspense!'

'Well, you know they're building those units across the street from me?'

Kat nodded.

'They had to get a crane in. And to get the crane in,

they had to cut down the tree on the nature strip.'

'Oh dear,' murmured Kat, fearing the worst. Betsy was even more passionate about her neighbourhood than Kat, and rather more inclined to participate in furious letter-writing campaigns, marches, sit-ins, rowdy Council meetings, and worse. 'What did you do?'

'I was so enraged I didn't know what to do. As soon as I saw them I tore out of the house—then I just stood in the street shouting, "BAD DECISION! BAD DECISION!"' Betsy's voice cracked on the last word and Kat burst out laughing. Leo looked up, grinning, wanting in on the joke; the rest of the patrons regarded them with alarm.

'Oh Bets,' said Kat when they'd both regained control of themselves. 'At least you didn't throw yourself in front of the chainsaw.'

'Might have, if I'd got there in time. Or attacked him with it. Arrived just a minute too late,' said Betsy, draining her coffee.

Kat gazed at her friend fondly. How many times had they sat just like this, in a café or a kitchen, talking about nothing in particular? Or about major dramas. Or thrilling triumphs. One of the nice things about getting older, she thought, was the comfort of it. A certain settled-ness. The history.

She remembered when Bets still wore bonkers plaits and pinafores and multi-coloured tights; when she rang at 2am to relate her first night out with Jim. When Leo's existence was first verified, when he was born. Holding that wrinkly pheromone-soaked lump and feeling a completely unexpected rush of love and longing.

And Kat's own highlights and lowlights, of course, also shared. Moments of horrible grief and humiliation, sometimes work-related, mostly bloke-related; things that were almost too awful to speak about but that Bets absorbed calmly and kindly, putting the kettle on or pouring some wine, knowing exactly when to deliver bracing advice, when to joke her out of the dumps, and when to say nothing. That absolute understanding was a priceless quality in a friend.

'Hello there. Are you still with me?'

Kat refocused with a start. 'Just taking a trip down memory lane.'

'Happy memories, I hope?'

'Oh yes,' said Kat, patting Betsy's hand. 'Very.'

5

The good thing about the suicide, Kat thought as she watched the contestants standing around chatting in knots of two and three, was that it promoted some serious team bonding. They'd just had their final briefing before shooting began, and already they were like family, or the survivors of some terrible ordeal, those people you see staggering from the smoke of a bomb blast or a burning building or hugging each other at a flower-strewn memorial.

And I suppose it was a terrible ordeal, she mused, a small frown creasing her forehead. For normal people. And they were, actually, the survivors of it. Survivors... God. Was BC evil enough to have orchestrated it? No. Of course not. But he must be counting it as a great piece of good luck. It certainly added a whole new dimension to what lay ahead for their motley crew.

Kat felt a warm, proprietary wash of satisfaction as they began to disperse by car, truck, tram and bicycle.

In reality television, casting was everything, and this time Cohen Clarke had outdone itself.

There always had to be one young, pretty woman, preferably blonde. That was Peru. There had to be a handsome love interest: Zane, a classic Alpha male likely to crack wide open once the going got tough.

One or two representatives of the older generation: they had mumsy Sally and butcher Phil. A villain. That would be Vanessa (although the poor thing had no idea that's why she was there). The usual mixed bag of twentysome-things: the greenie, the head prefect, Jake the slacker and Amber the party girl. Michael was the necessary gesture to racial diversity, while Nick was an interesting one, fresh out of three years in the Department of Prime Minister and Cabinet. Those skills could come in handy.

And finally, her favourite: gay farm boy Trent. Kat loved Trent. Then again, she loved them all, individually and as a group. She loved the awkwardness and affection and enmity that were already brewing between them. And she was loving in anticipation the way that would be shaped and reshaped as the series progressed.

Next week the competition proper would begin, with the dirty dozen spending their first days penniless and without employment or distraction, adrift on the streets of Melbourne. Tasked with finding shelter, food, money and work—privileges steadily withdrawn and contestants eliminated each week—until the final pair faced the ulti-mate challenge: living completely unassisted for five days. Or until emergency services had to be called. Whichever came first.

Kat still didn't really understand why people volun-teered for this kind of thing—the only prize was $100,000 to a charity of the winner's choice, the hardships and potential humiliation significant—but she was glad they did. It promised to be fascinating.

Before all that came to pass, though, there was today's big task: their first major tech reccie since the Lonsdale Street shoot. GC had crossed all the t's and dotted all the i's to ensure getting their mob back out and filming was legal and appropriate. Kat had exerted what charm and faux-sincerity she possessed to renegotiate the permissions that delay entailed.

Now Harry was signalling to her that everyone was on the bus and ready to go. Good, Kat thought. Let's do this.

She loved these days, even more than filming. With filming, things could go wrong. Obviously. Filming was largely out of her control. Tech reccies were hers. The one time she felt truly both part of the team, and boss of it. My chance to show off, she thought, taking her seat at the front of the bus. We all need one from time to time.

'Okay!' she said brightly. 'Everybody ready?' Various nods, grunts and thumbs-ups indicated this to be the case, so she gave the driver's arm a little pat, and they pulled away from the curb.

Sourcing potential locations for sleeping rough had been an equally fascinating exercise. And heartbreaking. She had certainly had to cultivate her own degree of un-reality, to keep a little distance, to not think too hard about the implications of the information she was seeking.

Their first stop, which she liked a lot but BC wasn't keen on (it didn't look quite gritty and urban enough) was under the network of walkways leading in to the Tennis

Centre. Her sources told her this was a place with few passersby, minimising the likelihood of being harassed or rolled. The big concrete pylons gave you some protection from the wind. Most importantly, it was a place you could leave a sleeping bag or a pile of blankets and still find them there at nightfall.

She explained this cheerfully to her captive audience.

'It looks too open,' grumbled BC from the back. 'It doesn't look like the city.'

'We will have some laneways, some doorways, that kind of thing. We'll look at those next,' she said. 'But I think this could look stunning. That network of concrete, the city rising up hard behind it, these tiny figures huddled at the base...' Kat caught Ted's eye, seeking support.

'I like it,' Ted said. 'Start with Rod Laver Arena, the place the rich people play. The lights of the city, the river. Twinkle twinkle. Then come down, like Kat said, through all that concrete. The tram tracks, the chain-link fence. Look at the size of that pylon, it's brutal. Some miserable sod huddled up against it.'

'I guess,' BC said.

Thank you, Kat mouthed to Ted. And they all piled out of the bus to take a closer look.

So the day progressed, tootling from one dismal location to the next: hidey-holes behind dumpsters, reeking doorways, nooks under railway overpasses, with a couple of hours' break for lunch in a nice Mod-Oz place at the top of Bourke Street (one hat in the latest *Good Food Guide*).

There the arguments continued. BC liked locations cramped and dank, but visually one small dark hole looked very much like another, and they were tricky to shoot. There was also the question of safety. While the contestants had emergency beepers, at night they'd be on their own, just them and their infrared handycams. The spots BC liked best because they looked lonely and dangerous *were* lonely and dangerous.

But by four o'clock, with the winter sun weakening and all tempers getting ragged, they made it safely back to the production office with a final list of locations and most of the technical specifications sorted.

Waving off the bus and driver, Kat sighed and rolled her shoulders. Tired but happy, she thought. Tired but happy. Slinging her various bags, satchels and assorted sheaves of paper into The Box, she made a quick detour into the coffee shop for one last refuel.

'Afternoon Wilson.'

'G'day Kat.' He looked up, smiling. He really does have a lovely smile, Kat thought.

She propped against one of the tables and watched him deftly blend a little milk with the coffee in the bottom of the cup before filling it with increasingly dense layers of foam, finishing with a flourish.

'Thank you,' she said, handing over some coins.

'My pleasure.'

She raised the cup to her lips and snorted with laughter. Carved into the top was not a heart, but a skull and crossbones.

6

'Had our first real tech reccie today,' Kat said, sipping her wine.

'Did you?' said Miles, intent on de-choking artichokes. They were Bonnie-free this week, which always made her feel somehow more grown-up—part of her mentally became four years old whenever Bonnie was around—but skittish, too, ready for fun. A good day at the office always helped. And while it was a splendid family home, with the toys stowed away, no half-eaten bits of fruit on the table, no miniature shoes and socks and jackets strewn around, the house looked even lovelier, sophisticated, filling her with pleasure.

Kat could never quite decide on her favourite room. She loved it here, in the kitchen, the obligatory box at the back of the house with the wall of glass and the bi-fold doors opening on to the deck. She loved the scrubbed table and the big red sofa and the stone counters studded with good things to eat and drink, the wine rack glowing. But she loved the front room, too, the Good Room, the only real remaining vestige of Victoriana with its tasteful, rather manly furnishings and walls of books and piles of scripts, the fireplace. And, of course, the enormous flat-screen TV. Perhaps they could retire there after dinner, read, talk, listen to some music. Or perhaps they could go straight to bed? She liked the bedroom too...

'We were looking at places to sleep rough.' Kat went and stood a little closer to Miles.

'Yep,' he said absently. He added a final squeeze of lemon to the artichokes and put the lid on the pot. 'Can you keep an eye on that? I just need to make a couple of calls.'

'Sure.'

He wiped his hands on a tea towel, patted her shoulder, and headed down the hall to the study. Kat stood duti-fully looking at the saucepan for a moment, which wasn't doing a great deal. Peeked in the oven, where fish wrapped in foil sat on one rack, potatoes with lemon and garlic braised on another. Thought about making a salad. Then thought, maybe not. Miles was fussy about his salads.

She wandered back to the table, took a seat facing the stove—where she could remain alert to any unruly beha-viour on the part of the artichokes—and sat idly twirling her wine glass. It had been a good day, she thought. But all the interesting and funny things that had transpired seemed rather less interesting and funny now. Her skittish mood had evaporated and she knew with a flat certainty that her fantasy of retiring early to bed, for any other purpose than sleep, was precisely that.

Sometimes, she thought, it was hard to accentuate

the positive. It was churlish, childish even, she knew, to expect Miles' mood to always match hers. To expect a romp midweek, especially when he was in the throes of a major new project. After two years it was only natural that a certain element of routine would set in.

And anyway—didn't she like routine?

Miles' placidity, his predictability, a sort of calm bordering on affectlessness: those were the things that had attracted her in the first place. Plus his reputation and accomplishments, of course. Kat didn't consider herself a shallow woman, but without doubt there was something sexy about a very successful man: the most in-demand director in Australian television and the only one to have won an Emmy. (He kept it discreetly hidden in a cupboard, naturally, along with his many AFIs. He'd never be so callow as to boast.)

And as for him? Well, he didn't give much away, but she suspected her gratitude at his sheer lack of awfulness was enormously satisfying to him. She certainly admired him (and he liked that), while her quest for peacefulness in her life outside work must have seemed to him like a perfect fit. She was undemanding, and she knew that was important to him.

Kat drank a little more wine, listened to the tick and murmur of the food cooking, the buzz of the refrigerator, the low rise and fall of Miles' voice from the other end of the house, and felt her eyes sting. She pinched the bridge of her nose angrily. She liked routine. She wanted peace and quiet. So why was she feeling so disconsolate?

Tapping herself lightly on both cheeks, she stood, swung her arms around, breathed deeply. Jogged from one end of the kitchen to the other. Lifted the lid on the saucepan, where the grey-green vegetables looked anything but appetising. Poured herself some more wine. Decided to set the table.

The thing is, she thought, wiping down the surface with a damp cloth, I have no idea what a functional relationship looks like. She counted out knives and forks. A succession of tempestuous affairs of varying duration with moody artistic types (she'd always had a weakness for them) had given her a fair idea of what a *dysfunctional* relationship looked like. The painter, the writer. The other writer. The musician. That stand-up comic. They were bad news. Charming, usually (except the stand-up comic). Terribly interesting, of course. Never a dull moment. But disastrous. And everyone except her had been able to see it a mile off.

Miles, though. Miles was a grown-up. Yes, he too worked in television. But he was a successful, professional man. He was intelligent. Creative. Generally considered good-looking. Generally considered a catch, a keeper, despite a romantic history almost as patchy as hers. And certainly Kat had not been able to believe her luck at the whirlwind courtship, the unexpected bonus of Bonnie, the precipitous shacking up.

So why—*why*—wasn't she happier? What did she want? What *do* I want? she asked herself with some urgency, putting a dish of salt flakes and the pepper grinder on the table. And could only answer herself, rather helplessly: More.

'Ah, thank you,' said Miles, re-entering the room and glancing at the table before moving to the stove.

'They tried to make a run for it at one point but I managed to corral them,' Kat said as he checked the artichokes. He threw her a puzzled glance, looked in the oven, then passed his wine glass to her. 'Would you mind? I'll just make a *salsa verde*.'

'Of course.' No salad then. She took his glass, refilled it, topped up hers—there goes the bottle—and said, 'Everything okay with *Mrs Miller*?'

He grimaced, shook his head, feeding basil, parsley, capers, oil into the blender. 'They fancy themselves as HBO but they've got more in common with your lot,' he said, furiously mulching everything into chunky green slime.

'You forgot the anchovies,' said Kat, passing him the jar. She wasn't especially fond of anchovies. Or artichokes, for that matter. But she knew it wouldn't improve his temper if he only remembered when he tasted it.

'Shit.' He chopped the anchovies, scraped them into the blender, gave everything one last whiz. 'They want more jokes,' he said bitterly.

'Jokes?'

'Humour. It needs to lighten up, apparently.'

'Ah.'

Miles took a deep breath, exhaling the sudden flush of anger. He'd been getting angry a lot lately. In his own quiet, pinch-lipped way. On set, his roaring temper was legendary. Kat thought he rather prided himself on it. At home, the reverse was true. At home he insisted on order and quiet. But over the last six months Kat had been aware of the bubbling tension he rigorously contained. Sometimes she wished he'd just let it out.

Now he simply said blandly, 'Let's eat,' and dished up the evening's creation onto large white plates.

They ate in silence for a moment, then Kat said, 'Well, sometimes disastrous things can be funny.'

He paused with his fork halfway to his mouth. 'Can they?'

She thought about mentioning Suicide Guy. Thought better of it. But persevered. 'Sometimes all you *can* do is laugh, surely?'

He shook his head. 'Some things just aren't funny. *Mrs Miller* isn't funny. There's nothing funny about it.' He chewed a mouthful, took a sip of wine, shook his head again. 'I am just sick of this relentless...'

As he searched for the word, Kat thought: Please don't say 'dumbing down'.

'Dumbing down,' Miles said emphatically. 'Always pandering to the lowest common denominator. This disrespect for the intelligence of the audience. People will watch serious drama, if we give them the opportunity to do so. But when do they get the chance? *Mad Men*. That's it. And does anyone in this country have the guts to try and do something like that of our own?'

'Well, there's humour in *Mad Men*.'

Miles gazed at her in genuine puzzlement. 'No, there isn't.'

Kat pursed her lips, attended to her plate, changed tack. 'In the end, though, that's a problem for the writers, for the producers, isn't it? With *Miller*?'

Miles sighed. 'You know how much of myself I've put into this project. You know how much it means to me.' And looked so genuinely crestfallen Kat reached out and took his hand, kissed the fingertips gently.

'All is not lost, sweetheart. You might be able to strike some compromise. You might be able to talk them round.'

'Maybe,' he said, resuming eating.

'You can be very persuasive.' She gave him her most

winning smile, and received a smile as her reward. 'And you're a first-rate cook.'

His face lightened. 'It is good, isn't it? I almost bought salmon, but then the swordfish looked so good. You don't think there's too much of the same flavour profile in the potatoes and the artichokes?'

'No, it works. The *salsa verde* really lifts it.'

Pleased, Miles sipped his wine.

After dinner Kat cleared away, stacked the dishwasher, washed the saucepans and the glasses while Miles returned to the study to resume negotiations. As soon as he left the room the heaviness in her chest returned. Her own day, with its small excitements and triumphs, felt a long way away. She resisted the urge to pour more wine and made coffee instead. Strong blacks with a dash of hot milk. What was that called? Macchiato? She'd have to ask Wilson. And smiled, thinking of the death's head on her latte. Wilson would like a drama with jokes in it, she thought. Wilson would be a *Deadwood* kind of guy.

Kat slid Miles' coffee onto the edge of his desk, turned to leave, then turned back. Okay, she thought. Once more into the breach.

She took a breath. 'Miles?'

He looked up, a little startled to find her still there. 'Hi.'

She perched on the edge of an armchair. 'Look, I know you're busy, but do you have ten minutes? To talk?'

He put his pen down. 'About what?'

'About us.'

'What about us?' His tone was not encouraging, and Kat blanched a little.

After a pause she said, 'Are you happy?'

'Of course.'

Now he was supposed to say: 'Aren't you?' But he just continued to look at her with a mix of puzzlement and impatience, forcing her to blurt out, 'I'm not!'

He looked nonplussed. 'Oh,' he said. Then, after a moment: 'Is there anything I can do?'

'I... Yes... Maybe...' Kat was struggling to find the right words, the diplomatic phrases. Be nice to me! Listen to me! Pay attention to me! She'd sound like a sulky teen. 'I sometimes feel like...you're not very interested in me, or my work, or how I feel,' she finally managed.

'Of course I am.'

'I don't *feel* like you are.'

'Well, that's hardly my problem, is it sweetheart?' he said mildly. Then, seeing her face, he moved his chair a little closer and took her hands in his. 'Look Kat, I'm sorry you're not happy at the moment. But we all get down from time to time. And we've had this discussion before. It really doesn't help to be constantly picking over the entrails. You say I don't do this enough, I say you do that too much. We both just end up feeling worse.' He squeezed her fingers. 'You'll be fine,' he said kindly. 'Don't dwell on it.'

They sat there for moment in silence, gazing at each other. Eventually Miles said, 'Go and put your feet up. Have another wine. I really have to...' He gestured at his desk.

Kat stood. 'I'm sorry. I know you're busy. But maybe when you've got some more time—maybe over the weekend...?'

47

He expelled a sharp breath. 'Kat. Darling. If there's something you need me to do, let me know,' he repeated, with some asperity. 'But don't ask me to waste the weekend—any weekend—pointlessly dissecting our relationship. Do we really need to go through all this *again*?'

Kat stood a moment longer, then nodded. 'Okay,' she said. 'I'll leave you in peace.'

Well, what did you expect, Kat?

It wasn't the first time they'd had that conversation, or variations on it. And maybe he was right. Maybe she was just in the dumps a bit.

She cleaned her teeth, washed her face, brushed her hair. Undressed and slipped into bed, thinking: Don't dwell on it.

1

Kat put The Box into reverse and backed out of the driveway.

'Do you know what this is about?'

'No,' said Harry, groping for his seatbelt. 'But I don't have a good feeling about it.' He buckled himself in. 'You know, every time I get in this car I want to light a cigarette.'

'Well don't! Anyway, it's only the ashtray. It's so glamorous, it's just begging to be used.'

Harry flipped the top, revealing a jumble of coins, hairpins and scraps of paper, and closed it again. 'You're right,' he said. 'I feel like I should be wearing a cravat and smoking. You also need a scarf around your neck. And larger sunglasses.'

'Probably should have put some lippy on, too.'

Harry reached for the radio—the Pressmatic Deluxe, another feature as far as Kat was concerned—then seemed to remember their only choices were talkback or easy listening, and folded his hands back in his lap.

'Do you even know who else is going to be there?'

'Core crew, I think,' Kat said.

'So we're re-shooting something?'

Kat pushed her modestly-sized sunglasses back up her nose. 'I don't know, lovely. I'll guess we'll find out soon enough.'

Bell Street was at a crawl. Kat saw an opening, turned right, headed south, glancing at the clownishly large clock on the dash.

'Are we going to make it?'

'We'll make it. You know no one knows more devious ways across town than me.'

'True.'

They drove in silence for a while, Harry rubbing his knuckles nervously. Eventually Kat said, 'Sweetie, whatever it is, you'll deal with it. You always do.'

Harry sighed. 'I know. It's just...I hadn't realised it'd be...'

'So full-on?'

'I guess. I thought I was more *ready*.'

'You are ready.'

He shook his head. 'They should have chosen you. It feels wrong.'

'Well, they could hardly choose me when I didn't offer. You know I've never had any ambition to herd cats.' Never had that much ambition at all, she thought, except for a peaceful life. To do her job well. But mainly to be left alone while she did so.

Harry, on the other hand, had a young man's hunger for success, position, to climb the ladder. Three years ago he'd been doing the coffee run and engaging in daily wrestles with the photocopier when Kat had invited him to join her as a scout. She'd liked his energy, his sense of humour, his sensibility. In an industry bristling with ego, where too many people took themselves far too seriously, she'd liked his attitude.

Like her, Harry was an unashamed enthusiast for television but not in any way blind to its foibles. It made him easy to be around. A kindred spirit. She missed those early years they'd spent in The Box, combing Melbourne and beyond, knocking on doors, exploring alleyways and byways and sub-suburbs they hadn't realised existed. And talking.

At her suggestion, he'd put his hand up for First Assistant Director on Cohen Clarke's 'groundbreaking new factual series'. He was now responsible for making sure all the key human components, but especially the contestants, were where they should be, when they should be. Herding cats.

But that combination of pragmatism, enthusiasm and humour was precisely what was needed to get the job done. And it was a combination that would stand him in good stead, Kat knew, when he achieved his ultimate ambition: to direct.

Like GC, Harry enjoyed people. And people reciprocated. He had an unassuming confidence that people responded to instinctively. A quiet extrovert, Kat thought, remembering a conversation she'd had with one of the *Big Brother* psychologists. There'd been the general misapprehension that residents of The House were all extroverted. Maddeningly so. But apparently the reverse was true. That a classic extrovert—like Harry, or GC—was chiefly concerned with what they thought of other people, while a classic introvert was obsessed with what other people thought of them.

Many extroverts certainly were gregarious. The loud extroverts. Like Miss Universe contestants, like Peru, they loved 'meeting people', and would enthusiastically work a room, never doubting for a moment that everybody in it would be delighted to meet them. Others were more like Harry, content in their own company but always interested in the people around them. It was a real virtue, Kat thought. A gift.

The *Big Brother* contestants, on the other hand, were desperately concerned with what other people thought of them and fed that by preening and parading and talking themselves up, often blithely unaware of their real effect on their interlocutors. The loud introverts.

And then there's me. Kat smiled to herself, turning at last onto the freeway, shifting up and putting her foot down, feeling The Box hum appreciatively. The old-school quiet introvert. The one who often couldn't even work out whether she liked someone because she was too busy worrying about whether they liked her. 'Though I am getting better,' she said, accidentally finishing her train of thought out loud.

'Every day, in every way.' Harry grinned.

'God. Sorry!' Kat laughed. 'I was just thinking how very good you are at herding cats. And, while I would be very bad at it, I'm not nearly as shy and awkward and dorky as I used to be.'

He shook his head. 'You know I just don't see that at all. I don't think anybody does except you.'

'Well, you have met me rather late in the piece.'

'If you were that shy and awkward and dorky you could never do this job. You could never handle Mr Whataboutourrevenue. Or Mr Fivefuckencoffees. Or BC and his "I want it darker! Darker! More urban!" And I'm pretty sure you could herd cats if you had to.'

'Think so?'

'I do.'

'Luckily, I don't have to. Or want to,' she added firmly.

Peeling away from the traffic on to Footscray Road, on the home stretch, Kat glanced at the clock again. What did BC want? What would warrant calling yet another production meeting, so soon after the last?

She pulled in to her regular spot in front of the office, dragged her maps and schedules and picture files from the back seat and locked her door, reminding Harry that one of The Box's other quirks was no central locking.

Upstairs, the usual suspects were gathered round the table, BC drumming his pen on the desktop, exuding his own unsettling kind of electricity. Only GC was missing, and as Harry and Kat took their places they heard her clattering up the stairs behind them. Kat shot her an enquiring look as she came through the door and received an indecipherable one in reply.

'Right,' said BC, jumping to his feet and grinning in a way that did not bode well. 'Great news.' Everyone sat up a little straighter. 'After our last session, I got thinking. *Survivor.* Why not go all the way.'

BC scanned each of their faces.

'So I called Burnett's office and put it to him. A whole

new take on the franchise. A whole new lease of life for, let's face it, a pretty tired idea. A whole new direction. *Survivor: CBD.*'

He paused again to let the full glory of it sink in. Kat made the mistake of meeting Harry's eyes for a moment and bit her lip, choking back a giggle. GC had her eyes on the notepad in front of her, Bev and Ted looked thoughtful. Everyone else just looked blank.

'It's provisional at the moment, subject to a bit of tweaking of the format,' BC said, resuming his seat. 'But Burnett loved the idea, loved the concept. Now it's up to us to make it work.'

There was a longish silence until Kat said, 'How far away are we able to move from the original Bible?'

'Great question,' BC said, jumping to his feet again. 'You and Ted both worked on *Celebrity Survivor*, didn't you?'

They exchanged looks, nodded; Kat pressed her lips more firmly together. In some ways, it had been a dream job. Months travelling outback Australia, the Barrier Reef, then on to the Pacific Islands, hunting up the perfect spot to maroon twenty C-listers for a month. Then micro-managing the locations for the challenges, the rewards, and the campsites.

But like any successful franchise, whether that was McDonald's or Jim's Mowing or a reality-television series, it came with a set of rules. A big set of rules. The Bible. For the series creator, maintaining the integrity of his vision was crucial. Any deviation, even slight, required extensive negotiation. Any mistakes could knock schedules sideways and send whole days of shooting sliding into the abyss. And that was for a series where the local incarnation had been doing pretty much exactly what had been done in the original.

This was a big deviation. A monstrous one. Kat strongly suspected 'tweaking the format' wasn't quite the right phrase. What was BC thinking?

'What I'm thinking,' BC said, 'is to stick with our format—living homeless. Don't worry about that. But we need to incorporate some of those classic *Survivor* elements.'

Well, if BC had made up his mind, there was no point arguing with him. Instead Kat plunged in. 'So, will you need me to—ah—tweak—the "sleeping rough" segments and establish two campsites?' she asked.

'Yes. Definitely,' said BC approvingly.

'Will we need to tweak the contestants' contracts?' Harry asked.

'We will,' said BC. 'But that shouldn't be a problem. I'll leave that to you and Gen.'

'I imagine we'll need to tweak what's required for set-dressing,' said Bev, getting into the spirit of things.

'And we'll have to tweak the site for the eliminations,' Kat said, envisaging a forty-four-gallon drum filled with burning shoes or car tyres in place of the traditional campfire.

'Yep,' said BC. 'And don't think I don't know you lot are taking the piss with all this "tweaking",' he said, pointing at them. 'But this is going to be great. We can do this.'

Bev would work with Kat on the look of the campsite and the hardware required. It'd probably be Bev's job to come up with something to replicate the *Survivor* bandanas too. *Maybe a kerchief on a stick?*

They were all charged with suggesting ideas for contestant challenges, appropriate to surviving in the CBD. Kat's mind immediately turned to the inappropriate and the illegal: drug dealing, prostitution, begging. Were you even allowed to busk in the city any more? She'd have to work on that.

When the meeting broke up Harry stayed back with GC to talk over the small matter of persuading the contestants to embark on something completely different from the show for which they'd signed on. Kat mouthed 'coffee' and pointed downstairs. Harry nodded and gave her the thumbs up.

In the café, Bev and Wilson seemed to be having quite the confab. Kat resisted the temptation to edge closer and eavesdrop. She watched with some interest the way in which Wilson spoke to the older woman, the subtle shifts in his face and tone. Eventually Bev finished. Wilson said a few words, and Kat was struck by the great kindness in his face. When the designer finally left after a brief goodbye to Kat, Wilson smiled and said, 'She's worried about her daughter.'

'Is she?' said Kat, with some astonishment. Who knew? Then: 'You should have been a barman, not a barista.'

'Thought about it,' he said. 'But making coffee, customers are less likely to pick a fight. Or vomit on you. And you don't have to work nights.'

'All good reasons,' said Kat.

'So you're a location person. Scout? Is that what they call you?' he said as he wiped down the machine.

'Yes. Or location manager. Depending on how pretentious you are. And if you have underlings, then they're the scouts and you're the manager.'

'You have underlings?'

'Not this time.'

For a moment the room was filled with the hiss of the water forcing through the grounds. When the coffee was brewed he said, 'Do you really just knock on people's doors? Ask to film their house?'

'Sure. That's part of it.'

'How do you even start doing something like that?' He passed Kat her coffee.

She sat down again, checked the top of her coffee—today, a simple fern pattern—took a sip. 'Well, I liked the idea of working in television. But for pretty much every-thing else—writing, directing, all the technical jobs—you actually need skills, training, that sort of thing. There's acting. You don't necessarily need training to be an actor, but you do need talent. And I have no talent. That left locations. All you need for that is a driver's licence. And I already had a driver's licence.'

Wilson grinned and leant one hip against the counter, crossing his arms on his chest. 'Enjoy it?'

'Yeah!' Kat said. 'I do. Exploring the city. Snooping around other people's houses. Getting access to places mere mortals can't. You know, Flemington, the MCG. That's cool.'

Wilson nodded.

'Can I ask you something?' she said.

'Go for it.'

'A short black with a dash of hot milk. Is that a macchiato?'

He smiled, inclined his head. 'It is.'

At that moment Harry stuck his head in the door, caught her eye. 'Sorry, love. You ready?'

'I am.' Kat gathered up her things. Wilson greeted Harry, glanced from one to the other curiously. 'Thanks,' she said, raising the coffee cup.

'No worries. See you next time.'

As she followed Harry out the door she paused, turned. 'Actually, there is one other thing.'

'Yep?'

'Do you like *Deadwood*?'

Wilson smiled in surprise. 'Love it.'

8

On her way to Betsy's, Kat turned off Sydney Road a block early and cruised past her old flat. This time of year the long avenue of elms was bare, the figs and pomegranates in front gardens leafless and pruned to stumps, but the lemon trees were glossy and bowed with fruit, lawns and nature strips neatly mowed, the odd plot of winter greens—kale, broad beans, parsley—brightening immaculate garden beds. Miles had herbs in pots in the courtyard, in summer a couple of tomato plants. But she missed having a proper vegie patch.

Number Twenty looked pretty much as it always did: tidy enough, but certainly the worst block in the best street. She remembered so clearly the day she bought the flat. Back then the fence had been falling down, the front garden beds choked with weeds, the guttering holed with rust and looped drunkenly along the fascia. Next door had been an empty lot, piled with rubble and refuse.

But inside Flat Four she'd discovered original parquetry floors, recently sanded and sealed. Fresh white paint. A wall of windows looking out onto a diminutive courtyard, full of promise. A proper bath in the neat little bathroom. And walls of bookshelves. She knew she was home.

At a time when the Melbourne property market had been enjoying a headline-making boom, when house hunters attended auctions week in, week out for twelve months or more before getting lucky, this unprepossessing place had been for private sale. The day after she inspected it she made an offer. The day after that she was signing the contract. She'd been actively looking for about ten days. By the end of the month she was—at thirty-seven, somewhat belatedly—a homeowner. It was fate.

She'd finally felt like a grown-up. She was working in a job she loved, not making big money but enough to fund a flat in Coburg. She'd rid herself of the last in a long line of terribly inappropriate boyfriends, and vowed never to go there again. And if her life hadn't quite worked out the way she'd anticipated (no husband, no kids, no Federation weatherboard with the picket fence), she finally felt it was, in its own way, working out. Her microscopic dream home was the 3D proof. And despite the excitement of moving in with Miles and Bonnie, it had been with real sorrow that she'd closed the door to her place for the last time and relinquished it into the hands of strangers.

The unit was set back so she couldn't actually see it unless she got out and snooped on foot. The tenants were still there. She decided to leave them in peace. But in one of her bags, among the sheaves of papers, was a letter from her real-estate agent. The premises were about to be vacated. Did she want them to go ahead and advertise it for lease?

It should have been a formality. But somehow she hadn't been able to bring herself to respond. Things had been crazy at work, of course. She'd had a lot on her mind. And she and Miles had talked, last year, about the possibility of her selling it, buying into his place. Maybe she'd just put in on the market. But as she sat there, The Box idling impatiently, she knew there was a darker reason for her hesitation. One she was loath to put into words, let alone seriously contemplate.

She took a long breath, then another, and put the car back into gear. No need to decide anything right now, Kat thought, pulling away from the curb. No need to think about it at all tonight.

Instead she drove the last hundred metres to Betsy's house, parked, tooted to alert Leo. He flung open the front door, presenting an odd sort of profile in the halo of the hallway light. As she got closer she realised he was wearing a costume. 'I'm an octopus!' he cried cheerfully as she bent to embrace him. He was dressed in a leotard with multi-coloured foam wands stitched around the waist, teamed with a pair of brown leggings and green-and-white-checked gumboots.

'You're a magnificent octopus,' Kat agreed, standing back to better admire the ensemble.

'Octo means eight,' Leo confided.

'It does. Shall we count your tentacles?'

'One. Two. Three. Four. Five.' The other three were awkwardly situated in the small of his back, resisting being counted off, so Leo cut to the chase. 'Eight!'

'Eight tentacles. Just as it should be.'

'Come in! Shut the door! It's freezing!' Betsy called from the kitchen, and the octopus stood back to let Kat pass.

'Darling,' said Betsy, drawing her into a sticky embrace.

Kat, returning the hug, nodded to Leo's outfit. 'Nice work.'

'Jim's work.' Bets released her and raised food-smeared hands apologetically. 'I've been slaving over a hot stove.'

'What demon possessed you to do that?'

'Thought I'd give the bloke a break.'

'And had him slaving over the Useful Box instead?'

'I thought it came up rather well,' said Jim, leaning in to peck her on the cheek. 'Drink?'

'Yes please.'

Leo was twirling aimlessly, muttering under his breath, intent on some imagined under-sea scenario. As Jim poured her a glass of shiraz, Betsy returned to her work.

'Sit down,' said Jim. 'Tell me about your day at the office.'

Kat sank into a chair at the dining table, sipped her wine. In her honour piles of newspapers, sketches, eccentric shopping lists (hummus, crayons, flea powder) and mini Tonka Toys had been pushed to one end, a small vase of flowers and a pair of candles placed in the centre, the surface wiped mainly free of food spills except for the fresh dribble of red wine recently applied by her host.

A large and slightly sinister tabby sat on Leo's raised chair at the head. Several sofa cushions bore a generous quilting of cat hair. Magazines, books, more sketches and a beekeeping manual kept company with discarded clothes and shoes on most surfaces. The walls were crowded with drawings and paintings, most provided by friends, some by Leo, some actually bought.

Kat felt her shoulders relax. Personally, she liked a touch more order. But there was always something so lovely about being here, somewhere you felt you could put your feet on the furniture, spill wine, talk loudly, say stupid things. Be fed generously. Be listened to. The pies were cooking, filling the room with meaty, buttery smells. Kat felt her melancholy steadily subsiding. It was good to be here.

After the meal Jim took care of bedtime duties while Kat helped Betsy clear up.

'How's Harry?' Bets asked, scraping congealed mashed potato into the compost.

'Good! Bit stressed, but good.' Kat took the plate and slid it into the dishwasher. Took a breath. 'I got a letter from my agent this week.'

Betsy raised her eyebrows. 'Since when have you had an agent?'

'Real-estate agent.'

'Oh.'

They continued cleaning in silence, washed the pie tins by hand, set the dishwasher going. When the kitchen was in order Betsy pulled another bottle of wine from the cupboard and raised it questioningly. Why not, thought Kat. I'll get a cab home.

'So,' said Betsy, filling fresh glasses. 'What did this letter say?'

'That my tenants were moving out.'

'Uh huh.'

Kat examined her hands intently. 'The thing is...'

What was the thing? She still couldn't bring herself to

say it, couldn't even bring it to the front of her mind. She was uneasily aware the whole evening had passed without mention of Miles, without her raising him, without Bets or Jim enquiring. Over the last six months or so her relationship was a subject on which none of them had anything to say. Miles had stopped accepting invitations to these dinners: pressures of work, he said, which was true. But they all knew the get-togethers, which were never unpleasant but always awkward, only highlighted the yawning gap in their sensibilities.

Initially, Kat had found that somehow endearing. Miles' earnestness. Now, like so much about him, about them, it simply brought on a kind of helpless lethargy. But even then, the thought of... Well, that thought had not crossed her mind. Until she got the letter from the real-estate agent. And now, the thing was...

'How do you know if you're happy?' she asked.

Betsy's eyebrows lifted again, but she considered the question seriously. 'Well, it depends what you mean by happy. Sometimes it's an active thing, isn't it? I'm in the middle of something, or I get into bed at the end of the day, or I'm looking at Leo or Jim, and I feel it. Like you would sorrow. Or fear. As a physical thing.'

Kat nodded, studying her wine glass.

'But other times—most of the time—maybe what you're talking about is contentment? Not that...rush of joy. Just that feeling that everything's okay.' Betsy paused. 'Are you unhappy, my friend?'

'I don't know! Not all the time.'

'Well, that's something.'

'I don't know, Bets. I don't know what to expect. Things aren't horrible. Not at all. I mean, they're fine.

And I know... Or at least... It's almost three years now. We've been living together for two. I know it can't be all wine and roses. But I guess I'm wondering: Is this it? Is this as good as it gets? Is this just what it's like?'

'You're bored.'

'Oh Bets. I'm bored off my tit.'

Betsy gave a spurt of laughter. 'You're just impossible to please, aren't you. Psycho Glenn too exciting. Worthy Miles too boring. Fussy, fussy, fussy.'

'You know that's *exactly* what I'm thinking.'

'I do know that, my love.'

There was another silence, then Kat said, 'It's not just that, though. The thing that worries me—and please don't laugh—but I'm thinking more and more that Miles, and Glenn, and Pete, and all the rest, *all of them*—they're not that different.'

'Ah,' said Bets.

'I mean obviously Miles doesn't...you know...'

'Good.'

'He's not unfaithful.'

'Excellent.'

'At least, as far as I know.' Kat took a sip of wine. 'It's just something about his attitude. His attitude to me. It's starting to feel, oh...*familiar*. In a horrible way.' She paused again, then said: 'There are all kinds of ways of being disrespectful.'

Betsy reached out and squeezed her hand. 'Yes,' she said. 'There are.' Then, after a moment: 'Have you talked with him about any of this?'

'Yes. Or, I've tried. He doesn't believe in it.'

'Doesn't believe in what? Respect?'

'Talking. About relationships. Says it just makes things

worse. Doesn't believe in saying "I love you" either. Says it's meaningless. Says the only thing that counts are actions.'

'Oh dear,' said Betsy mildly.

Kat tightened her grip on her friend's hand. 'What am I going to do?'

'Well. In the end you'll do the thing you think is best. I can't instruct you. But I would, respectfully, suggest that two years, or even three years, isn't all that long in the scheme of things. Every relationship has its road bumps. And the day-to-day business of living together is not exciting. Or romantic, especially. On the other hand... Kat, you deserve to be loved. And valued. That is absolutely *not* too much to ask. You don't have to be there if you don't want to be. You are a free agent.'

Kat propped her head in her hand and gazed at her friend for a long moment. I am a free agent, she thought. I am the master of my own destiny. The notion filled her with dread.

'You don't just throw things—people, relationships—away because you're bored.'

'No. They're not just for Christmas.'

'On the other hand, I don't want to... I don't want to just *settle* anymore. I don't want not-awful. I want more than that.'

Betsy made no response.

'On the other *other* hand...' Kat had been making an effort to keep her tone light. But suddenly she could feel the pain in her chest, tightness in her throat. She closed her eyes for a moment and swallowed. Tried again. 'On the other hand...' Her voice jerked unevenly on the last word. Betsy reached out again to clasp her hand. A minute

66

passed, then another. Kat struggled to re-find her voice.

Betsy squeezed her fingers and said, 'On the other hand, there's Bonnie.'

'People stay together because of the kids all the time.' Kat could hear the desperation in her own voice, hating it.

Betsy nodded. Topped up their wine glasses. The silence extended. Eventually she said, 'But I don't think you stay in a relationship because of someone else's kid.'

9

'Kat?'

'Yep?'

'I need you to find us a dumpster.'

'Isn't that Bev's department?' Kat said, tugging The Box one-handed against the curb.

'A dumpster-dumpster,' said BC impatiently. 'Not one of ours. Something in situ. Behind a Safeway or something. Something they can feed out of.'

'You're sending them dumpster-diving?'

'It's perfect. I don't know how we didn't think of it before. Can you imagine? Peru arse-up in a skip?'

Kat rubbed the centre of her forehead, weighing up the pros and cons. 'It's a fantastic idea,' she finally said. 'But we might be better off getting Bev to organise the bin and the contents, and I'll find a spot for us. A great spot. Using an actual dumpster might pose a few problems.'

'We have to use an actual dumpster. This is supposed to be reality, isn't it?'

'Well, yes,' said Kat, thinking of all ways in which this show was already a million miles from reality. 'But our dumpster would be a real dumpster. And the stuff in it would be real. And the location would be real. It just wouldn't be...*real* in the same way.'

'Exactly. That's why we need a real one.'

'And you really want them to eat out of it?'

'Of course. That's the whole point.'

'Don't you think that might be...?' *A lawsuit waiting to happen? An absolute nightmare for me to organise?* 'What if someone got sick?'

'Great! I mean, don't deliberately make someone sick. I'm not suggesting that. But if they did? Great telly. It'd make it seem really...'

'Real?'

'Exactly. We need to arc this up. We need some drama.'

You want drama? Kat spent a couple of seconds thinking of the ways in which she'd like to give BC a bit of drama. Then said: 'Well, we'll have the abseiling challenge.'

'That's a stunt. And viewers know it's a stunt. A great stunt, don't get me wrong. But we need to keep this real.'

'CBD?' sighed Kat.

'Of course CBD.'

'Vic Market?'

'Great. By Monday.'

BC hung up. Kat sat listening to the dial tone for a moment, put The Box back into gear then sat at the curb, riding the clutch, listening to the uneven revs and thinking, Must make time to drop the car in to Ange this week.

69

Clean out the car. Maybe fill up that skip. Drop the car in to Ange. Buy Bonnie's birthday present. Presents. No kid got just a single present these days. Sort out a high rise for the abseiling challenge. Talk with the lawyers about the begging thing. She was sure it was illegal. And find a food-filled dumpster. But not—not!—by Monday. Sheesh.

Switching off the engine, she made one firm decision. Coffee. There was a place a couple of blocks away that wasn't too bad. And where nobody gave you the evil eye if you spent an hour making phone calls.

Beyond the snug confines of the car the wind bit through her coat, worked its way through the loose folds of her scarf, trickling icily down her back. But the sun was shining and where it hit the back of her head and shoulders she felt the tension in her neck slowly dissolve.

Around her inappropriately dressed teenage girls, insulated from the weather by youth, vigour and the intoxication of school holidays, clattered in packs, exclaiming excitedly at nothing in particular. That'll be Bonnie one day, she thought, driving her hands deeper into her pockets, smiling. In a state of permanent semi-hysteria. It's all so important. Everything. Every slight, every compliment, every glance. Every small win a world-crushing triumph, every minor disappointment a catastrophe. I wonder what teenage girls will be wearing in 2026? Sequinned bikinis? Or perhaps there'll be a revolt. Perhaps the next generation will be anti-flesh. Perhaps they'll get about dressed like Quakers.

We live in hope, Kat thought, making further efforts to ensure not a millimetre of her own flesh was exposed to the elements, and began tramping up the hill.

Inside TwoForty the odour of slightly scorched coffee

70

grounds didn't bode well. She found a seat in the corner, placed her order, levered the various bags and satchels off her shoulder one by one and retrieved her phone from her pocket. Then sat tapping it gently against her lip. One step at a time, she thought, and dialled.

'Bev?'

'Hello sweetheart. What bizarre command has BC issued this time?'

'How did you know?'

Bev just gave a short laugh in reply.

'He wants them to go dumpster diving,' Kat said. 'At Vic Market.'

'Sally arse-up in a skip?'

Kat grinned. 'Peru arse-up in a skip, actually. But yes, that's the general idea.'

There was a pause. 'It's not a bad idea.'

'It's a great idea. It's making it happen that's giving me spasms. He wants a real skip. With real rubbish in it.'

'To keep it real.'

'Were you eavesdropping?'

'Do you know how many years I've been working with BC?'

'So you can imagine the conversation,' said Kat. 'Now the thing is, what do we do about it?'

'Well, having worked with BC for so long, I can guarantee he won't know the real from the unreal as long as you and I do our jobs properly, and no one tells him. You find the spot. I'll get a dumpster.'

Kat pinched her lip for a moment. 'You know what? The abseiling challenge. Why don't I have a look at the old YMCA building, the one near Franklin Street. We can push them off the side of that in the afternoon, then get them over to Vic Market in the evening for some delicious refuse. You can do the food as well as the skip?'

'I can do the food.'

'Bev, you are a champion.'

'I aim to please.'

Kat put down the phone, flexed her wrist, took a sip of her rapidly cooling coffee which, as she'd feared, was not first rate, not Wilson-standard, then slopped a dollop of it into her lap when the phone rang again. GC.

'Hi!' she said brightly, rubbing at the murky stain on her skirt.

'Kat. How are you, my lovely?'

'Good! Busy. Glad you called.' Kat filled her in on the latest directive from her co-producer.

'Of course. You and Bev do what you think best. Let's just keep the wheels turning. I'll look after things my end. And look, darling, I have some good news for you.'

'Uh huh?'

'It seems ridiculous for you to be one-out on such a big project. I've managed to find a few extra dollars in the budget to get you a helper.'

'That *is* good news. Anyone I know?'

'Well, no. She's quite a young girl. But very bright, and very keen. You will need to show her the ropes initially, but I know she'll be a tremendous help to you once she settles in.'

'What's she worked on before?'

'Well, just bits and pieces really.' Nothing, Kat thought. She's worked on nothing before. A work-experience kid. 'But, as I said, very bright. Her name's Heidi. Can you come by in the morning and meet her? Take her out on rounds with you?'

'Of course!' said Kat, her heart sinking. Heidi? Dear God. As if this job wasn't already complicated enough, now I'll be babysitting a goatherd too. Although Heidi wasn't the goatherd, was she? That was Clara. Still. 'Eight-thirty?'

'Perfect. See you then.'

'See you then!'

The phone quivered in her hand, then made its cheerful Tinker Bell announcement that a text message had arrived. From Miles.

Caught up here. Can you get B?

She gripped the phone, glanced at her watch. Three o'clock. Dialled the kindergarten. 'Samantha? It's Kat Kelly. Bonnie's…'

'Hi Kat. Miles just called. Are you on your way?'

'I don't suppose Bonnie could stay with you for a bit longer? I have some work to finish up.'

'Of course.' Kat could feel the disapproval. 'How much longer?'

'Just a couple of hours?'

'A couple of hours.'

'I'm sorry. Please tell Bonnie I'm sorry. And I'll be there as soon as I can. As close to 5pm as I can.'

'Of course. But please remember. We close at 5.15 sharp.'

'I'll be there by 5. Thanks.'

Dropping a couple of coins next to the dregs of the coffee, Kat hauled her baggage back onto her shoulder, buttoned her coat, and headed back to the car. The sun had disappeared and the wind was whipping through the city canyons, making her nose drip and her eyes stream.

By the time she reached The Box, her face and fingers were numb. Fumbling, unwilling to remove her gloves, she retrieved her keys. That's one thing you can say for a classic European auto, Kat thought. Great heaters. She unlocked the passenger door and dumped her bags on top of the rubbish on the seat, which scrunched and rustled and, disconcertingly, squished.

She sat for a minute while her fingers defrosted, listening to the emphysemic rise and fall of the engine—what was the problem there?—then pulled out into the thickening traffic and headed south down to Elizabeth Street, practising her lines as she went.

I'm with Channel Five. We're producing a great new reality series. Have you seen *The Apprentice*? *Survivor*? *Filthy Rich and Homeless*? No. No one except her and Harry and that bird from *The Age* had ever seen *Filthy Rich and Homeless*. And maybe stop with *The Apprentice* too. People didn't seem to like it. *Jamie's Kitchen*, about the homeless kids? That had a feel-good factor. Made the show sound like a public service. Or that singing one. *Choir of Hard Knocks*. Maybe start using that.

Have you seen *Survivor*? *Choir of Hard Knocks*? It's like a mix of those two, but something totally new. We're highlighting the plight of Melbourne's homeless, but in a family-friendly competition format. And we'd like to use your building. We'd like to use this *terrific* building—it's so quintessentially Melbourne...

On the passenger seat the phone rang again. 'Stop it! Leave me alone!' Kat shouted at it. Then took the call, pressed speaker.

'Yes?'

'Is that Miss Kelly?'

'This is Kat Kelly.'

'Miss Kelly, this is Bernard Toohey. You used my doorway for your TV show.'

'Yes, of course, I remember you.'

'You said $500?'

'That's right.'

'You said there'd be $500 in my account by Friday, but I just checked my balance and the money isn't there.'

'I'm sorry, Bernard. I'll chase that up for you right away. Let me just make a call to our producer. I'll call you back in five minutes.'

She hung up, turned right into Elizabeth Street, dialled GC.

'Kat. Everything okay?'

'Yep, just chasing up a payment to one of our locations. Bernard Toohey? The money was promised for Friday; it hasn't arrived.'

'Paperwork in?'

'It should all be in order, I did it on the day—that would have been Block Two.'

GC spelled out the name, Kat confirmed it. 'Hang on,' said GC. Kat hung on. 'Okay, sorted. The money should be there tomorrow.'

'Fantastic. Brilliant.'

Kat scrolled back through the calls, dialled, heaved her bags onto her shoulder, locked the car.

'Bernard? It's Kat Kelly from Channel Five. Just wanted to let you know the money should be in your account by Monday... No, no bother at all. Okay. Bye. Bye.'

'Now. Shut up,' Kat said sternly to her phone, switching it to silent. She pushed through the doors of the YMCA and approached the desk. Three-forty. Time for some fast talking. Vic Market would have to wait.

'Hi,' she said brightly. 'My name's Kat Kelly, I'm with Channel Five. Could I speak with the manager?'

10

'You're late.'

'I know I am, sweetheart. I'm sorry.'

'Daddy said you were on your way. Ages ago!'

'Daddy didn't realise I had work to do. Are you all set?'

Bonnie nodded, her ridiculous afro bouncing. Kat felt a pleasant tightening in her chest, crouched down and hugged her, inhaling playdough and orange and residual No More Tears. 'Let's go then.'

'Are we in The Box?'

'We are in The Box, my petal.'

'Is it going?'

'Like a dream. And it's warm as toast.'

Taking Bonnie's bony hand in hers, Kat crossed the road and unlocked the rear door of the car. 'In you hop. Need a hand with your seatbelt?'

Bonnie shook her head, curls jiggling again, and clambered into the booster seat. 'I can do it.'

Sliding behind the steering wheel, Kat felt the phone buzz in her pocket. She hesitated, turned the key in the ignition, grimaced as the engine reluctantly groaned to life, then pulled out the phone and, without looking to see who was calling, switched it off. I'm in a meeting, she thought. An important meeting.

Pulling out into the street, she caught Bonnie's eye in the rear-view mirror. 'So, my angel. What happened at kinder today?'

With a little prompting Bonnie began relating the important events of the day, with many extravagant hand gestures and much rolling of eyes. Life at four-and-eleven-twelfths wasn't as simple as grown-ups seemed to think.

Trying to avoid shifting down out of third—the old girl was running like silk in the higher gears, for some reason—Kat negotiated the back streets of North Fitzroy as the daylight faded, keeping one eye on Bonnie's vivid face and making appropriate expressions of delight or outrage as required.

Does she look like me? Kat wondered, not for the first time. She does look like me. We both have curly hair. Only hers much more so. She almost has my eyes. She does have my eyes. People often said, 'You have your mother's beautiful eyes,' and Kat and Bonnie would exchange conspiratorial looks.

Of course, they resembled each other mainly because Kat and Bonnie's actual mother resembled each other. Kat hadn't known whether to laugh, or just run, the first time they'd met. It was like staring at a glamorous younger sister. Miles seemed to have simply exchanged one diminutive blue-eyed brunette for another. And while Kat liked to think her and Victoria's personalities were poles apart, sometimes she wasn't so sure. Kat hoped she would never descend to Victoria's petty vindictiveness—the snide comments, her unsmiling blankness—but there was no question passive-aggressiveness had been Kat's stock in trade for years, especially in emotionally difficult situations.

Until I grew up. And on the upside, it comforted and pleased her to an inappropriate degree that she and Bonnie looked like blood. That she could gaze into those peculiarly all-seeing four-year-old eyes and see herself, feel connected.

'What?' said Bonnie.

'What?'

'You're looking at me funny.'

'Am I? I just like looking at you.'

Bonnie folded her hands in her lap. 'Well I am quite pretty,' she said contentedly.

As they neared Alexander Parade their progress slowed. Kat felt dwarfed by the broader streets with their lavish upholstery of Japanese four-wheel drives and tank-like Aussie classics, several complete with venetian blinds in the rear windows. Bonnie would be tall when she was fully-grown, but for now she was tiny. Kat was never going to be anything but tiny. The Box was deliciously tiny. For the first time that day she felt pleasantly invisible, creeping along in the shadows of the other vehicles, in no particular hurry, forced to slow down.

After two years it was also, finally, starting to feel like home. She was no longer bewildered by the labyrinth of one-way streets and secret laneways. She knew which pubs to visit, and which to avoid. Which cafes were overrated, which unfairly neglected. She even knew some of the neighbours. Up in Edinburgh Gardens she and Bonnie commiserated politely with the older residents about the invasion of their bocce court and bowling club by the impossibly cheerful hip young things.

The elderly weren't invigorated by mingling with the younger generation. They were exhausted by it. Kat knew how they felt. Bonnie tolerated endless hair-tousling and cheek-pinching as these serious matters were discussed, the same conversation each time, the same helpless shrugging and raising of hands. What could you do? They meant no harm, the young ones. The last thing these gentlemen in their shirts and ties and cardigans and caps would do is be impolite. But still.

Turning into Moor Street, Kat was surprised to see the lights on, and glanced at the clock on the dash. Not quite 5.30. She and Bonnie said in unison, but with markedly different emphasis: 'Daddy's home!' After squeezing The Box into a parking spot, Kat grabbed her luggage, took Bonnie's hand, and began the march to the front door.

Inside, she dumped her bags in the Good Room, switched the phone back on, glanced at her messages, while Bonnie thundered down the hallway and into her father's arms. Kat took a moment to compose herself, then made her own way into the kitchen where Miles, his hair on end, was wielding a large knife, his daughter on his hip, her legs dangling to his knees.

'Hello darling,' she said, kissing him briefly. And then, not able to help herself, 'I thought you were caught up at work.'

'I was never going to make three o'clock pick-up,' he said cheerfully, letting Bonnie slide to the floor. 'Script meeting that just wouldn't quit. But we finished up early so I stopped by Vic Market on the way home and got dinner sorted. Bought you some flowers, too.'

'Vic Market?' said Kat faintly, turning away to unbutton her coat.

'Duck,' he said. 'And I'm thinking braised lettuce. Maybe lentils?'

But Kat had wandered back down the hall to where her bags lay, one of them spilling sheaves of paper in a wide arc over the floor. On a side table were 'her' flowers, a rather stark arrangement of spiky natives she would never have chosen for herself in a fit. Shrugging out of her coat, she knelt and began stroking the paper back into some semblance of a pile, keeping one eye out for something in the stack that was urgent. But these were just maps, heavily annotated, already scoured and plundered for an increasingly outrageous roster of stunts and set-ups.

She slid them back into the appropriate satchel and remained resting on her heels, scrolling through the calls she'd missed. Again, the usual suspects. And one number—no name—that was vaguely familiar. Another location that hadn't been paid? Or one who'd changed their mind? Maybe to a yes? She needed a break.

As she pressed dial, Bonnie came trotting in, saw her squatting next to her bags and squatted down beside her. Kat smiled at her and reached out one hand to gently stroke her back, holding the phone to her ear with the other.

'Belt and Smythe!' said a woman brightly. Kat's hand on Bonnie's back went still. She resisted the urge to hang up.

'This is Kat Kelly. Someone from your office called earlier—about an hour ago?'

'Do you know what that might have been regarding?'

Achingly conscious of Bonnie next to her, listening

with interest, Kat said, 'I think it's probably my rental property—20 Addison Avenue.'

'And are you the owner or the tenant?'

'Owner,' said Kat dully.

'One moment, please!'

Shifting to sit cross-legged, she pulled Bonnie onto her lap and cradled her there as the young gentleman who managed her unit came on the line and asked, very politely, if and when they might expect advice on whether to re-let the property. 'I'm sorry. I did get your letter. Things have been crazy with work...'

He made understanding sounds.

'And things here are a bit... I'm not quite sure yet, about the property. About what I want to do next. Can I call you back in a couple of days?'

'By the end of the week?'

'I'll call Friday. Absolutely. Sorry to keep you waiting.'

He assured Kat it was no problem, while leaving her in no doubt it was in fact a great inconvenience, and both parties bid each other a cordial farewell.

'What are you girls up to in here?' Miles appeared in the doorway.

'We're talking about Kat's house,' Bonnie said instantly.

'What about Kat's house?'

Bonnie shrugged, having reached the limit of her intel on the matter, and struggled to her feet. Kat also rose, saying, 'Something smells good!'

'Duck,' said Miles again. Then: 'What about your house?'

'The tenants are moving out.'

'Is that a problem?'

'No,' said Kat. 'No.'

He looked at her for a moment. 'You shouldn't have any problem getting another tenant.'

'No.'

There was a silence, during which Bonnie looked from one to the other curiously.

Eventually, Miles said: 'Who's hungry?' And they all trooped back down to the kitchen.

After the dishes were cleared and Bonnie put to bed, Miles topped up their wine glasses and he and Kat sat down at the long table. Outside the wind was thrashing the denuded Japanese maple against the side windows but there was still no rain. As she smiled absently at the man across from her, Kat wondered idly about the extent to which they'd have to factor weather into the abseiling challenge. Was Harry coordinating with the stunt guy? Or GC? She mentally added that to her to-do list for the next day.

Now frowning slightly, she raised her eyes from her glass and took a breath, about to ask Miles if he had any experience with high altitude stunts, when he asked, 'Is there a problem with the unit?'

Unit? Oh. *Her* unit. Not now, she thought. But added Pleasant Young Gentleman to her mental Friday to-do list. She shook her head.

'No problem.'

'Are you thinking about selling it?'

She shook her head again, more emphatically. 'I don't know what I'm thinking. There's so much going on at work at the moment...'

'There's no reason why you couldn't just let it again,

and if you decide you do want to sell, you could always sell it tenanted,' he said with his usual calm. 'At some future date. Or wait till the next tenants move out. There's no rush.'

Kat gazed at him, thinking: *At some future date*. And suddenly knew with absolute certainty that she would never, ever sell her flat and buy into his house. Or any other house with him. At any future date. Everything else in her life, in her mind, might be uncertain, be in chaos, but she did not want to be here, with him, pinned by the weight of mutual assets, at some future date.

As for what she wanted tomorrow, and the next day, and at various more proximate dates...that was far less clear. Swallowing, she said mildly, 'No. There's no rush.'

Later, as Miles got ready for bed, then got into bed, then slept, she sat in Bonnie's room by the ghoulish glow of the nightlight (a giant mushroom, green and sickly, but Bonnie seemed to like it) and watched her breathe. The faint, warm scent of her made Kat's throat contract. She looked at the mad curls (*must organise a haircut for her*), the serious brows, the silky curve of her cheek. And thought: At some future date...

11

Kat knew GC and the work-experience kid were waiting for her upstairs, but she couldn't face either of them without chemical assistance. Wilson was out from behind the counter, sitting on one chair with his feet on another, a large book open in his lap.

'Aristotle?'

'Agassi,' he said, swinging his feet down and standing, the chair legs—long since missing their rubber stoppers—scraping painfully on the floor.

'He looks a bit like you,' she said, picking up the book and examining the cover.

'Same hairdresser.'

Back behind the counter, tamping the grounds into the filter, Wilson glanced at her. 'Everything okay?' Meeting his eyes—not brown after all, she realised, but hazel—Kat had a sudden temptation to unburden herself of the whole lot: *Survivor*, Miles, Bonnie, the flat, her growing conviction that despite spending more than four decades on this earth and to all appearances having achieved a successful professional if not personal life in the process, she had absolutely no idea what she was doing. With any of it. He should have been a barman.

Instead she shrugged lightly and said, 'About to start training up a new girl.'

'An underling?'

Kat grinned, nodded.

'So a promotion then. Congratulations.' Not getting much of a response to this, he added, 'Or maybe just a doubling of your workload?'

She exhaled, exchanged coins for the coffee. 'That's what I'm thinking, yeah.' Today the creamy foam on her latte was decorated with a smiley face. She glanced at him again. 'You know, that's just a little bit creepy,' she said. Wilson smiled to himself but made no further comment.

Draining the last of the coffee and dropping the empty cup into the bin by the door, Kat looked through the glass front of GC's office and caught her first glimpse of her new protégé. *Hello Heidi*. Not blonde, but in almost every other way exactly what she'd expected, a standard-model, well-to-do, twenty-first century twentysomething. Tall. Short skirt. Low-cut top. Lots of dangly jewellery. Legs-legs-legs and about a mile of cleavage. (Real? Kat wondered. You never knew any more, even with the kids.) Long glossy brown hair hanging loose, guaranteed to be an object of much flicking and fussing and endless finger grooming over the coming weeks. She would have a tattoo somewhere. Along with a large tote. An iPhone.

Impractical shoes. And an irritatingly high-pitched voice.

Exhaling another long breath and relaxing into her most welcoming smile, Kat waved cheerfully, tapped lightly on the doorframe and walked in. GC rose from behind the desk, saying, 'Kat,' with her usual warmth and gesturing to the bright young thing who had also risen, towering over her in, yes, wildly impractical platform pumps. 'This is Heidi van Doort. Heidi, our wonderful location manager, Kat Kelly.'

With a great clanking of costume jewellery the two women shook hands, Kat—if nothing else, an expert dissimulator—masking her rising dismay. Van Doort? Daughter of the legendary director? That explained a lot. Instead she simply said, 'Heidi. Lovely to meet you.'

'Great to meet you too!'

There was indeed a tattoo—Asian script—on the inside of Heidi's right wrist, but her voice was in fact a pleasant contralto, and when she dropped her hand and stood awkwardly, smiling but clearly at a complete loss as to what to do next, Kat felt a surge of warmth towards her.

The jewellery reminded her irresistibly of Bonnie, who last night had adorned herself with the entire contents of her own jewellery box, before declaring with satisfaction, 'There. Now I look grown-up.'

Heidi may turn out to be a complete waste of time when Kat had precious little to spare, but she was also just a big gangly kid. That impression was confirmed when she followed up the handshake by saying enthusiastically, 'I am so stoked to be working with you. I really, really appreciate it.'

'My pleasure,' Kat said. 'It's a fascinating shoot. And I could certainly use some help.'

'So,' said GC, gesturing for them all to sit. 'How do we play it from here?'

Heidi looked at Kat, tense with pleasant anticipation.

'Well, I thought for today Heidi could just ride shotgun with me. We can chat in the car. You can tell me about whatever experience you've had so far. I can explain the kinds of things I do and the things I'd like you to be able to help me with. I need to go by Unit sometime today, so I can introduce you to some people there. How does that sound?'

'Great!' said Heidi.

GC nodded. 'Terrific. Do you need anything from me?'

Kat shook her head. 'Not right now. Do we have a stunt guy on board yet?'

'Working on it. It'll have to be someone who can squeeze in the occasional consult—I don't think we're going to be able to get someone full time. All these damn cop dramas. And the movies in Queensland.'

'Right. Shall we hit the road?'

Heidi leapt to her feet, retrieved her own bag (yes, a large patent tote, also jangling with decorative baubles and a metallic plaque displaying the name of its fashionable manufacturer). In her flat Camper boots Kat's head barely topped the girl's shoulder.

'Do you have a coat?'

Heidi shook her head.

'Well, there's a good heater in the car.'

The enthusiasm of her puppyish new friend suffered its first setback when she set eyes on The Box.

'Wow,' she said. 'It's like—an antique.'

'With cars, you call them vintage.'

Heidi nodded. 'Cool.' Then: 'We could take my car, if you like?', gesturing to a late model Prius parked a few spaces down. 'My dad bought it for me,' she added, with faint embarrassment.

'Twenty-first?'

'Eighteenth.'

Kat smiled at her. 'I'm kind of used to mine. And I'll be driving for now. It's nicer than it looks.' At least she'd remembered to clear a couple of weeks' worth of fruit scraps, water bottles, coffee cups and sandwich wrappers from the front seat, and squished the booster seat into the boot.

Kat pushed the passenger seat back as far as it would go, manoeuvred her bags onto the back seat, and slid behind the wheel. Heidi climbed in next to her, her own bag clutched nervously on her lap, and took in the glory of The Box's dash. 'Wow,' she said again. With a silent prayer Kat turned the ignition and in answer her old friend started first time.

'Am I right in thinking your dad's Gert van Doort?' Kat asked casually as they pulled out onto Footscray Road.

'Yep,' said Heidi.

Kat shot her a glance. 'Is that a blessing or a curse?'

'Um, both probably.'

'Which part's the blessing?'

'Well, he's a great dad. And, you know, he has interesting friends. You get to meet a lot of famous people. Travel a lot. I went with him to the Oscars last year. That was cool, even though we didn't win.'

'And the curse?'

There was a brief silence, then Heidi said, 'Like, no

offence or anything, but sometimes people think I only want to work in film and TV because Dad does. That I expect special treatment or something. That I'm, like, a bit of a princess or something. And I'm so not!'

'Plenty of people go into the family business.'

'Exactly! And Dad won't let me work on his own shoots. But we've known Genevieve for, like, years. And she said she'd give me a shot. So here I am.'

'She's a nice person.'

'She is. And she said you're a nice person too.'

Did she now, thought Kat.

Ice broken, Heidi proceeded to embark on a detailed rundown of her ambitions (producing), experience (zero, but a life spent hanging round shoots big and small), education (expensive private school, enrolled in film school next year). It was a recital that carried them all the way to Elizabeth Street.

Squeezing The Box into a space behind the market redundantly marked 'Small Car', Kat outlined her mission for the morning. To discover who owned the Vic Market dumpsters, when they were emptied, what was required to gain access to the spaces, and firm up a date when they could film the stunt.

'I actually know a couple of freegans!' Heidi volunteered, her excitement levels rising again.

'You do?' Kat said with some astonishment.

'Yeah! I could ask them, like, when they go diving, where the best spots are.'

'Do they come here?'

'Oh yeah. This is, like, David Jones Food Hall to them.'

'Have you ever done it?'

'Omigodno! Eew!'

'But your friends do?'

'Well, not friends exactly. But a girl I used to hang out with at school. She and her boyfriend are, like, throwing off the capitalist yoke and all that. I've got her number. She probably won't be awake but I can text her right now…'

'Could you? That'd be great.'

Kat sat and watched her expertly tap out a message on her phone to a friend who was obviously not so anti-capitalist that she didn't have a mobile. Kat could feel her own phone buzzing in her coat pocket, glanced at it, decided it could wait. When Heidi was finished she said, 'Thank you. That's great. We need all the help we can get.'

'No, thank you. Seriously. It's so great you're letting me tag along with you. I really, really appreciate it.'

As they wriggled out of the car, retrieved their bags, locked the doors, Kat asked, 'Why me? Why not G— Genevieve? Especially if you're interested in producing.'

Heidi leaned towards her earnestly. 'I think it's really important to start from the ground up, don't you?'

12

As Kat slid the phone back into her pocket it finally started to rain in a half-hearted manner, just enough to blear the already dust-smeared windshield. She switched the wipers on, then off, then on again. One of The Box's manifold period features was, of course, no intermittent option on the windscreen wipers. Not that it mattered, especially. That unconscious flick of her finger as she drove—on, off, on—was as automatic to her as changing gears. And tonight, even that persistent hiccup when she was idling or in first gear hardly penetrated. She was on autopilot: driving, at work. The whole external world had become a blur.

Heidi, bless her, was a high-energy kind of companion. She loved a chat. Indeed, she seemed compelled to chat whenever a silence of more than twenty seconds opened up between them. Inevitably, the content of those chats was often inconsequential, bordering on inane. She hadn't quite shaken that teen tendency to self-obsession. Kat had no particular desire to share personal details with her new offsider, but over the course of the week had become aware that while she was now fully across Heidi's family, friends, lovers, ambitions, favourite foods, health concerns and body issues, Heidi knew nothing about Kat beyond her name, job description, and how she took her coffee.

Still, as she'd said to GC in her debrief, Heidi was at least a narcissist with *potential*. She'd spent her life around film and television sets and people. She had a rudimentary understanding of the various players and their tasks, and was quick to pick up and assimilate the detail Kat had provided while they'd cruised inner Melbourne, attended meetings and short bursts of filming, and shuffled Council paperwork back at the office.

In another week or so she'd probably be able to undertake some real work, unsupervised. Kat couldn't wait. She longed above anything to have The Box to herself again; her own warm, quiet bubble; her purring, undemanding friend. She longed for silence. For solitude. Or as much of either as she was likely to get, neck-deep in a production as chaotic as this one was turning out to be.

At its best, TV was like an old-fashioned watch: dozens of tiny cogs and springs and wheels whirring, locking, releasing with a rhythm that was somehow both frantic and soothing. Now someone (well, BC) had prised off the back and started fiddling with the mechanism, and bits (budgets, schedules, locations, people) were flying loose in every direction. As it was BC doing the fiddling, Kat held out hope that he'd eventually manage to fiddle all the bits back into place and get the damn thing working again. In the meantime...

She was exhausted, and there was one task left un-ticked on her Friday to-do list. She chose Brunswick Street, knowing the end-of-week peak-hour would delay her homecoming by a good twenty minutes. Flicked the wipers on, then off, then on. And let the dark undercurrent of thought she'd been unable to examine all week slowly bubble to the surface.

As Miles had said, there was no rush. There was no reason she couldn't just re-let the unit and take her time, see how things evolved. Because—it was one of the things she kept coming back to—Miles was not a bad person. He cooked for her and, as often as not, did the dishes too. He uncomplainingly made up the financial shortfall between her contribution to the household and his. When she made a special effort with her appearance, he noticed. Sometimes he bought her flowers, more often a book or DVD he thought she might like.

On the downside, they were mostly books and DVDs he liked. And when she scrolled back through their history to the time when she was actively happy—or at least thought she was—those lively conversations seemed much more like her listening, entranced, as he told tales of his creative plans and exotic past. She had loved his seriousness, his earnestness, his high-mindedness. His sheer lack of cruelty had seemed to her, at the time, the very definition of love.

She had even quite liked his teasing her for her own lack of earnestness and high-mindedness. She didn't mind playing the fall guy to his straight man; she was simply giddy with the idea of them as a team. And of course, in the beginning, the sex had been great. Until he seemed to decide that the time for regular, sweaty, delirious romps had passed; that they should settle down. He seemed to think assuring her that he found her attractive was an acceptable substitute. What he didn't seem to understand was that she wasn't seeking reassurance. She simply wanted sex.

Sighing, Kat shifted up into second at a longish break in the crawl of traffic and crossed Gertrude Street. You're just a slut, she told herself. Slutty, and irredeemably lowbrow. The teasing had gradually become more pointed, more critical. For a while Miles had encouraged her to go after a different kind of project. And she certainly had no objection to twenty-two episode ABC dramas. But not only were they few and far between, she actually liked the work she did. She liked the energy of it, the not-too-seriousness of it, the fact that millions of people actually watched it. And in this respect, she knew, she had gravely disappointed him.

Despite his protestations, she knew Miles had no interest in hearing about her day at work. Kat suspected it was both inconsequential and faintly embarrassing to him. He felt the same way about most of her friends. With the exception of Harry. Everyone liked Harry. The thing is, she thought dolefully, echoing her barely articulated complaint to Betsy, Miles and I have nothing in common.

Worse, she was increasingly made to feel that lack of commonality was a failing on her part. That she had disappointed him—continued to disappoint him. That she was, to put it bluntly, not good enough. He still implied that she could be good enough, if she'd only make the effort. And a few years ago she might have seriously taken that on board. Accepted she was at fault. Tried harder. Tried to change. Tried to be worthy.

But Kat was pretty sure she *was* worthy. And now, idling at the pedestrian lights outside the Asian grocer, the darkest part of that dark undercurrent—like a corpse that kept threatening to break the surface—came bubbling into her consciousness. That there were only two real reasons she was delaying the decision to re-let her unit.

One. She loved Miles' house. Loved the bathroom and the kitchen and the furniture and the fireplace and the central heating and the light fittings and its all-round perfectness. It was, somewhat in miniature, a *Brothers & Sisters* house, a *Parenthood* house, the quintessential middle-class creative's house. On a bank executive's budget. If she were scouting for a house for a character that was her, Miles' house would be that house.

Two. She loved Bonnie. She loved Bonnie more than the house, and Miles, and her job, and The Box all put together. That was a lot of love. A whole city, a continent, an entire planet of love. She would give up all those things, every other thing she loved, every friend she had, every ambition, every man, present and future, in an instant for Bonnie. But unlike actual parental love, when you were allowed—indeed, were obliged—to love like that, she wasn't supposed to love Bonnie that much.

She was not Bonnie's mother. Bonnie had a mother who, despite a habit of delivering her daughter every second week accompanied by a suitcase full of dirty laundry, seemed to love Bonnie with precisely that extravagance. Even Miles, in his rather bloodless way, adored her: her regular messy presence in his otherwise impeccably ordered life was testament to that. Kat's overwhelming love was not only surplus to requirements, it was quite out of order. And while Kat had spent pretty much all her adult life enmeshed in inappropriate orgies of love, this was different from all the years spent enslaved by a variety of Mr Wrongs.

Because, she thought, drawing a ragged breath, kids belonged to you. Despite the oft-quoted epithets of Kahlil Gibran, there was a bond between parents and children that was like ownership, an unbreakable contract that existed in no other relationship. And it was a bond she had come to realise she would never have.

That cruel thought rose up to torment her, closing her throat and making her eyes sting. *I will never know what it's like to grow another human being.* Miles had made it clear another child was not on the cards. At the time she'd been okay with that. They had Bonnie. Now, thought Kat, I'm racing towards my mid-forties and in a relationship that's on the rocks. Even without Miles, the hard lonely road of deliberate single motherhood was not for her (and certainly not the agony of IVF). She'd always wanted the package, the family. Now it was too late.

The reality is, she said to herself, my time is up. I will never be connected to another human being by blood. There is no one in this world that is mine, and there never will be. I will never be anybody's mother. And while I can love Bonnie with a ferocity that's terrifying, I am not Bonnie's mother. I never will be.

Now Kat was crying so hard she couldn't see the road in front of her; just a wavering blur of tail lights and streetlights. Her arms and legs were trembling. She forced herself to indicate, shift down, and pull over into a loading zone, eyes and nose streaming. The Box gurgled and hiccupped. The windows first fogged then started to drip as Kat sat there with her hands gripping the steering wheel, mouth pulled into an open grimace, shuddering with grief.

Eventually her gasping abated. She took one deep breath, then another. Groped in the glove box for tissues and blew her nose noisily, twice. Mopped her eyes and face. She breathed again, inhaling leather and wood and motor oil and all that old-car smell, as distinctive and intoxicating as new car smell. Oh Mum, she thought. What am I going to do?

Kat sat for a long time, breathing, letting her heart rate gradually subside, until she felt she had command of herself, of her voice.

Fished her phone out of her pocket and dialled. After four rings it was answered: 'Belt and Smythe!'

13

Over dinner, her lack of appetite was so marked that even Bonnie commented on it. ('Did Dad cook yours wrong?') Miles had given her a long look but said nothing. The emotional force field with which he surrounded himself was increasingly oppressive.

A week had passed since she'd made the call to her real-estate agent, a week in which she had several times picked up the phone—even dialling the number on a couple of occasions—desperate to take it all back. But each time she hadn't made the call. She was, she knew, not so much desperate to take it all back as desperate for things to be different. Desperate for Miles to be a different person, to be the friend and soulmate and true partner she wanted so badly, and had tried to create in him by sheer force of will and deluded optimism.

While she blamed him for wanting her to be someone she was not, Kat knew she was just as guilty. And just as her steadfast refusal to morph into someone both more ambitious and more acquiescent had clearly become a source of growing irritation to him, his absolute inability to be the funny, listening, supportive lover she yearned for was something she knew she couldn't continue to live with.

It wasn't his fault. He was who he was. If his refusal to even have the conversation, to discuss how they might be happier together, frustrated her mightily, she knew unequivocally that, should they have that conversation, his list of demands for her would be as impossible to fulfil as hers for him.

That was what she kept coming back to, over and over again. Neither of them was going to change. If all they had been was lovers, it would have been so simple.

But it wasn't that simple.

Nor was it even a question of: How much am I prepared to sacrifice for Bonnie? If Bonnie had actually needed her, there would have been no question at all. If one or both of her actual parents had been derelict, Kat would have sacrificed everything, have happily tolerated any slight or insult, have endured a lifetime of Miles' special brand of emotional neglect, in order to care for her.

But Bonnie didn't need her. She needed Bonnie. Or at least felt like she did. And that, Kat knew, was neither right nor healthy.

Which brought her to now, this evening, another rainy Friday and a rising tide of nausea so powerful she'd hardly been able to look at her dinner, let alone eat it. Leaving Miles to clear up, she took Bonnie to the bathroom to wash her face and clean her teeth, then tucked her in to bed. During the ordinary routines she'd managed to maintain her usual cheerful demeanour. They read a book together, then another. Kat would have read a third, and a fourth, kept on until dawn, but Bonnie yawned and pushed *Pippi Longstocking* to the floor. 'I'm sleepy,' she said.

Kat felt tears sting her eyes. I will miss you so much, she thought. I will miss every single thing about you. I will miss sponging goop from around your mouth and dragging a brush through the birds' nest of your hair. Sitting on the edge of your bed. Reading you stories. Bonnie would go back to her mother in the morning. Kat hadn't given a great deal of thought to what she'd do in the weeks until her flat was vacant, but she knew she couldn't stay here indefinitely. *By the time Bonnie comes back, will I be gone?*

The pain in her chest was choking her. She stretched out on the bed and wrapped her arms around the girl. 'I love you,' she murmured raggedly.

'Mmm,' said Bonnie.

Kat laid her cheek against Bonnie's cheek, breathed deeply, hugged her closer.

'You're squashing me,' said Bonnie, elbowing her in the ribs. Kat made a spurt of sound, half sob, half laugh, and slid off the bed. Kissed her cheek. Stroked her hair. 'Sweet dreams,' she whispered.

'Night,' murmured Bonnie, and burrowed down under the doona.

With Miles ensconced in the study Kat locked herself in the bathroom, ran the tap, and wept as quietly as she could for as long as she dared. Then rapped sharply on the study door, opened it without waiting for a response, and said, with rather more authority than she was used to employing with him, 'I need to talk to you.'

'Can it wait? I need to finish this.'

'No.'

Miles sighed, laid down his pen, and removed his reading glasses. 'What is it?'

Kat took a breath. 'I've decided not to re-let the flat.'

Miles' eyebrows shot up. 'You're going to sell?'

'No. I'm going to move back in myself.'

'*What?*'

Kat recoiled a little. 'I'm...I'm going to move back into my flat.'

'You're *leaving* me?'

'I...I guess. Yes.'

'You *guess* you're leaving me.' Miles straightened in his chair, directing her the kind of look he usually reserved for his least competent underlings.

'I... Yes.'

'Right. Just like that. Did it occur to you it might be polite to discuss it with me first?'

'I... You... We don't... I know you don't like talking about things...'

'So this is my fault?'

Yes, thought Kat. 'No,' she said. 'Of course not.'

'There's someone else.'

'No!'

'Then what? When did you come to this unilateral decision you thought I wouldn't be interested in discussing?'

Kat felt her face flush, her hands start to tingle. *I have not really thought this through, have I?* She had, bizarrely, not thought for a moment about how he might feel about it all. Mainly, she thought, because she'd got used to the idea that he wasn't feeling much at all when it came to her. She had certainly rehearsed her opening lines. And then imagined something along the lines of sleeping on the couch for a while followed by staying in Betsy's guest room for a week. She thought Miles might be sad. She had not expected this. This rage.

'Well?'

'It wasn't an easy decision to make,' she said, struggling to stay on script, hoping by keeping her voice down she might encourage him to lower his.

'Is that supposed to make me feel better?'

'I'm sorry.'

'Well obviously you're not. How long have you been living here, under my roof, hatching your escape plans?'

'Only... Just this week. I got the notice from the agents, I thought about it—a lot, I really did.'

'But you never mentioned it to me.'

'I did mention it to you.'

'Not, "Miles, my flat's empty, I'm leaving you."'

'I never thought about it like that.'

'How did you think about it? "Thank God. At last I can get out of here."'

Kat held out both hands placatingly, hating every second of this, casting a worried look at the door, where Bonnie slept across the hall.

'I just felt... I just felt like we weren't really working as a couple any more,' she whispered.

'And whose fault is that?'

'It's no one's fault.'

'It's always someone's fault. Really, Kat, I thought you were better than that shit. Not working as a couple? What are we—in a scene from *Neighbours*?'

'I don't think you love me any more.'

'Love!' Miles jumped out of his chair. 'You're always banging on about love. Can you at least spare me the fucking clichés, Kat? What about respect? What about a bit of respect for me?'

'Dad...?' came Bonnie's querulous voice from the other room.

'Go to sleep!' snapped Miles.

'Keep your voice down,' hissed Kat.

'Don't you dare tell me what to do. Don't you dare tell me how to speak to my daughter.'

Kat flinched. Now Miles was standing over her, flushed, his hands balled in his pockets. 'After all I've done for you. I cannot believe your gall.'

Kat straightened a little. 'I did try to talk with you about this. And you told me to get over it.'

'That's exactly what you should do. Jesus wept, Kat! Can't you just be thankful for what you've got? I took you in, I paid your bills, I cooked your meals, I put up with your low-rent friends and your shitty job, and all I ever asked for in return was a bit of peace and quiet, and a bit of respect.'

'Miles!' Kat sobbed, horrified.

'Dad? Kat? Dad?'

'GO TO SLEEP!'

'Miles, for God's sake...'

'Get out. You don't want to live here anymore? Get out.'

Kat rose shakily from her chair and backed out of the room. In the bedroom, sobbing now, she fumbled with her overnight bag, stuffing in the first clothes and underwear that came to hand, grabbing odd items from the bathroom. Miles thrust her handbag into her free hand as Bonnie appeared in the doorway.

'Kat?' She took in Kat's tear-streaked face, the fixed look on her father's, the bags. 'Kat! Kat!'

'I have to...'

'Kat's leaving. Go to bed,' said Miles.

'Miles, please...'

'Get out. Now.'

'I want Kat! I want Kat!' sobbed Bonnie, struggling to get past her father's legs as Kat backed out the front door. For a moment she stood on the path, facing them, father and daughter silhouetted in the light from the hallway, Bonnie still wailing Kat's name.

'Bonnie,' said Kat as evenly as she could, crouching down and stretching out both arms.

'Don't. Touch. Her.' Miles pushed Bonnie back behind him and slammed the door.

14

'Jesus. Where did you spend the night? Under a bridge?'

Kat held one hand up tiredly. Not now. Opened the fridge, pulled out a bottle of water, drank extravagantly. 'In the car,' she croaked. Her throat was raw, her eyes burning. She felt sticky and grubby and suspected her hair now resembled a late 1970s disco fro. And not in a good way. It was possible she didn't smell that great either, but that was the least of her worries.

Wilson had started to smile. Then realised she was serious. 'Oh dear,' he said. And made them both a coffee.

She finished the water and tasted the coffee, which hit her stomach with a gurgling protest, loud in the almost-empty room. There is no end to my glamour, Kat thought dolefully. Eventually she cleared her throat and gave him a halting, expurgated version of her big Friday night.

Miles' unexpected fury. Her own foolishness in not thinking things through. Bonnie's hysteria. A scene worthy of the most overwrought midday movie.

Seeking the meagre comfort of The Box, she had sat in the car and cried. Again. Then fallen asleep.

At dawn she woke, stiff, sore and horribly dehydrated, and cried a little more, but without real enthusiasm. She needed water, and coffee, but nothing would have induced her to brave the Brunswick Street crowd. The early dog walking, jogging, outdoor-yoga strangers would have been bad enough, but running into someone she knew? Intolerable. Not to mention the straggling Young Things heading home for the night. *No. No. No.*

Nor did she want to sit parked outside Miles' house a moment longer. So in lieu of a firm destination she'd started up The Box and cruised aimlessly for an hour until she found herself drifting towards Footscray, and the office. Her second home. It had not occurred to her that Wilson might be in business on a Saturday morning. But she was here now. And almost glad, although she was at a loss to explain why.

Wilson offered no comment. Just removed their empty cups and handed her a muffin, which she picked at un-enthusiastically, while he made more coffee. When he was seated opposite her again, he said, 'You can't keep sleeping in your car.'

Kat nodded mutely.

'Can you stay with a friend?'

'I can't face anyone right now,' she whispered. 'I just… I need some time alone.'

'You need a cave to hide in,' Wilson said, watching her over the rim of his cup.

Kat nodded again.

'Can you afford a hotel?'

'A cheap one,' she murmured.

'They're the best kind,' said Wilson, pulling his phone out of his pocket and initiating some kind of complicated search-and-rescue manoeuvre. After a longish period of stroking, pinching and tapping the screen, he found a pen on the counter and scribbled on the margin of the page of a newspaper, tore it neatly, and handed it to her. 'Footscray Best Western. Cheaper by the week. It's just over on Barkly Street.'

She took the slip of paper. 'Thank you.'

He stood and laid a very large hand briefly on the top of her head. 'You're welcome,' he murmured.

The sun was fully risen now and last night's drizzling rain had vanished. It was going to be a beautiful winter's day. The combination of fatigue and caffeine was making Kat's hands tremble. She clasped them together, for a moment unable to even form the thought of movement, let alone enact it.

Eventually Wilson said, 'It's about to hit rush hour here. I can't have you sitting there looking like the Wicked Witch of the West. You'll frighten everyone off.'

Kat managed a smile and pushed herself to her feet.

'Rush hour? Really?'

'Really. Saturday morning's how I pay the rent for the week.' He looked at her kindly. 'Eat something. Have a shower. Go to bed. Things won't seem so bad tomorrow.'

Kat looked around vaguely, patted the pockets of her coat. 'I've left my purse in the car.'

'It's on the house. Now go away.'

'I owe you.'

'See you Monday.'

Wilson was right, thought Kat, dumping her bags on the bed. Cheap motels are the best kind. Tiny soaps and thin white towels in the bathroom, an electric jug and a neat collection of teabags on the counter, long-life milk in the fridge. Everything wrapped in waxy paper for hygiene purposes, though she'd never been clear what particular sanitary benefits waxy paper bestowed.

On some jobs they put you up somewhere ritzy but Kat could never relax. They weren't the kinds of rooms you felt like you could put your feet on the furniture. In a cheap motel you felt okay about sitting up in bed in the middle of the day watching telly, and leaving your wet towels on the bathroom floor. Ritzy places made her slightly anxious. Cheap ones calmed her down. You were invisible in a cheap motel. You had nothing to prove. No one expected anything of you. It was, indeed, the sensible alternative to a cave or a cupboard. 'Thank you,' she murmured.

Putting the kettle on, she emptied out her holdall. All things considered, she'd done all right. There was a change of clothes that would do for work on Monday, some clean underwear, basic toiletries, but no toothbrush, and no tights. She could get both at the 7-Eleven later. For now, she stacked her work things neatly on the bench, switched off her mobile (no charger), shook out her day clothes and hung them in the wardrobe. Made a cup of herbal tea, which she left to steep while she stood under the shower. The water felt good on her swollen eyes and crazy hair. Then drew the curtains and lay down between the thick, rough sheets in the half light, and waited for sleep to come.

15

Kat was surprised by the physicality of it. She felt constantly nauseous, although if she remembered to eat the food went down okay. All she really wanted to do was lie quietly on the nondescript nylon bedspread in her darkened motel room until there was nothing left of her but a shadowy outline (she was sure she'd seen that in an old *Twilight Zone*). But while pining away might be all very well for Victorian heroines, Kat just didn't have that option.

The great, shuddering machine that was *Survivor: CBD* rolled on and at the moment she was one of the central cogs. Having scrambled half-cocked into production, much of what they'd already filmed was going to be trashed. Despite its manifest *un*reality on many levels, it only worked if they began properly at the beginning. Kat and Ted had warned everyone weeks ago that remaking the series as *Survivor* was going to entail starting completely afresh. Sure enough, they were back at square one. While the producers and director frantically scouted for a host, she and Heidi had spent the week trawling the city's most obscure quarters looking for three permanent locations: the campsites for the two teams of contestants, and an urban equivalent of Tribal Council.

The latter was less of a problem. It would have been nice to leave something set up, but she and Bev had agreed that it wasn't too big an ask to dismantle and reassemble their old oil drum, milk crates and beat-up sofa once a week, and if they shot in the dead of night the local Council was relatively tolerant.

The campsites were another matter entirely. The Council had unequivocally objected to having two groups of over-excited middle-class homeless people camped in old shipping containers for an indefinite period. So the sites would have to be on privately owned ground. Somewhere they could actually get the containers in and out, too. The logistics of it all made Kat's eyes water.

Still, if all they'd wanted were domestic kitchen and bedroom scenes they probably wouldn't have bothered hiring her. Weird shit was her speciality, and she took pride in that. And although getting out of bed every morning was an almighty effort—as was attending even partially to Heidi's incessant chatter—it was good to be busy, to have company. Kat's fatigue had reached new, rare levels but the frenetic activity ensured other less fruitful thoughts were mostly crowded out of her mind.

And today... *Well, today just might be a good day.* Yesterday, while Heidi had sat on one side of the desk filling out interminable permission forms, Kat sat on the other painstakingly crosschecking promising slivers of land with title deeds. To her amazement she'd unearthed a handful of locations—more like a pinch, really—that seemed to be private easements, not public thoroughfares. So she was almost smiling when she stopped in for a coffee before going upstairs to collect her helper.

'You're looking better,' Wilson said. 'How's the Footscray Hilton?'

'Perfect. Feels like home.' She strategically sipped the foam from the top of her cup to obscure the smiley face he'd carved into the crema. Having discovered how much she disliked it, Wilson had felt compelled to include it as a final flourish whenever the opportunity arose. It was a small price to pay for his kindness in her hour of need, and she said now, 'I haven't had the chance to say how much I appreciate...everything. You weren't a social worker in a previous life, by any chance?'

'God no,' he said. 'A chemist.'

She laughed. 'Really? In the white coat? Behind the high counter?' It was an image almost too ludicrous to entertain.

'You're thinking pharmacist. Yes to the white coat, but no to the high counter. A chemist. A scientist.'

It was still a perfectly ridiculous idea. Kat looked at him through narrowed eyes, trying to picture it. 'With microscopes and things.'

'Yes. Microscopes. Test tubes. Bunsen burners. All the regulation gear.' He smiled at her scepticism. 'I had hair then. And glasses. I know it's kind of hard to imagine.'

Kat flushed. 'I wasn't thinking anything of the kind.' Although, of course, she had been. It was like casting Michael Chiklis as a friendly GP. Although he had gone straight from brutal cop in *The Shield* to suburban dad in *No Ordinary Family*, so maybe it wasn't so crazy after all. She said: 'That's a real career switch.'

'Not really. They say making coffee's an art, but actually it's a science. The more you know about molecular biology the better you are behind the Gaggia. Plus, I needed to get out of there. It's true what they say about scientists.'

'What do they say about scientists?'

'They're weird.'

'Unlike TV people.'

'TV people are kind of interesting-weird. And can form whole sentences. Scientists are more...'

'*Big Bang Theory*?'

'My second-favourite show. Yes. Exactly.'

'So which one were you? Sheldon? Leonard? Howard? Or Raj?'

'None of the above. I was the cool motorbike-riding astrophysicist Penny dated in season one, of course.'

Now *that*, thought Kat appreciatively, I can imagine. But she simply said, 'Of course you were', and drained the last of her coffee.

Upstairs, Kat shuddered a little at Heidi's outfit. She wasn't sure of the protocol or even the ethics of instructing the girl on the way she dressed. Her fair-minded self told her it was none of her business. And if you couldn't dress the way you wanted in this line of business, when could you? Her professional, grumpy-old-woman self felt irritated and faintly embarrassed at dragging Disco Bratz around after her, especially when she had serious business to conduct. Appearances mattered when you were trying to persuade someone to do something not even slightly in their interests. If they took one look at them and shut the door it would be disastrous.

Then again, said her fair-minded self, depending on who answered the door Heidi's acres of flesh and predilection for glittery things might as easily swing the deal. So Kat swallowed her qualms and ushered her young friend down to the car.

Handing her the *Melways,* she said, 'I'll need you to navigate for me today.'

Heidi looked at the tattered, bent-spined book warily. 'Read a map?'

'That's right,' said Kat, passing over a list of addresses.

'Don't you have GPS?'

'Nope.'

'They're pretty reliable these days, you know. If you use them properly. Or I have Google Maps on my phone.'

'It's not about just getting from A to B,' said Kat. 'You want to develop a feel for the place. A context. Alternative routes in and out. It's about the location, remember, not just the destination.'

Heidi bit at her lip anxiously. There was a moment's silence. Then Kat switched off the engine, reached for the book of maps and said tartly, 'Here. I'll show you how to do it. It's easy.'

Fortunately for both of them Heidi mastered the arcane art of looking up streets in the *Melways* relatively easily. If she had to keep turning the map around to work out left from right and east from west... Well, that was okay. So did Kat.

Finding where they needed to go was less straight-forward, especially as Kat, on high alert, kept detouring down promising laneways in the hope of finding something useful, better, more interesting. Laneways that more often than not ended in abrupt dead-ends or walkways so narrow not even The Box could squeeze through. After being sent out to scout ahead for the fourth or fifth time, Heidi returned to the car with bad news, muddy heels, and in a rising temper. 'Why can't you just go where I tell you to go? I thought that was the whole point? We're spending the whole morning driving round the city backwards!'

Kat leaned out the driver's window and took a couple of quick photos of a building she liked the look of, crisscrossed over five floors by an ancient wooden fire escape. There was a challenge for the Survivors in that, for sure. Although shooting it might be a problem. Jotting down the address in her notebook, Kat became aware of Heidi's glare.

'Mistakes,' she said blithely, grinding The Box into reverse and taking a quick look over her shoulder, 'are simply the opportunity for creativity.'

Heidi refastened her seatbelt and turned her face towards the window, grinning reluctantly. 'Whatevs,' she said.

Back on Little Collins Street, idling in a loading zone, Kat handed her the *Melways* again. 'But you're right. We need to get these sorted. Can you get us back to that first one from here?'

Sighing theatrically, Heidi took the book. 'What would you do without me?'

'I'd be lost, my dear. Completely lost.'

After only half-a-dozen more wrong turns they found themselves at their first location. Kat parked and got out of the car with a growing sense of excitement. The backs of old Victorian buildings rose up on all sides, the entrance a scant car's-width. But the square itself—half cobbled, half broken concrete—was substantial, and while the direct egress was narrow, that stretch of the laneway was blessedly short. Kat judged you could crane in a container without too much difficulty—a couple of hour's work, at most.

Identifying the barred door that should, according to her research, give access to the owner of the land, Kat took a deep breath and turned back to face the car. Heidi was looking at her expectantly. The girl really wanted to be part of this. And she had to learn sometime. Kat supposed there was no real harm in letting her tag along. Maybe even some good, if the owner happened to be either a fifteen-year-old with raging hormones, or a sixty-year-old perv.

She opened the passenger door and leaned in. 'Okay. You ready for this?'

Heidi straightened, and Kat was reminded yet again of an oversized puppy. 'Yesss!'

'Want to spit out that gum?'

'I'm okay.'

'I meant get rid of the gum.'

'What are you, my mother?'

'No, I'm your boss. Spit it out. That constant chewing makes you look like a moonling.'

'What's a moonling?'

'Look it up.'

Heidi immediately pulled out her phone and started tapping through to Google.

'Not now, you goose!'

'Jeez!' said Heidi, jerking her head away, sudden tears

in her eyes. Kat's first impulse was to reach in and shake her, but instead she crouched down by the car. Took the phone and slid it into the side pocket of the door. Then took Heidi's hands loosely in hers. They were both uptight. Someone had to be the grown-up here.

'I'm sorry. But this is important. I want you to come along, but it's not a training exercise. It's not a test you can get half right and still pass. We've got one chance on this, and if we blow it you know we don't have a lot of other options.'

Heidi nodded glumly.

'We're about to ask this person to let us invade his life for at least the next two months. We have to look professional. And trustworthy.'

'Don't I look professional?'

Kat paused for a beat. 'The gum...isn't great.'

Heidi nodded again. 'Okay.'

'Now, this time, I don't need you to say anything. Just say hello when I introduce you, shake hands. Then just observe, and if I need something—the pitch, maps, job sheets, contracts—pass them to me. You have all that stuff?'

'Maybe I should just wait in the car...'

'I'd like you to come in,' said Kat, with more conviction than she was feeling. 'There's no need to be nervous. All you have to do is watch. If you do think of something that I've forgotten or that you think might be useful, have a quiet word in my ear. But you don't have to do anything. Just watch. I think you'll find it interesting. This is the most challenging part of the job, but the most satisfying too.'

Heidi was silent.

'Okay?'

'Okay.'

A moment later, Kat was knocking at the door. What a letdown, she thought, if there was no one home. But after a moment a figure appeared in the shadows of the hallway.

'Mr Bradley?'

'Yes?'

'I'm Kat Kelly. This is my colleague, Heidi van Doort. We're from Channel Five.'

16

Heading back to Wurundjeri Way, towards the office, Heidi was literally bouncing in her seat. 'That was so cool,' she said for the third or fourth time. 'That was so cool.'

Kat grinned at her. 'Told you.'

'You were totally awesome.'

'You were great.'

'I didn't do anything.'

'You did everything I asked you to.' Kat smiled a little more widely. 'And we got a result. Three results! That's what counts.' Thinking: I am. Totally. Awesome.

Sure, they'd got lucky. All three owners being present and free to talk was one of the big hurdles, potentially one of the real time-wasters, and they'd cleared that effortlessly. But there had also been moments when she'd had to bring all her professional wiles and diplomacy to the task. And she'd got a result. Three, in fact. Two campsites, and a Tribal Council. Awesome.

They travelled in silence for a moment, The Box gurgling audibly in the early peak traffic, then Heidi said, 'What else should I do?'

'What do you mean?'

'Well, I've been thinking about shoes.'

'Shoes?'

'I really like wearing high heels. But is that professional?'

'Oh,' said Kat. 'It depends. At a meeting, in an office, totally. But when we're scouting or shooting, it's not that it's not professional, it's just not practical. Even GC, or the PR girls, you'll see them wearing flats when we're shooting.'

Heidi nodded gravely. 'What else?'

Kat shot her a look. 'It's not that you don't look nice. You do. You always look beautiful. But I would say, as a general rule: tits or legs. But not both.'

Heidi flushed, and tugged at the hem of her skirt.

'I don't want to tell you how to dress,' said Kat, untruthfully. 'And—while it's probably not really PC to say it—looking attractive certainly helps get the job done. But you want people to focus on what you're saying, not your body. It's about compromise. Striking the right balance. So that top, for instance, but with a pair of jeans. Perfect. Or that skirt, but with a high-necked jumper.'

Heidi absorbed this silently for a moment, then said, 'Is that one of your favourite outfits?'

'Why?' asked Kat, surprised.

'Like, no offence. You look really pretty. I've just noticed you wear it almost every day.'

Kat laughed, glancing down at what was indeed almost her winter uniform: low-heeled, knee-high boots, skirt, jumper, overcoat and scarf. Every other day she swapped the skirt for jeans. 'You don't have to go to quite these extremes,' she said. 'I haven't been paying *enough* attention to the way I look lately.'

But Heidi was right. She only had one change of clothes, and while dully rinsing out her knickers and tights had become part of her numb nightly routine, she really had to retrieve her things from Miles' house, and she probably had to do it today. Bonnie would be back in Fitzroy from Saturday (Kat still had her schedule memorised), and though she should be in kinder or day care on work days, Kat would rather not risk it. Glancing at the dashboard clock, she said, 'Would you mind if we took a little detour?'

'Will it mean driving backwards?'

'No. All main roads. I promise.'

Heidi shrugged. 'Sure.'

At that hour they made good time to Brunswick Street, and Kat was relieved to see it was still well before 5pm as they pulled up in Moor Street. Sitting two doors down from the house, she suddenly felt herself bobbing in a violent wash of longing and sorrow and fear. The ache in her chest returned, making her heart beat in painful, irregular thumps and her breathing shorten. Muttering, 'Two minutes', she snatched the keys from the ignition and scrambled from the car. Heidi, engrossed in an extended text conversation, simply nodded.

Kat closed her eyes for a moment as she slid the key into the lock, praying that Miles wasn't unexpectedly home. But when she pushed open the door the house was dim and silent. She closed it gently behind her and stood in the hallway, eyes closed again. Then reached out to shut the door to Bonnie's room, before making her way down to the kitchen for garbage bags. It was, as always, immaculate. And painfully familiar. While she could quite honestly say that along with the hurt and the anger, leaving Miles also entailed a pronounced element of relief, she missed this, achingly. The house. The kitchen. The scents and textures of it all, the quality of the light. And everything it embodied. The family.

Resisting the temptation to take a quick swig from the capped bottle on the counter—a nice Heathcote shiraz she was particularly partial to—Kat found what she needed and headed to the bedroom. Her toothbrush, she noticed, had already been disposed of, and if she'd left any toiletries behind they were gone too. But her clothes and shoes were all in place and she stuffed them methodically into the bags, going through the cupboards and drawers one at a time, making sure she left nothing behind, leaving everything closed and as she found it, smoothing the bed covers back into order.

In the Good Room she retrieved a meagre collection of books and DVDs from their gulag in the farthest, darkest corner (Miles had always been faintly alarmed at the idea that a guest might spot them and think them his). She then stood back in the hallway with the bags at her feet, thinking: *How little there is. How little of me was ever in this house. What a tiny, imperceptible dint I have made in their lives. It's like I was never here.*

This thought, and the weight of the self-pity that accompanied it, dizzied her, and she stretched out a hand to steady herself. Her palm came to rest against the plaque on Bonnie's door—a rabbit in a tutu—and the cool ceramic at first shocked, then soothed her. She laid her forehead against it, trying to soak it with love, wanting to leave something behind, some invisible evidence, some aura. Concentrating fiercely, she turned her head and pressed her lips to it. Then told herself: *Enough. This is getting silly.*

Gathering the bags, Kat pulled the house key from her key ring, left it on the hall table, opened the front door again, and stepped out into the street.

Heidi was now sitting up, gazing down the footpath expectantly. Without meeting her eyes, Kat opened the boot of The Box, stuffed the bags in, thumped it closed, and resumed her seat behind the wheel. Then sat there for a long moment, swallowing hard on tears.

Heidi gazed at her. 'Are you okay?'

Kat drew a long breath. 'I used to live here.'

'What happened?'

After a pause, Kat gave her the Twitter version: 'Broke up with my boyfriend.'

Heidi exhaled noisily, reached out one arm, and drew Kat towards her. Caught off-guard, Kat leant without resistance into the embrace.

'Men!' said Heidi.

And with her head cushioned on Heidi's pillowy bosom, a cloud of scent making her eyes water even more freely, Kat found herself smiling in spite of herself.

17

'Have you heard?' Harry stepped into Kat's office, glancing over his shoulder furtively, and shut the door.

Kat glanced up from her sketches, eyebrows raised. 'Heard what?'

He leaned across the desk with a look of mingled glee and disbelief. 'They've just signed the host,' he murmured urgently.

'And...?'

He clasped her hand, hard. 'Dare O'Donnell.'

Kat rocked back in her chair. 'Oh. Em. Gee. Seriously?'

'Seriously.'

'Dear God,' she said, choking on a laugh.

'I know.'

Casting Dare O'Donnell in the Jeff Probst role was a stroke of dangerous, perverse genius. Brilliant. But how much was he going to cost them? And *what* did the contract look like?

'The contract,' said Harry, gesturing with his fingers to indicate a pile of documents the size of a local Yellow Pages. 'Don't know the price tag. *Strictly* confidential.'

Kat nodded, digesting the news. In so many ways, he was perfect. Famous enough to only require a one-word moniker. (Although people referred to him as simply O'Donnell, rather than Dare, as was the custom with footballers, ex and otherwise.) Possessed of the kind of charisma generally associated with profound narcissistic disorders. Ridiculously handsome, in that smoky, sleepy Don Hany style. (The Don Hany of *Offspring*, not the bearded *East West* Hany.) But bigger, built, about six-four and with a playing weight, apparently, of around 100 kilos.

Then there was the back story. Kat didn't know how much was true and how much apocryphal, but that hardly mattered. According to legend—a legend he traded off relentlessly, in his self-deprecating style—O'Donnell had not been one of the golden boys, and was certainly never a No. 1 draft pick. While other sons were being groomed by obsessive parents, AusKick mentors and lavish govern-ment-funded sporting bodies, Kid O'Donnell was stealing food from Frankston Safeway, rolling punters exiting the 21st Century Club in the small hours, and lifting boots and balls from the Rebel store at Southland (generally after hot-wiring a car to get there in the first place) to keep body and soul together, and his AFL dream alive.

Home—according to legend—meant ceaseless thrash-ings from his alcoholic father, now conveniently deceased, unable to confirm or deny. Forcing the boy onto the streets and into bad company, and worse habits. It was only his staggering talent, and the sheer blind luck of being spotted while training solo at a suburban oval by a

Draft Camp scout that saved twenty-year-old O'Donnell from multiple seasons in the Big House, and had him as a surprise inclusion on that year's rookie list instead.

The rest, as they say, was history. Legitimate history. His record on the field was indisputable. When he retired, twelve years later, the bidding from all the networks (and radio, and newspapers) to take him on as in-house talent had been fierce.

Five had missed out, not having nearly deep enough pockets.

And then watched with, no doubt, considerable *schadenfreude* as O'Donnell proceeded to rapidly and publicly unravel. He was great in front of the camera, one of those rare people who made it look effortless, who made it seem as if they were speaking to you personally, sharing a private joke only you were clever enough to understand. Trouble was, you could never be sure he'd actually be in front of the camera when he was supposed to be. Or if he was, if he'd be sober. And then there were his antics off field, as it were.

Long before his monstrously profitable three-year contract had run its term O'Donnell was in rehab. Then out of rehab. Then in rehab. Then at the Logies, causing mayhem. Then in rehab. Kat had lost track of where he was on the rehab carousel right at the moment, but he'd been out of the papers for more than six months and had clearly accrued sufficient day leave to make filming a twenty-episode reality series possible.

Kat drew a deep breath. 'My dear boy,' she said, meeting Harry's eyes. 'You are going to have your work cut out for you.'

'I think it'll be okay,' he said, with more hope than

conviction. 'We all had a meeting yesterday. He seemed like a very rational, together sort of bloke. Humble.'

'But darling. You know that's his *shtick*. The sorrowful eye contact. The *mea culpa*. And then...' She mimed emptying a bottle of grog down her throat.

'I know, I know. But everyone deserves a second chance, don't they?'

Kat refrained from pointing out that O'Donnell had already, in fact, had multiple second chances, and blown all of them.

'Plus...' Harry leaned forward again, unable to keep the smile off his face. 'He's perfect for us.'

Kat couldn't help smiling back. 'He is. Absolutely perfect.'

At his best, O'Donnell would handle those contestants like a master mesmerist. He would work the camera like nobody's business. She was prepared to wager a large sum that he'd watched a fair few episodes of *Survivor* in his time. And God, the press they'd get just from having his name attached to the show—not to mention the way his life story mirrored their brief.

'Anyway,' said Harry briskly. 'Just in case.'

'Yes,' Kat said, suspiciously.

'GC asked me to have a quiet word with you.'

'About what?'

'Well, you worked on *Celebrity Survivor.*'

'Sure.'

'I know you were just...'

'Just the location scout,' Kat said dryly.

'Yes, but you know how this works. On the ground. You know how it's put together.'

Kat waited.

'We'd just like some idea of how much of him we can shoot in blocks, pre-shoot, kind of thing.' Harry paused. 'Just in case.'

Kat grinned again, more saturnine this time. 'Humble,' she said pointedly. 'Rational. Together.'

'He is. He really seems...okay. But...'

'Just in case. I know.' She scratched her head with her pencil. 'Once we're underway, there's really not much you can do. He has to be there for the long haul. I mean— what?—we get to the finale and someone else is hosting the last Tribal Council?'

Harry shrugged. 'I think what they're thinking is if, say, he needs to take a break...'

'For God's sake.'

'No, really. I'm not saying... All I'm saying is... You know what it's like once shooting's underway. It's punishing. Is there any way we can start with a bunch of challenges and Councils? Then give him, say, two to four weeks off while we shoot the day-to-day stuff. Then shoot a second block with O'Donnell...'

'No,' said Kat emphatically.

'No?'

'No way. You have the challenges? Then people voted out? Then bring them back to make-believe with the scheming and the politicking? Darling, we've already had this conversation, and paid the price. It completely undermines the integrity of the game.'

Harry gave a shout of laughter.

'What?'

'The integrity of the game. Kat, only you would say something like that.'

'You know what I mean! All the pieces have to work

together. Who's good at scavenging? Maintaining the shelters? Who's good at keeping the team together? Who lies around moaning and doing fuck all? Monsters the challenges? Who's persuasive? Who gets everyone offside? Then—someone gets voted out. It's how it *works*.'

Harry held up his hands. 'I know, I know. It just sounded funny.' He rubbed the top of his head resignedly. 'It really can't be done, can it?'

'No. Besides, I reckon it'd actually be tougher for him having to shoot long days, out of sequence, than just dip in and out of the action on a regular basis. If fatigue is really what you're worrying about, and not something else.'

'Obviously everyone's worried about *everything*. It's a high-risk play.'

'Well, having made the decision to take the risk, they really just have to go with it.'

'And now everyone's madly trying to cover their arses,' Harry sighed. He stood to leave.

'Seriously, though, if you're after arse-coverage, keep him out of this first block of shooting as much as possible until we see how it plays,' Kat said. 'It's like the extended warranty.'

Harry raised one eyebrow.

'You know, those extended warranties they try and sell you on your fridge or whatever. An extra $150 for an extra three-year's cover. Pointless. Either you've bought a lemon and it breaks down in six months, or it's okay and works for years. There's no point angling for an extended warranty. Shoot this first block without letting O'Donnell in the same frame as the contestants. And let's see if we've got a lemon.'

'Okay,' said Harry. 'I'll pass that on.'

Kat sighed, reading the subtext.

'Harry, have you spoken to Ted about this? He was on Vanuatu too.'

'BC talked with Ted this morning.'

'And what did he say?'

Harry grinned. 'Same as you, boss. Same as you.'

18

It was well and truly dark by the time Kat made her way downstairs. She'd had a long meeting with Bev that afternoon, nutting out the logistics of the campsites and Tribal Council, Bev knitting madly the whole time. It had been decided their contestants would wear beanies rather than the traditional kerchief, and that it would be quicker and undoubtedly cheaper to have Bev produce them herself. So she had clacked on steadfastly while they discussed everything from whether they could really ask their contestants to live in large appliance boxes (shipping containers were out) to where one might find the extra rats, spiders and cockroaches BC thought they might need.

Now the office was long deserted, but the lights were still on in the café. On impulse Kat stuck her head around the door.

'You still open?'

'For you? Sure.' Wilson smiled.

Kat hesitated in the doorway. 'If you're closing up...'

'Come in. Shut the door. It's cold.'

Kat did as she was told, took a chair off one of the tables and swung it to the ground.

'Do you drink?'

'Of course.'

'Whisky?'

'Certainly.'

'Good girl.'

He took a bottle from the bottom cupboard, poured generous shots into two latte glasses and sat down opposite her. 'I have actually cleaned the machine for the day,' he said, passing her one. 'This do instead?'

She took a sip, stretched out her legs. 'Oh yes,' she sighed. 'This your usual end-of-day routine?'

Wilson shook his head. 'Not really. Sometimes a mate drops by, and we might sit here for a bit.'

She gazed at him. She supposed he did. Have mates. Family, even. A life outside this room. She was so used to him only existing in this context it was hard to imagine him anywhere else (she'd been trying to imagine him in a lab coat, without success). Did he live in a house? She couldn't really imagine him in a house, with a backyard. Despite his quotidian appearance there was something very un-suburban about him. Maybe a flat?

She tried to conjure the *Wilson: Domestic* location. At first it was some kind of West Melbourne high rise with chunky leather sofas and a wetbar. But that was probably just the influence of the whisky. Unless he was independently wealthy—and he certainly did not look independently wealthy—it was more likely to be some sort of 1960s number in Richmond, kitted out from

Furniture Galore. But that didn't feel quite right, either.

Maybe a caravan. Like McDreamy's, in *Grey's Anatomy*. That would sort of fit, although he looked nothing like Patrick Dempsey. And living in a caravan in Melbourne would be absolutely nothing like living in a trailer in that mysterious Seattle forest. She wondered idly where that location actually was. Did they have to travel sixty kilometres out of town to shoot those scenes? Or was there somewhere close at hand where a neurosurgeon could feasibly live and still make it to work on time?

'Yes...?' Wilson, smiling, broke her train of thought.

'Just wondering where they filmed those scenes from *Grey's Anatomy*—the ones around Derek's trailer.'

He nodded slowly. 'Of course.'

She grinned, and doodled one finger through the air. 'Just one of those, you know, strange trains of thought.'

'I guess it's an occupational hazard.'

'Strange trains of thought?'

'And constantly wondering where things were filmed.'

'Mmm,' she said. 'It is.'

They were silent again for a moment, until he said, with a degree of gentleness that caught her off-guard: 'How are you travelling?'

Kat was going to say what she always said to that question. Brightly: 'Good!' Or, sometimes, 'Terrific!' Instead, in the warm quiet of the near-empty room, the whisky tingling pleasantly in her face and hands, she just sighed and shrugged.

'It's a funny feeling, isn't it?' he said.

She looked away, nodded silently.

'Have you talked to anyone about it? Friends?'

She met his eyes. 'You know what? I haven't told anyone.'

'Except me.'

She smiled wryly. 'I know. Weird. Except you.'

'It's not so weird. Strangers are easier, somehow. You don't have to... I don't know. You don't have to *care* about them.'

'You're not really a stranger, though.'

'No. Not like some completely random guy sitting next to you on the tram. Telling *him* your problems *would* be weird.'

Kat laughed.

'It's more about someone who's not invested in you or your problems. I think that makes it easier.'

Kat found the idea that Wilson wasn't invested in her or her problems strangely upsetting. But she just nodded and said, 'I guess that's why people go to therapy.'

'Or bars.'

'Or bars.' She twirled her glass between her palms for a moment. 'Voice of experience?'

'A few of us have been there, mate. Although I have to say—in my experience—it's usually the bloke who's chucked out on the street in the middle of the night.'

'I like to challenge the stereotypes.'

'You still in Footscray? Still okay there?'

'Why are you being so nice to me?'

'Because I have been there. And I know how much I appreciated people—sometimes the people you least expect—helping out. Listening. Buying you a coffee.'

'Or a whisky.'

'Or a whisky.' He smiled at her.

What very kind eyes you have, Kat thought. Aloud, she said: 'Well, I think you're a very decent human being.'

'Oh no,' Wilson said, adding a splash more to their

glasses. 'Don't make that mistake.' He grinned at her. 'I have it on good authority I'm a complete arsehole.'

'I'll bear that in mind.'

He looked at her over the rim of his glass. 'But you know—when you're ready—your friends will want to help too.'

Kat sighed. 'I know.'

Was she ready? She hadn't said anything to Harry, but then they rarely discussed her private life. Other friends—well—these days months could go by without contact between them. Everyone was busy. So much of her time was spent with her colleagues she forgot they weren't really her friends. So many of her actual friendships, Kat thought, almost with surprise, seemed to continue on the basis of quarterly visits and sporadic flurries of emails. That just seemed to be the way life was.

But Betsy... She hadn't spoken to Betsy in three weeks, responding to her calls with texts, assuring her they'd catch up soon. Bets was used to her getting caught up in work. But she was also very familiar with the way Kat went to ground when things got bad and, knowing what she knew about the state of things between Miles and Kat, she'd be getting worried.

At first Kat had been so wounded, so incapacitated by grief she couldn't face the thought of saying the words aloud. Once the grief started lessening, the rest of her life was so chaotic it was just simpler to stay put in her cheap motel. Now, though...

Kat rubbed a hand through her hair and smiled ruefully. The only other person she'd mentioned it to, apart from Wilson, was Heidi. Another almost-stranger. Maybe it was time to come out of the cupboard, she thought. To come out of her cave. Apart from anything else, the bill from the Footscray Best Western, modest as it was, was quickly burning through her savings.

In another week she'd be able to move back into her flat. For the first time, she realised the idea didn't fill her with dread. And before she did that, she really had to talk with Bets.

Tilting her glass, Kat held the last of the whisky in her mouth for a moment and swallowed.

'Thank you,' she said.

'You're very welcome.'

Wilson stood when she did, briefly laid an arm around her shoulders and gave them a squeeze. And Kat was struck, just for a moment, by how well they fit together despite the vast difference in height and bulk: his hip into her waist, her head into the hollow of his shoulder. She could have happily stood there, snugly supported, for an hour. But he released her almost instantly and stepped away, so she just said, 'For a complete arsehole, you're not too bad.'

Afterwards, Kat sat in the cosy confines of The Box for a moment, engine running and that fabulous heater kicking into gear, then pulled out her phone.

'You home at the moment?'

'Yes—where are you?'

'Just leaving the office. Can I drop round?'

'Of course,' said Betsy.

'See you soon, then.' Kat tossed the phone on the passenger seat, took a breath, and put the car into gear.

As soon as Betsy heard The Box in the driveway she

flung open the front door. '*Where* have you been!' she exclaimed as Kat extricated herself from the car.

'Oh Bets,' said Kat, clattering up the front steps and giving herself over to her friend's stern embrace. Betsy led her down to the back of the house, pushed her into a chair, and poured her a glass of wine.

Seated again at the kitchen table—was it really only four, five weeks ago she was here last?—Kat felt a slightly bewildering mixture of relief, happiness, embarrassment and anxiety, wondering what to do or say next. Wilson was right. Strangers were easier. You didn't care about strangers. You didn't really care what they thought about you, and you didn't care about their feelings either. You didn't care if they were worried, or upset on your behalf, or angry, or if they pitied you.

Kat cared about all those things with Betsy, cared all the more because they had had this conversation, in various permutations, so many times. Apart from all the other things she cared about, she cared about maybe Betsy being sick and tired of Kat sitting at her kitchen table pouring out her woes.

So there was a silence of some considerable length before she could even begin to speak. And then, because Betsy wasn't a stranger, the telling also took rather a long time. You didn't give strangers all the minute details. You didn't explain to strangers the complicated miasma of emotion these events precipitated. Talking with strangers, you tended not to take regular breaks to weep helplessly before picking up the story again. And when the damp and comprehensive narrative (minus Wilson's interventions) had concluded, the two of them sat silently for several more minutes, Kat dabbing periodically at her nose and massaging the centre of her chest, where the pain had returned with startling ferocity.

'And how long ago was all this?' Betsy asked eventually.

'Three weeks.'

'You know I've been really worried about you.'

Kat breathed through pursed lips. 'I'm sorry. I am. But you know me, Bets. I like time to process things. And to be honest, until now I couldn't talk about it. Literally. I only had to think about…about…' Kat found she still could not say Bonnie's name out loud without difficulty. 'I'd just start weeping. Talking about it would have been impossible. I would have just been sitting here sobbing hysterically. And I don't need company for that. I can do that alone.'

'And have you been doing that?'

Kat nodded.

'Well,' said Betsy. 'That's something, I guess.'

Another silence. Then: 'And Miles?'

'What about him?'

Betsy looked hard at her friend. 'Do you miss him? Have you heard from him? Do you want to hear from him?'

'He called. The next day.'

Betsy waited.

'He… He got quite angry again.'

'You did kind of spring it on him.'

'I know. Only—not really. I'd tried to have that conversation, Bets, I really had. He just wasn't interested. And then, when it came to it… I was never going to threaten him. I was never going to say, "Do this or I'll leave". I mean, what kind of relationship is that, if you have to have your bags packed before he'll even talk with you?'

Bets nodded.

138

'Anyway...' Kat sighed. 'No, I don't miss him. I'm amazed at how much I don't. I'm amazed at how relieved I feel about all that part of it. And when he called...'

Kat sighed again and rubbed her temples. The memory still made her feel a little sick.

'I'm sorry,' he'd said. 'I shouldn't have lost my temper.'

'You scared me.'

'I'm sorry. But Kat—really—I expected more of you. Don't you think this is all a bit...adolescent?'

Kat had been speechless.

'So now I'm getting the silent treatment?'

'I just don't know what to say,' she'd finally managed.

'Look, I forgive you. You haven't been yourself. Let's just forget about it. Come home.'

'Miles, no,' Kat had said, trying to keep her voice steady. 'I'm sorry I upset you. I could have handled things better. But I'm not coming home.' Adding baldly, 'I don't want to be with you any more.'

Then Miles had fallen silent for a long moment before saying, with a hard edge to his voice, 'Well. That's that, then.'

'Miles,' Kat had said quickly, before he hung up, before she lost her nerve. 'I hope we can stay in touch, though. I hope...' Her throat had tightened, her voice trembling. 'I'd like to stay part of Bonnie's life. I'd like us to be friends.'

He'd given a harsh bark of laughter. 'Are we friends, Kat? Have we ever been friends? I feel like I don't know you at all.'

'Bonnie...'

'The less Bonnie sees of you right now, the better,' he'd snapped. 'Do you have any idea how much you've upset her?'

'And then...' Kat turned to Betsy and grasped her hand, her eyes filling with tears again. 'And then he said, "You're not her mother. You have no place in her life."'

Betsy winced and moved closer, wrapping Kat in her arms. For a long moment the two of them sat there in silence, then Bets said, 'You'll stay here tonight.'

Kat nodded. 'Yes,' she said meekly.

'I'll make up the bed.'

As she rose, Betsy stopped, stooped to lay her palm against Kat's cheek, then gripped her hand. 'You know I love you.'

Kat nodded again, silently returning the pressure of her fingers. *Yes. I know. But it's not enough. Not nearly enough.*

19

Monday morning was bright but icy, a wind whipping straight off Antarctica and howling through the CBD lanes. Dare O'Donnell had been kitted out in an old-fashioned Bluey, a hand-knitted scarf in blues and greys (more of Bev's handiwork?), dark jeans and Blundstones. He looked, Kat admitted guiltily, sensational: his hair ruffled by the wind, a little dark stubble on his chin. Beside her Heidi had also done her best to costume for the occasion: polo-neck knit that made her breasts seem more enormous than ever, skinny jeans, Ugg boots.

When Harry saw The Box pull up he jogged over to meet them. 'Good timing, chief,' he said, opening Kat's door for her. 'We're expecting the cavalry in about fifteen minutes, but Dare wanted to get here and have a look at the lay of the land first. Can you talk him through it? I've just got to nip over and pick up the contestants.'

'Sure,' said Kat, hauling out a clattering stack of witches

hats and two hi-vis vests. She righted the pile of orange cones and handed one of the vests to Heidi, a garment she received with a mixture of disbelief and disgust.

'Put this on, love, and can you start marking out the ends of the block with those?' Taking note of Heidi's crestfallen face, she added: 'After you've met O'Donnell, of course.'

Kat slipped her vest on, Heidi draped hers carefully over the witches hats, and Harry led them both to the end of the street where the former footballer was sheltering in a doorway, bouncing on his toes, his hands deep in his pockets.

'Dare, this is our location manager, Kat Kelly, and her assistant, Heidi van Doort.'

'The director's daughter?' asked O'Donnell, stepping into the street and extending his hand to Heidi, manfully keeping his eyes on her face.

'Um, yes,' murmured Heidi, her shoulders bunched under her ears, a noticeable flush spreading from the top of her collar to the edge of her hairline.

'*Don't Ask, Don't Tell* is one of my favourite films,' he said, then—receiving no response—added, 'And I loved *3121* when I was a kid. Watched it every Thursday night, without fail. It was one of the reasons I wanted to play for the Tigers.'

'I wasn't born,' Heidi managed, turning an even darker shade of pink.

O'Donnell soldiered on. 'Well, I am getting on a bit. I'm not surprised you weren't around for it, but you should check it out sometime. What will you be doing here today?'

Now rendered entirely speechless, Heidi cast Kat a desperate glance.

'Heidi's already done a lot of the hard graft on this location, organising all the permits,' Kat offered. 'But it's her first time hands-on at a shoot. Right now we've got to close off the two ends of the block and put dibs on parking for the crew. From there we'll wait till the director arrives and see what he needs.'

O'Donnell smiled at Heidi. 'Well, it's my first time on location too. Hope I don't stuff it up!'

Heidi gargled helplessly, at which point Kat said briskly, 'Thanks Heidi. Can you make a start? I'll be with you in a sec.'

O'Donnell turned his attention to Kat, his eyes smiling into hers, and she felt a sudden burst of warmth in her belly. Jesus, Mary and Joseph, she thought. This man is catnip. Kat had always favoured slender men, but suddenly—first Wilson, now this—she was understanding the allure of the very large bloke. As O'Donnell towered over her, she had a powerful compulsion to just lean in to that vast expanse of chest and rest there. Instead she said, 'I wouldn't have picked you for a fan of Gert van Doort.'

'I've had a fair bit of time for DVDs these last couple of years,' he said, smiling crookedly and pushing his hands back into his pockets. 'Watched a lot of things—and read a lot of things—I never thought I would.'

'So it wasn't all bad?'

'There's always a bright side,' he said. 'And I reckon I managed about eight seasons of *Survivor*, so I'm raring to go on this.'

'Well, sorry we couldn't organise a tropical island for you, but it still should be fun. How much have they told you about what we're doing today?'

Digging her own hands into her pockets, as much

143

to prevent herself from reaching out and stroking him as for warmth, Kat explained the rundown for the day. Contrary to her advice, it was going to be a long one, and O'Donnell was going to be there almost every step of the way. They had, at least, filmed the packages without him. But today the contest started in earnest, with two earlier segments reworked to provide a new first episode. It began with them all trooping up to the roof of the original YMCA, whereupon the contestants would abseil down the side of the central tower—added in the 1980s, Kat guessed, by the look of it—to where their host and taskmaster awaited them.

First two to the roof would then select their tribes from the rest of the rabble. Once that was done, O'Donnell would explain the next phase of the competition. The tribes were then to be shipped off to the campsites, followed by the second crew while First Unit broke for lunch. Then at dusk they'd all be back for the dumpster diving, overseen again by O'Donnell.

'Have they given you a script?' Kat asked as Harry pulled up in the mini-van.

'I've worked on something with the guys,' O'Donnell said. 'Obviously there's stuff I have to say. But for a lot of it—especially once I get the hang of it—I hope I'll be able to just wing it.' Seeing the shadow of scepticism that passed involuntarily over Kat's face, he threw a casual arm around her shoulders, gave her that deadly self-deprecating smile again, and added: 'Don't worry. If there's one thing I'm good at, it's bullshitting.'

Ignoring the sudden pounding of her heart and tucking her elbows in closer to her sides, Kat said dryly, 'Let's hope so.'

She would have loved to have watched Harry introduce their man to the contestants, but she had to check on Heidi and found, having used all the witches hats to form an impenetrable cordon across both ends of the laneway, she was now at a loss as to how to mark out their reserved parking bays. Heidi was darting madly along Elizabeth Street (still sans vest), shooing away slowing motorists.

'Where's your vest?' shouted Kat.

'I don't know!' wailed Heidi.

'All right. Wait there. Don't get run over, for God's sake.'

Kat bolted back to The Box, retrieved the portable No Parking signs from the boot, scooped up as many cones as she could carry on the return trip, and herded Heidi back to the curb. 'Go and find your vest,' she said. 'You'll get yourself killed. Plus, you look like a crazy lady.'

Kat flung the metal A-frames into place and sprinted the length of the block, dropping witches hats haphazardly as she went. As she more slowly retraced her route, catching her breath and creating a more orderly DMZ, the first of the big trucks started rolling in.

Spotting Ted, she flagged him down madly.

'Ted, you and your boys need to turn left here—I'm sorry, there's forty thousand witches hats blocking your path, and if you could not run over them I'd appreciate it. And if you could get me a...' Kat gestured wildly in the vicinity of her ears.

'Headset? Walkie talkie?'

'Yes, both, if you could do that for me—two sets—I will love you forever.'

'No worries, mate. No need for sexual favours. Always happy to help.'

Back in the laneway O'Donnell was still standing surrounded by his twelve disciples. Kat glanced at her watch. Harry really needed to get them upstairs. Heidi stood to one side, talking animatedly into her phone. Stalking up to her, Kat took the phone from her hand.

'Is someone on their way to hospital?'

'No—what? Why?'

Ending the call, Kat slipped the phone into her pocket, holding one hand up to silence Heidi's protests.

'My love, we have work to do. Sorry I didn't explain to you more clearly what you needed to do this morning. You only use a couple of those witches hats at each end of the street. It's just a gesture, not a physical barrier. And we need to be able to move them easily so the trucks can get in and out.'

'Sorry.'

'That's okay. You didn't know. But you must—*must*—keep your vest on.'

'It's so ugly!'

'I know. Too bad.'

Ted appeared with their comms gear.

'Thank you, darling.'

'Don't mention it,' he grinned.

Kat showed Heidi how to strap the unit round her waist, the headset over her ears, how to use the controls.

'Keep an ear on what's happening, by all means, but pay particular attention to when I yell "Heidi!". Okay?'

'Okay.'

'All right. Let's find that bloody vest, then I want you to go back out and make sure all those vans have permits on their dashboards. And when the paramedics and the abseiling guys arrive, I need you to direct them down here and let me and Harry know they're coming. You good with that?'

Heidi nodded. Kat gave her a brief hug. 'It's all right. It's your first time. And in fifteen minutes we'll just be standing around again. But when things happen—they happen.'

As it turned out, finding Heidi's vest was a simple matter of retrieving it from where she'd stuffed it behind a dumpster. Suitably clad, Kat sent her back out onto the street, then jogged down to where Harry and O'Donnell still—still!—stood in the centre of an animated throng.

'Were you waiting for me?' she said, catching Harry's eye. 'Sorry, I thought I'd said I'd unlocked those doors for you. You can go up any time you're ready.'

Harry glanced at his watch. 'Shit. Yes. Okay. Well, people. Are you ready?'

The twelve sent up a half-hearted cheer.

'Then let's get this show on the road.' He glanced down the laneway to where the crew were moving purposefully towards them. 'Kat, can you look after things down here while I get these guys up top?'

'Sure.'

Harry herded his charges towards the lift.

'And what do I do again?' asked O'Donnell.

'You, sir, follow me,' said the director, disappearing into the stairwell. O'Donnell turned, smiled at Kat, gave her a brief wave, and did as he was told. Kat's headset buzzed.

'Kat? Can you hear me?'

'Yep, loud and clear.'

'The ambulance is here. And the climbing guys.'

'Thanks Heidi. I'll come out and meet them.'

In a black van with the word JUMPS stencilled *A-Team* style on the side was a serious-looking crew of six men and a significant quantity of ropes, harnesses and other rather frightening paraphernalia. Kat lead them the few steps to the building entrance, saw them into the lift, pushed the correct button for them, and wished them luck.

She then turned back to Heidi. 'How are you going? Get all those permits done?'

'Yep.'

'Wonderful. Thank you. Would you do one more thing for me?'

'Sure.'

'Could you do a coffee run?'

Heidi nodded. 'No worries.'

'And leave your vest on!'

Heidi grinned at her, and headed back down the lane.

Half an hour later a handful of them stood braced against the arctic breeze, six storeys above the city. Behind them was the CBD proper. To either side, a jagged line of apartment buildings and smaller office towers rose like broken teeth. Peering over the edge, Kat's thoughts turned irresistibly to the last 'first' day of shooting, the day in Lonsdale Street, the day their man had jumped almost exactly this far into the middle of the street.

Poor Suicide Guy, she thought. What happened to you? What was so bad, so unfixably bad, you'd do something like that? Kat shuddered slightly, thinking: *I hope I never get there. I hope I never get to that place.* A sudden gust buffeted her and she stepped a little further back from the edge.

Even higher above them were the Survivors. Kat craned her neck but, eyes watering in the wind, all she could see was a blurry blob. Directly in front of them, against a brilliant sky, was the central tower of the Jasper Hotel, grey-brown and grimy, while in the foreground O'Donnell stood grinning maniacally, one foot propped on a large heating vent, the other planted firmly on the pebble-deck of the roof. On cue he wordlessly threw out his arms, and behind him came cascading, one after the other, twelve shrieking, flailing contestants, twisting in the wind.

20

Early Sunday afternoon in Coburg, and as the kebab shops fired up their charcoal grills it smelled like the whole suburb was having a barbecue. The four—well, five—of them had convened in Betsy's driveway, Leo standing beside Wilson's silver HiLux, hands clasped reverently. (He'd learned early on that the things you most wanted to touch tended to be the things you weren't allowed to.)

Continuing to undermine his own emphatic claims to aresholedom, Wilson had instantly volunteered himself and his ute on hearing Kat mutter, in an unthinking aside, that finding a man with a van to get her stuff out of storage was Just One More Thing! she had to attend to. Now here they were, including the real-life Wilson, the person who existed beyond the confines of the café. The Wilson who had mates who drank whisky with him, the one who actually lived somewhere (a trailer was still not out of the question), the one who drove—no surprise, really—a large four-wheel-drive utility with a capacious tray.

Yesterday Kat and Betsy had done a preliminary run, installing clothes and kitchenware in the flat, still reeking of fresh paint and two-pack epoxy. Now it was the furniture and white goods; an unquantifiable number of boxes of books, CDs and DVDs; and the mystery boxes which she and Bets had turned around and around, vainly trying to find some kind of label or any indication of what they might contain. (Obviously, thought Kat, the ones packed last and probably full of miscellaneous treasures she felt at the time she could not bear to part with and which had now passed entirely from her consciousness.)

She was glad Wilson was here, and not just for his muscle. Betsy had been determinedly upbeat, but of course both of them were thinking of the last time they'd packed up together, before she moved in with Miles. The excitement and optimism and pleasant melancholy of those days, the feeling that Kat was stepping into her future. Now, Miles was history.

Kat was certainly well and truly ready to be out of cheap motels and other people's guest rooms, to have privacy, to have her own turf. But along with the regular washes of sorrow she felt any time anything reminded her of Bonnie was a dreary undercurrent of falling back into her past, of having landed on the biggest snake on the board, of having slid right back to Go.

Wilson, though, with his stranger magic, was distracting all of them from the metaphysical aspects of the move. He was not part of their shared history. He was purely present. And today that was a good thing.

The Box was having the day off. With preliminary

151

introductions taken care of, and having agreed to leave coffee for now, brisk discussion was underway regarding how best to team up in the two vehicles to get the job done.

'I want to go with the man,' Leo announced suddenly.

Kat grinned at Wilson. He cast a glance at Betsy and said, 'Sure. If it's okay with your mum.'

'The man's name is Wilson,' Bets said. 'And he might not want a little boy riding shotgun.'

'Really, it's fine. If you don't mind him travelling in the front seat. We can get that booster seat in. And there are twin airbags. Although I'll try not to crash.'

As Leo started hopping from foot to foot in excitement, Betsy said, 'We could just chain him up in the back like a kelpie.'

'Can I ride in the back?' Leo's voice went up an octave.

'No!' said all four adults in unison.

Leo grinned, and tried a different tack. 'Can I touch it?'

'Sure,' said Wilson. 'As long as the engine's not running you can touch it.'

'Can I see the engine?'

'Yes. But later. When we've finished helping Kat.'

Recognising the voice of authority, Leo merely stepped forward and laid one hand first against one of the enormous Desert Duellers, then stroked the silver duco appreciatively. 'Good car,' he said to Wilson.

'It is a good car. It's called a ute.'

'Ute,' murmured Leo thoughtfully to himself, trying out the shape of the word. Then: 'Kat has a good car.'

'She does,' said Wilson. 'But not as good as mine.'

Kat propped herself against Jim's Camry as he and Wilson wrestled the booster seat out of one car and into the other, Leo offering advice as they went. Like everything else he did, Wilson managed the manoeuvre without fuss, talking easily with Jim as he did so. He radiated a kind of calm competence that Kat found herself more and more drawn to, wanting to soak up a little of that peace, that feeling of all rightness. When they were done, Wilson straightened and met Kat's eyes with a half smile.

'Want to ride in the back?'

'Tempting,' she said. 'But I'd better set a good example for the boy.'

For the rest of the afternoon they travelled in easy convoy between the storage centre in Fitzroy and the flat, seeing Kat's hired bunker slowly empty and the flat first become homelike, as the furniture was assembled and put in place, then devolve into chaos as box after box was stacked on the shelves, on the floor, under the bed, until moving anywhere meant turning sideways, breathing in, and inching slowly through the maze.

Leo made the trips with Wilson, riding high in the big truck, chatting animatedly the whole time, Wilson chatting back. He found jobs for Leo to do, carrying lamps or one end of a dining chair or a box. Clearly able to bear twice the load, Wilson waited patiently until Leo's tiny hands were in place, shuffling slowly backward as the boy gripped the object, then thanking him gravely once it had been loaded into the tray.

It made for slow going, but by the end of the day Wilson seemed as unruffled as he had been at its beginning. And while Betsy and Kat found the box containing bed linen and performed the last crucial task, he took Leo back outside, as promised, hoisted him up on to the front bumper, and popped the hood.

'I like him,' said Betsy as they smoothed sheets over the mattress.

'Wilson?'

'No, my husband. Of course Wilson.'

Kat, tugging the doona from its box and releasing an unattractive odour of dust with undertones of mildew, said nothing.

'He's been magnificent with Leo,' Betsy persevered.

'Well, Leo is adorable.'

'He is not. Well, he is. But he's also a bloody nuisance. That man has the patience of a saint.'

'Me?' said Jim, sticking his head round the door, a six-pack of Boags in one hand.

'No, Wilson,' said Betsy.

'God yes,' said Jim. 'Does he have kids of his own?'

Does he? thought Kat. Have kids? And a wife? And...? No. Surely not. 'I have no idea,' she said. 'Why don't you ask him?'

Jim looked at Kat quizzically, exchanged glances with his wife (who rolled her eyes), before leaving the room, saying, 'Well, he's certainly earned a beer.'

When Kat and Betsy had finished making up the bed they joined the two and a half men in the backyard where Leo was sucking thoughtfully on a fruit box and inspecting the filthy state of his hands with considerable satisfaction. Jim and Wilson were talking footy.

'Thank you. So much,' said Kat, sinking into a chair.

'No worries,' said Wilson, passing her a beer.

'Really,' said Betsy, accepting her own beverage. 'You were absolutely fantastic.'

Wilson flushed slightly and waved one hand, shooing away the compliment. 'Happy to help.'

'We're going to get Leo home and cleaned up, then have a feed. Just a pasta or something. You're very welcome to join us.'

'Thanks!' he said to Betsy, pleased and surprised. 'That's really nice of you. But I have plans, I'm afraid. I'd better make tracks.'

Kat didn't know whether she felt sorry or relieved. Wilson drained his beer and stood. Jim stood with him, shook his hand. Betsy embraced him, kissed him on the cheek, saying: 'You were so great with Leo. We really appreciate it.'

'I'll walk you out,' Kat said.

As they stepped back out on to the street, Wilson said, 'I like your friends.'

'They like you!'

'You going to be okay here? Sorting all this out?'

'Oh sure. It looks much worse than it is.' She stopped and turned to face him. Lacking Betsy's elevation, a casual kiss on the cheek was out of the question without a cherry picker. But she laid one hand on his chest and said, 'It really was fantastic to have your help. It made it all so easy. You made it fun. It was incredibly generous of you.'

He gazed down at her for a long moment, his face unreadable. She was deeply conscious of the heat of his skin through his T-shirt, the faint beat of his pulse, the smell of him. What was supposed to be a friendly pat had suddenly turned, quite unexpectedly, into something else entirely and she could feel her own pulse quickening, her colour rising. Oh dear.

She stuffed both hands into the pockets of her jeans, saying, 'Thanks again!' a little too loudly.

He stepped back and opened the driver's side door.

'No worries,' he said lightly. 'See you tomorrow?'

Kat raised one hand. 'See you tomorrow.' Then turned and walked back down the driveway, her thoughts in considerable disarray.

Faces and hands washed but their clothes still covered in grime, the four of them sat down to heaped bowls of fettuccine bolognaise, three accompanied by very large glasses of red wine. Kat's hands, forearms, biceps, neck, back and legs had all started to ache and she could tell from the rigid way Jim was sitting that he wasn't entirely comfortable either. Leo had a glazed look, the precursor to either a bout of delirious high energy, or total collapse. Only Betsy seemed buoyant.

'That's that done,' she said with satisfaction.

'Thank you, guys. You've been absolute champions.'

'Our pleasure,' said Jim, refilling her glass. 'And Wilson doesn't have kids of his own. He's not married, either. Single, in fact.'

Kat coloured and looked at him crossly.

'Wilson's nice,' piped up Leo, unexpectedly emerging from his stupor.

'Wilson *is* nice,' said Betsy firmly.

Leo swung around to look at Kat. 'Is he your boyfriend?'

'No!'

'What is he?'

He's just the coffee guy! thought Kat desperately. Then: Well, obviously that's no longer quite true. He knows some of the most embarrassing details of my private life. He's helped me move house. He's met my closest friends. He's put the bits of my bed together and used my bathroom.

And yet... I don't know the first thing about him. Except that he used to be a chemist. He makes great coffee. And, despite being an arsehole, he is one of the kindest people I've ever met.

'He's a friend,' she said eventually.

'He has spectacular guns,' said Betsy.

'He's just a friend,' said Kat sternly.

'Why didn't he show me his guns?' asked Leo, peeved. Jim burst out laughing.

When the meal was over Kat said goodnight and walked the short block back to her flat. Despite the cold she stopped for a moment, propped against The Box, and contemplated the shadowy silhouette of the building. When I bought this place I was working on, what? *City Homicide*? Kevin Rudd was prime minister for the first time. Leo didn't exist. Twitter didn't exist. Heidi was starting high school. It didn't feel that long ago. But the world felt entirely changed. And me? she thought. Am I changed? Or the same?

Kind of both, she thought, sighing and groping in her pocket for her keys. Same but different. Old Kat would never have left Miles. Old Kat would have hung on for dear life. Old Kat would have gone on pretending she was happy because she was too scared to contemplate the alternative.

But somehow, despite New Kat's many admirable qualities, her resilience and her courage and clearer sense of self, New Kat had ended up right where Old Kat left off. She opened the front door, stepped inside, closed it gently, then turned to look into the chilly gloom of the hall.

'Hello,' she murmured. 'I'm home.'

21

Just as Kat eased into her usual parking spot, O'Donnell emerged from the café, cup in hand.

'Nice,' he said, nodding toward The Box.

'She's lovely,' said Kat fondly, closing the door and giving it a pat.

'Not flashy, but stylish. Real wood dash?'

'Oh yes. And steering wheel. Real leather, too.'

'You an Alfa girl?'

'Not really.' Kat leant against the bonnet and let her bags rest there for a moment. 'This one's a bit of a family heirloom.'

The ex-footballer walked around the car slowly, admiring its humble lines, peering in the windows. Kat felt a faint flush of embarrassment. No matter how often she tried to clean it out, the debris seemed to accumulate at an exponential rate.

'Nineteen-seventy-two?'

'My mother bought it new in 1970. But good guess. Are you an Alfa guy?' *I've never met a bloke more Alpha.*

'I like cars. These Italian jobs are a bit small for me to actually get around in, but they're beautiful machines. Especially when they're mint like this one.' He smiled at her and once again Kat felt the full physical force of it. 'Would you take me for a spin sometime?'

'Sure,' said Kat weakly, glad she had the car for support until the rush of blood to various extremities had passed.

'Great! Well, I'd better get upstairs. But I'll keep you to that.'

Kat raised one hand in farewell, then, when he was safely inside, gave herself a shake and patted her cheeks briskly. When she looked up she saw Wilson watching her through the window with evident amusement.

Dear Lord. Since the day of the move she had found herself periodically haunted by the memory of her hand on his chest, his proximity, the heat of his body against her palm, and had, on occasion, struggled to maintain her composure during such simple exchanges as saying hello or ordering a coffee. He, on the other hand, had continued to appear his normal, placid, friendly self.

Now Kat resisted the urge to run straight upstairs and hide in her office. Apart from anything else, she'd found herself more and more enjoying—and more and more relying on—the comfort of Wilson's company. She really didn't want a girlish crush to spoil things. So she simply took a breath, picked up her bags, and went in to say hello.

'Was that who I thought it was?'

'It was. Haven't you introduced yourself yet? Asked for his autograph? I thought you were a big Tigers man.'

'Too shy,' said Wilson, setting up the machine for her coffee. 'Unlike you, apparently.'

Kat laughed. 'It really is remarkable. My rational, mature human brain knows he's a lech and a scoundrel. But something about him just fires up that sort of ancient, reptilian part of my brain. I can't help myself.'

'It's funny to see you going all silly.'

'I did not go "all silly"!'

'You couldn't see yourself.' He passed her the coffee, today decorated with some kind of oval. She looked at him, puzzled.

'It's a Sherrin,' he said. 'Getting the stitching right's kind of hard.'

'Cheers. Had your fun?'

'Just getting started! What did he ask you?'

'How do you know he asked me anything?'

'You seemed to get a little flustered. He either paid you some outrageous compliment, or asked for some small favour.'

'And you think I don't deserve an outrageous compliment?'

Wilson propped against the far counter, grinning. 'I think he knows exactly what he's doing. He might compliment you on your work, in the appropriate circumstances, but not excessively. He knows that would embarrass you. Or make you suspicious. Or both. But asking for something? That gives you a little power. Or at least the appearance of it. It's a good strategy.'

Kat flushed. 'Stop it. Dare is *not* interested in me. I am certainly not interested in him.'

'Whatever you say, Kat. Whatever you say.'

Exasperated—at least in part because she suspected his

analysis of the transaction was shockingly accurate—Kat simply rolled her eyes, paid for her coffee, and left, hoping she wouldn't run into O'Donnell again upstairs.

But he was locked in conference with the production team, Heidi milling around outside the office in a not-so-subtle attempt to catch Dare's eye. Kat swallowed a smile, gestured to her, and walked into her own office. The small influence Kat had established over her assistant's sartorial decisions seemed to have evaporated with the arrival of O'Donnell. The one concession Heidi made was to trade her skyscraper heels for ballet flats, but otherwise the full smorgasbord of her flesh was once again on display.

It was nobody's business but her own, Kat reminded herself, especially now all the key locations had been sewn up. And if a bit of tricky business comes up, I can always make her wait in the car. 'I want to go by Unit today first,' she said to Heidi. 'I need to talk with Ted about the next challenge. But after that I thought you might like to just drop by the campsites with me and watch them film for a while. What do you think?'

'Will Dare be there?'

'I'm pretty sure Dare's office-bound—or at his leisure—between challenges and Council now. But you've got a shooting schedule. Have a look.'

Heidi didn't bother to look. They both knew perfectly well what the schedule was for the next week. Nor did she take Kat's question as anything but rhetorical. Instead she shrugged, murmured, ''kay', and picked up her bag.

'Just give me ten minutes,' Kat said, which Heidi took as permission to go and loiter in Dare's general vicinity for a little while longer.

After clearing her emails and phone messages, Kat

collected her charge and drove over to the car park on Spencer Street where the crew had set up base for the duration. At least on this shoot they hadn't had to make room for wardrobe and make-up trucks or trailers for the stars. O'Donnell was happy enough to be kitted out back at the office and have his nose occasionally powdered on location, while as for the contestants—the scruffier they looked, the better. Still, months of production required a lot of infrastructure, not least keeping the crew fed round the clock. And while this patch of gravel was neither cheap nor, as it turned out, especially well located, Kat was still pretty happy to have found anything with a 3000 postcode.

Harry, she discovered, had headed up to Bunjil campsite himself (after endless discussion, the two teams had been named after Wurundjeri totems, Bunjil and Waa). Ted was drinking International Roast from a stained mug and leafing through that morning's *Mail*.

'Morning boss,' said Kat, dropping her folders on the table.

'Wish my actual underlings had a bit of your respect,' he replied. 'What nightmare have you got for me this time?'

'Ted, you know the nightmares aren't my creation. I'm just following orders. And yes,' she held up one hand to snuff out the inevitable rejoinder, 'I know that's what the Nazis said. Anyway, not too much of a nightmare this time, I think.'

'No stairs?'

'No stairs. And no cranes. Not even any alleyways to speak of. In fact, the nightmare's all at my end this time. They're going busking. Midday, on Bourke Street Mall, and then around sixish, the Arts Centre underpass.'

'Nice one!' said Ted. 'You're closing off Bourke Street?'

'Well, no. A, that would be impossible unless we got Spielberg to pull some strings. And b, they're going to need some actual passersby if the busking is to have any effect.'

'Fair enough. Still, main roads. That's a result.'

With Heidi sitting by paying a reasonable degree of attention, Kat and Ted discussed the finer points of the upcoming challenge, from the need for a field producer to handle the permissions from anyone and everyone caught on camera, to the logistics of moving principal photography across town in peak hour. Plus, of course, the inevitable parking issues. When they were happy that the set-up was doable and had set a date for a reccie, Kat said, 'Thought I'd take Heidi over to Bunjil camp for a squiz. Okay with you?'

'Knock yourself out,' said Ted. 'And while you're there, keep an eye out for a spot for the wildlife pick-ups, will you? Bev's hunting up vermin as we speak.'

'What are "wildlife pick-ups"?' asked Heidi as they walked back to The Box.

'You know how on, say, *Survivor South Pacific*, they intersperse the action with quick shots of a snake twisted round a tree branch, or a giant tarantula, or a—I don't know—crab crawling along.'

'Sure.'

'Well, we need some of those. You and I need a couple of locations where Bev can release our wildlife, and one of Ted's boys can shoot them.'

'What kind of locations?'

'I'm not really sure. But if you see something you think might do the trick—where we can get some nice close shots that sort of fit with the show—let me know.'

By now The Box almost drove itself to the two campsites, and Tribal Council. Kat wasn't there much these days. Most of the filming was done by eminently portable two-man crews who required nothing of her. But it had taken so long to get everything established she felt she could still get there from any point in the city with her eyes closed.

Even her favourite park was waiting for her, she noted with satisfaction. Getting out of the car she spotted Harry loitering on the corner and murmured to Heidi, 'There's no problem with us being here, but they are filming pretty much constantly so remember to keep your voice down. And don't slam the car door. That kind of sound really carries.'

Heidi nodded, closed the door softly, and tiptoed down the lane to where Harry had turned and waved.

'You on duty?' Kat asked.

'Yeah. We're breaking the fourth wall today.'

'What are they up to?'

'See for yourself,' he said, stepping back and gesturing for the two women to move forward.

Poor Vanessa (the villain) had already been voted out, even earlier than Kat had anticipated. But otherwise, Bunjil remained intact, having won the next two challenges. As Kat stepped out of the side street and into the strange anteroom that a century of haphazard building had created, she realised what was happening.

In the background, Fiona the greenie sat huddled in one of the big cardboard boxes, protected from the elements in a rudimentary way by a large sheet of plastic Phil the butcher had managed to scavenge from somewhere. Phil was tending the fire, something he had done almost single-handedly since day one. On either side of him squatted the two young professional men, Nick and Michael, both already sporting impressive facial hair, chatting in a fake-casual manner, periodically passing him thick twists of old newspaper. In the foreground was Peru, the resident hottie, alternately picking at her dirty fingernails and gazing doe-eyed into the camera.

Harry passed Kat a headset, and she picked Peru up mid-sentence.

'...hard enough!' She gestured to the campsite extravagantly. 'I mean, shouldn't we all be working together? Phil says we should all pull together, and I agree. Anyway, Waa are hopeless, they'll never get immunity. We'll win. So I think they should just be nicer.'

Harry stepped forward. 'Thanks Peru,' he murmured. 'Great. Terrific. Can you send Michael over?'

'Okay,' she said, beaming at him with her full two-forty volts.

A moment later Michael and Peru passed each other, faux-smiles at five paces, and Michael took his place on the upturned milk crate. As soon as Harry gave him the go-ahead he hissed, 'This is ridiculous! Haven't any of these people ever watched *Survivor*? Sooner or later we're going to lose a challenge, then they'll vote me out. Then Nick out. And then they'll be stuffed. We're supposed to strategise! We're supposed to outwit! That's the whole point, isn't it? If we're going to win this, we have to get rid of Fiona. She's a complete waste of space. You don't keep someone on the team just because she likes animals. We all like animals, for Chrissakes. Just because Nick and I don't go gaga over kittens doesn't mean we don't like animals.' Realising he'd somewhat lost the thread,

Michael took a breath and continued. 'Then Phil says we've got to look after the girls. No, we don't! That's exactly what we *don't* have to do! It's not how the game's played. I mean, I can't trust Nick either, obviously. Last night he...'

But whatever Nick had done last night was destined to remain a mystery. At that moment a needling scream had them all on their feet, Kat tugging off her headset and spinning around to clap a hand over Heidi's mouth.

'What are you *doing*?' she hissed. But Heidi continued to gurgle and gesture frantically towards the crumbling wall against which she'd been resting. Framed by a faded advertisement for a business long since defunct, his head poking out of a gap in the brickwork, was a very large rat. In his jaws was a struggling cockroach, also of considerable size, and from the hollow in which the rodent crouched scuttled a steady stream of the insect's friends.

Thrusting Heidi back down the laneway, Kat directed the disoriented cameraman's attention to this gruesome tableau before pulling her phone out of her pocket. 'Ted?' she said, choking down her laughter. 'I think we've got our wildlife pick-ups sorted...'

22

Cruising the aisles of Coburg Woolworths, Kat experienced one of those surprising moments of culture shock that continued to catch her unawares. She'd never felt entirely at home in Fitzroy, always keenly aware of her lowbrow middle-classness and her recent tenure in what was at that stage still the Outer North. At least to Fitzroy types. Miles' faint disparagement hadn't helped, of course, but in a milieu where seventy per cent of the population was absurdly young and the rest way too cool for school, Kat had felt a savage resurgence of teenage self-consciousness.

Here though, most days, most times, she felt completely at home among the Burg's allsorts, where fat Greek nonnas and heavily draped twentysomething mothers shared space with sharp young men in their pimped-up Holdens and Fords and people like her and Betsy and Jim, refugees not from some Middle Eastern hotspot but the skyrocketing prices of the inner suburbs.

Yet at midday on a Saturday it wasn't the sight of a woman in a full-face burqua soothing a toddler by thrusting a well-chewed Spongebob doll at her that brought Kat up short but the contents of some other mothers' trolleys. Mountains of homebrand white bread, tens of litres of soft drink, biscuits, chips, massive bags of chocolates, instant meals, with a six-pack of floury, marked-down apples the one gesture to a balanced diet.

Almost invariably these mothers and their overloaded trolleys were accompanied by rotund children with pasty skin, reminding her irresistibly of those unfortunates in *Honey, We're Killing the Kids*. Kat had complicated feelings about her reaction to all this, knowing it was at least in part a vestige of that strange protectiveness she felt these days towards all children, all of whom she knew were not her responsibility.

It was a powerful thing, though, this urge to interfere. She wanted to tap them on the shoulder. Say: You can't raise a child on a diet like that. She wanted to go through the weekly shop with them and help them select good food, appropriate food, Fitzroy-approved food. She wanted to have the authority of a *Biggest Loser* trainer, or that strange woman from *You Are What You Eat*, the one obsessed with examining people's faeces. Not that Kat wanted to examine people's faeces. Merely bring a bit of tough grocery love before more lives were ruined. It was, she knew, absolutely none of her business. But sometimes the impulse to reach out a hand and say, *No!* or *Don't!* was almost overwhelming.

Two young men who looked like they were subsisting on nothing but tinned soup and English muffins, or the woman with a basket full of cat food and Lean Cuisine made her smile. But those extravaganzas of processed food in the groaning family trolleys? Won't somebody think of the children! She tried to turn her attention away from other people's shopping and back to her own.

Assuming everybody else was as obsessed with other people's groceries as she was, Kat felt her Noah's Ark selection marked her out indisputably as a new arrival. It had been a long time since she'd faced a larder that was literally bare. And quite a while—given Miles' iron rule over the kitchen—since she'd prepared anything more adventurous than cereal, toast or alphabet spaghetti. But after a fortnight spent alternately raiding the catering at Unit and trawling the kebab shops and curry houses of Sydney Road, it was beyond time to restock.

So here she was in the supermarket, dividing her attention between the social failings of her neighbours and trying to imagine what she might require to eat for a week, along with questioning seriously whether she really needed such 'basics' as flour.

It made for slow going. But she comforted herself with the thought that at least eating was no longer something she had to force herself to do. The constant nausea had subsided. She had, first, begun to feel hungry again, and was now actively taking an interest in her next meal. The ache in her chest, too, had diminished. She was beginning to feel whole again, if not precisely brimming with joy. No longer did every child under ten stop her in her tracks with a savage stab of loss; just the ones who actually bore a resemblance to Bonnie. A thick head of curls, maybe, or those gangly arms and legs.

And rather than every resting moment being a swamp

of grief and pain, Kat had begun to monitor her own recovery with a disinterested curiosity. Appetite back? Check. Uncontrollable sobbing under control? Check. Weird behaviour around small children—a kind of maniacal friendliness that had mothers gathering their offspring protectively to them—in abeyance? Check.

Being back in the flat was a mixed blessing. While every spare moment had been spent unpacking boxes she'd felt okay. Busy was good. Once everything was in order there'd been an unexpected resurgence of grief. Everything was the same, but different. She was different, irrevocably. She felt not-at-home in her own home, strangely adrift despite its narrow confines and profound familiarity. But even that was beginning to wear off, or wear in. It felt normal now to be putting her key in the front door every night. And even, sometimes, comforting.

It does get better, she thought. You feel it never will, but it does. I wonder if anyone told Suicide Guy that?

Sure, the fact that she was constantly assessing her own state of mind indicated that she wasn't quite out of the woods. (*Huh. I actually enjoyed that for ten minutes*; or: *Why am I feeling so dreadful? Oh. That's right. Bonnie's gone.*) The idea of just living her life without being constantly braced against pain still seemed like fantasy. But she hadn't fallen to pieces. Well done, New Kat, Kat said to herself. You might just make it.

'Just moved in?' asked the checkout chick brightly. Although 'chick' wasn't quite the right appellation for the weatherworn middle-aged woman pushing her purchases rhythmically past the scanner.

'Yep,' said Kat.

'Like it here in Coburg?'

'I do. I used to live here. I've moved back.'

'Where'd you go?'

'Fitzroy.'

'Oh,' said the woman, clearly expecting something more exotic. Then: 'What's this?'

'Celeriac.'

She found it on the electronic page, selected it, weighed it, still eyeing the vegetable suspiciously. 'What do you do with it?'

'You can roast it. Like potatoes. Make a soup. Braise it with leeks. Bit of white wine and olive oil. That's nice.'

'Hmm,' she said, clearly not convinced. 'Expensive.'

Kat offered no opinion on the pricing.

'Eat a lot of this in Fitzroy?'

'They do,' said Kat, biting her lip against a smile.

Silence fell between them for a moment until the woman, noting the price on Kat's bag of carefully selected apples, said: 'You know, you can get six Royal Galas for half that price.'

'I like the Pink Ladies. They're a bit crisper.'

'Some people like to know about the specials,' she said without malice.

'Thank you,' said Kat, thinking her apples and celeriac were barely a drop in the oceanic total accumulating on the checkout screen. But that maybe next week she'd consider the sweet potato, which she had noticed was a fifth of the price of today's snooty vegetable selection.

'Pet food,' said the woman unexpectedly.

'Pardon?'

'You should see what some people spend on pet food. First thing out of the trolley, and I could feed my whole family for a week on what it costs. Makes you wonder, doesn't it?'

'Mmm,' said Kat. Clearly she was *not* the only person who took an unnatural interest in other people's weekly shop.

Transaction complete, the woman handed Kat her docket, met her eyes, and said, smiling: 'Welcome back.'

'Thank you,' said Kat. 'It's good to be back.'

23

Heidi beamed at Kat, bouncing on her toes, and Kat couldn't help grinning back. Behind them, the icy night air nipped at their necks and the darkness in the alley was disturbingly complete. Before them, however, was a bizarre tableau: a blazing fire in a metal drum and a dilapidated sofa on which the remnants of Team Waa were huddled; in the foreground, O'Donnell, one foot propped on an old crate; and as a backdrop three pock-marked brick walls jagged with bits of iron, casting macabre shadows in the flickering light.

'Zane?' said O'Donnell briskly, and the young man lifted a handsome, surly face to the camera. 'What's the animosity level right now?'

Zane puffed out his cheeks. Shrugged. Cast a glance at the people sitting either side of him. 'High,' he offered.

'What's got you all so uptight?'

'Like, I don't think you can just elect yourself leader.'

'I didn't "elect myself leader"!' protested Trent, at whom the accusation was clearly levelled. Of the motley crew on the sofa, the good-natured farm boy was clearly holding up the best. But even he seemed to have lost much of his sunny humour.

'What do you call it then?' piped up party-girl Amber.

'None of the rest of you ever *do* anything,' countered Trent, clearly exasperated. 'Except bitch and moan.'

'Ooooh,' said Amber. 'Nasty.'

Trent folded his arms across his chest and pressed his lips together.

'Okay,' said O'Donnell. 'I think it's pretty obvious Team Waa is in trouble. This is the third time you've been up at Tribal Council. Jake, why is that? Who's not pulling their weight?'

'Zane,' said Jake promptly, a comment that brought the other man instantly to his feet. O'Donnell stepped forward, laid a large hand on his shoulder, and gently pressed him back into his seat.

'Why do you say that, Jake? Trent says you're not really contributing either.'

'I don't think Trent appreciates what we do,' interjected Amber. Trent rolled his eyes. 'Like, Jake and I do heaps. And then Trent says we can't have any food!'

'I didn't say you couldn't have any food! I said we had to ration the food! And then you went and stole it anyway.'

'We didn't steal it! It's our food too. We were hungry.'

'I don't know why. You never get off your arse.'

'Okay, okay.' O'Donnell raised placating hands. 'Zane? Are you pulling your weight?'

'Of course I am. But Trent's right about one thing.

174

Jake and Amber do fuck-all except complain.'

Amber leant over and lightly smacked the side of Zane's head.

'Is this *Survivor* or *Jerry Springer*?' Kat murmured to Harry, as O'Donnell once again intervened to prevent an all-in brawl.

'Amber, I think even you'd have to admit that Trent was the only one really kicking goals in the last challenge.'

'Well, he's from a farm! What do you expect?'

'I don't think anything in the last challenge was really farm-related.'

'I mean, he's used to, you know, doing stuff. I'm creative. I'm artistic. They're my strengths. But no one appreciates that.'

'Zane, do you think Amber's creativity has been a benefit to Waa?'

'No,' said Zane bluntly, then ducked as Amber's hand swung out again.

'Dare?' murmured the director into O'Donnell's earpiece. 'I think you're enjoying this way too much. No fisticuffs please. Start bringing them home.'

'All right,' said O'Donnell. 'We all know why we're here. Amber, do you think you should go home tonight?'

'No! No one's given me a chance. I could, like, really contribute. I just want to be able to prove to the others what I can do!' Her voice broke slightly on the last sentence and her eyes filled with tears, but her teammates appeared unmoved.

O'Donnell said, 'Trent? How about you? Should you be the one going home?'

'They can send me home if they like,' he grunted. 'Love to see how they go without me.'

'Zane? Do you think you'd get by without Trent? Or should you be the one to leave?'

'I should be leading this team,' Zane said, straightening his impressive shoulders. 'I want to win this. And I think the rest of these guys know I can. If I go home tonight, it'll be because I'm a threat.'

Trent coughed pointedly. Amber regarded Zane with new interest.

'And that just leaves you, Jake,' said O'Donnell, as the second cameraman moved into position.

One of the reasons Kat had chosen this spot for Tribal Council was the dead-end that ran off one of the near walls. Shaded at one end by an old awning, it provided the perfect location for the casting of secret ballots. It was even lit by a ghoulishly flickering neon strip. Bev had provided scraps of torn cardboard and sticks of charcoal for the inscribing of names and an Oscar the Grouch-style bin to receive the nominations. Now, with the cameraman standing on a crate and pressed flat into one corner, the members of Waa slowly made their way down the alley, made their marks on the cardboard, and shuffled back out again.

'Creative, my arse,' said Trent, dropping his vote through the slit in the top of the bin.

'Sorry mate,' said Jake, when his turn came.

Zane scrawled with particular vehemence, saying, 'We'll get along just fine, mate.'

Amber merely sniffed and rubbed at her nose with the back of one hand, scribbling awkwardly with the other.

As soon as the votes were cast, Bev scuttled in to retrieve the bin and placed it next to Dare. 'Team Waa,' said O'Donnell, standing with legs spread and hands clasped behind his back. 'Whoever goes home tonight, you're now down to just three members. I hope you've chosen wisely.'

Then he began the process of counting the votes, by now a pretty meagre enterprise he tried to imbue with as much gravitas as possible.

'Trent. One vote.' And laid it to one side.

'Trent. Two votes.'

Retrieved another piece of cardboard.

'Amber. One vote.' Long pause. 'As you know, in the event of a tied vote, the two nominated teammates will face off in an individual challenge to decide who goes home.'

'God, I'd love to see that,' murmured Harry, during the even longer pause that followed. 'Do you think it'd be something creative?'

Kat shot him a brimming look.

'Trent. Three votes.' O'Donnell announced eventually. 'Trent, the tribe has spoken. Please remove your beanie.'

Kat had to admire the fact that, yet again, O'Donnell had managed to pronounce those words without appearing even slightly ridiculous. Amid half-hearted back-pats from his teammates, Trent stood, pulled off his beanie, and passed it to O'Donnell, who reached out to shake Trent's hand.

'Trent, how are you feeling right now?'

The big blond nodded reflectively. 'Well, I'm not surprised,' he said.

'Do you think your teammates appreciated what you brought to Waa?'

'No.'

'What will you remember most about your *Survivor* experience?'

Trent grinned ruefully and ran a hand through his hair. 'I'll tell you this, mate. I won't forget any of it in a hurry.'

'Trent, thanks for being such a great competitor. It's time to go.' And O'Donnell extended his hand once more, before guiding Trent into the blackness of the alley.

Off-camera, Harry said, 'Well done, mate,' clapping an arm around his shoulder.

'Fuck me, I need a shower. And a beer,' said Trent.

'You got it,' said Harry, and led him back down the lane.

As the remaining members of Waa trooped back to another cold, miserable night at camp, O'Donnell approached Kat.

'First time you've stayed for the duration?'

Kat nodded. 'I've seen the rough cuts, but this is the first time I've hung around for the live show.'

'Enjoy it?'

'Oh yes.'

'No script,' said O'Donnell, holding out both palms. 'Told you I could bullshit with the best of them.'

'You were fantastic,' Kat admitted. 'But—Lord!—what are those three going to do with themselves now?'

'Well, Zane'll elect himself captain, obviously.'

'Of a ship of fools.'

'Not my department,' said O'Donnell. Then: 'You come here in that sweet little Alfa?'

'I did.'

'Don't suppose you'd let me drive you back to Unit?'

Kat hesitated, throwing a look at Heidi, who was watching them with a mixture of curiosity and disapproval.

'The back seat's chock full of crap,' Kat said, 'and I drove Heidi here.'

'Heidi can come back with us in the truck,' offered Ted, in a decisive yet expressionless way that made Kat suspicious. But before anyone—particularly Heidi—could protest, he'd placed a hand in the small of her back, said, 'Come on, love', and begun ushering her back down the lane.

'So that's a yes?' O'Donnell said.

'I guess that's a yes,' said Kat, and reached into her bag to fish out the keys. 'Be gentle with her.'

It took considerable jiggling and manoeuvring to get the seat back far enough for O'Donnell to actually fit behind the wheel, matters not helped by the mountain of miscellany piled on the rear seat. But eventually he was in, and Kat found herself in the rare and not entirely pleasant position of being a passenger in her own car. She clasped her hands in her lap, and O'Donnell glanced at her, smiling, and turned the key in the ignition.

'It's all right. I do know how to drive. And I have a current licence.'

'It's not that.'

'I know. It's your baby.' He paused and listened to The Box idle. 'Carburettor trouble?'

Kat made a small tsk. 'I know, I know. At least, I don't know exactly what the problem is. I keep meaning to take her in to Ange—my mechanic—but I haven't got round to it.'

'How's she run in top gear,' he asked, revving gently.

'Lovely. No problem.'

'If I get the chance, I'll have a look at it, if you like. I'm not a mechanic, but I might be able to spot something obvious.'

'Thank you!'

He ran his hands over the steering wheel, reached out to stroke the dash and brush his fingers against the speedo, the clock. Big hands. Long fingers. Could hold a Sherrin like it was a tennis ball, thought Kat, feeling her breath catch a little.

'She really is beautiful, isn't she?' said O'Donnell. Then he put The Box into gear, and they pulled out from the curb.

Distracted by the unfamiliar sensation of riding shotgun—and the enormous man squeezed in beside her—it took Kat a moment to realise they were heading not down towards Spencer Street but out towards the Arts Centre.

'Shouldn't we...?'

He shot her a smile. 'I didn't say I'd drive you *straight* back to Unit. Can't expect me not to take her for a proper spin.' He shifted up into fourth and accelerated smoothly. 'What's her top speed?'

'Honestly? I don't know. She's pretty happy sitting on seventy—you know, 110 k's.'

He gave a short laugh. 'How long did you say you'd had her? And you've never done more than seventy?'

Kat flushed faintly.

'That is a crime. You know these little ladies were built for speed, don't you?' And he gently but steadily depressed the accelerator.

A protest caught in Kat's throat. Part of her wanted to wrench the wheel out of his hands. Part of her was desperately anxious about cruising police cars. She had never had a speeding ticket in her life, and she dreaded to think what would happen if those flashing lights appeared in the rear-view mirror. Would he even pull over? Would she find herself caught up in some hoon scandal with a disgraced former footballer?

But another part of her, some visceral deep-in-her-gut part, watched the needle on the speedo wobble and climb—edging over a hundred, what on earth was that in k's?—with a mad kind of joy. She dug her fingers into the stiff leather of the seat, breathed deeply, and hung on.

They whipped around the Botanic Gardens and down on to Alexander Avenue, the river glinting and shimmering as The Box took the curves like a pro. In what seemed like seconds they were roaring onto CityLink, the big freeway almost empty, the pylons and sidings—and the other cars—blurring past the window at a thrilling rate.

Kat could feel her pulse in her hands and face, feel her heart pounding, almost hear it over the high whine of the engine, part excitement, part panic. Weirdly, it wasn't crashing and dying that was needling at her. Instead, every time they passed a toll point she winced. Surely some, if not all, were also speed cameras?

But it was way too late to worry about that now. They were up and over the Bolte Bridge, the light flickering wildly.

'Westgate or Eastern?' Dare asked, grinning.

'Uh...'

'Westgate it is,' he said, cutting madly across three lanes to take the right-hand exit.

Now Kat's chest was actually aching, her fingers gripping the seat, as they almost two-wheeled it along the exit and entrance roads and roared up onto the bridge.

'Slow down!' she suddenly exclaimed. Then, more quietly, 'I want to look.'

So he obliged, dropping gradually back to sixty, then fifty—eighty k's, but it felt almost like walking speed— and they cruised quietly up and over the long sweep of the Westgate, the great blanket of the city stretching away to their right, the industrial edge of the river and the bay to their left.

'It's a beautiful place, isn't it?' he murmured.

'It is,' she said.

Indicating sedately, he took the Williamstown Road exit and said, 'Do you need to go back to Unit? I just realised I left my car at the office.'

'No. Footscray's fine,' said Kat. And sat in a pleasant stupor, the adrenalin gradually receding, as he drove—in her preferred style, right on the speed limit—back along near-deserted streets to the darkened production offices. That, she thought, was strangely sexual. No wonder all those young blokes couldn't help themselves.

Pulling up next to the looming bulk of his Jeep, Dare switched off the engine and they sat there quietly, warm and still, listening to The Box tick and settle.

Then he said, 'Like a drink?'

They gazed at each other for a moment in the gloom. Kat could feel the warmth of him, smell the wool of his coat and the scent of his skin and hair. He really was extraordinarily large.

'Not now,' she said softly.

'Soon?'

'Sure.'

Kat was dimly aware that he appeared to have just asked her for a date, but not at all sure why, or why she seemed to have said yes, or how she felt about that, or what might happen next. It had suddenly become a most unexpected evening.

'Well, thank you,' he said eventually. 'That was fun.'

24

'Thank God you're here!' Kat shut the door firmly and stood in the doorway, almost shaking with a vertiginous mix of shock and pain and mirth.

'I take it this is a whisky visit, not a coffee visit?'

'It's a *Wilson* visit!' she cried, advancing into the room and sinking into a chair.

'Well in that case...' He flipped the sign from Open to Closed, and locked the door. 'What have you done this time?' Then, looking at her face more closely: 'Are you about to cry? Or laugh?'

'I don't know!' Kat was aware she was speaking in a succession of exclamation points, her voice half an octave higher than usual. 'Laugh. I think.' She took a breath. 'In a crying sort of way.'

'Glad to have that cleared up.'

Wilson inspected two latte glasses for cleanliness, retrieved the bottle from beneath the counter—Macallan this time, Kat noted distractedly—sat down opposite her, and poured them both a generous slug. When Kat had calmed her nerves with a gulp of it, she took another breath and met his smiling, curious eyes.

'This has to remain *strictly* confidential,' she said.

Wilson crossed his heart gravely, then stretched out his legs and leaned back in his chair with the air of man settling in for the long haul.

'It all started last week,' said Kat. 'When O'Donnell asked if he could drive The Box back from Tribal Council...' She related the wild ride along Melbourne's plentiful freeways, the terror and the rush of it.

'Kind of sexy, isn't it?' Wilson said.

'Yes,' said Kat. 'Yes it is.'

Wilson cleared his throat. 'So... Then you slept with him?'

'No!'

'Really? No?'

'No, I really didn't.'

'Huh.' Then, seeing the expression on her face: 'That's not about you. It's about him. He's just that kind of person. Blokes want to be his mate, women want to have sex with him. That's the O'Donnell magic.'

'Well, it's funny you should mention that.'

Wilson narrowed his eyes at her. 'What have you done?'

'Nothing. Truly. But he did ask me out.'

'Did he now,' said Wilson blandly.

Kat went on to explain Dare's mild proposition before they parted company, and the turmoil that ensued.

'Because the thing is, you're right,' she said. 'He is one sexy dude. And once he'd put the idea in my head—not that he came out and suggested we have sex, of course...'

'But it was implied.'

'Yes. Or...' She looked to Wilson for confirmation. 'I think that would be a fair assumption, don't you?'

He inclined his head. 'I do,' he murmured.

'Well, once I started thinking about it, I couldn't stop thinking about it. It was ridiculous. It was like being sixteen again! I was blushing, I was stuttering, I felt sick, I couldn't sleep...'

Wilson was very still, his face impassive.

'Sorry. Too much information?'

'No,' he said politely. 'Keep going. I understand.'

'He was in the office all the time, but he was always with people, or I was busy. Sometimes he'd just look at me, the way he does. But we'd just say hello, nothing more than that.' Kat paused and drained her whisky.

Wilson stood abruptly. 'I want another one. How about you?'

'Yes, please.'

He took his time refilling their glasses, his back to her.

'It was a relief, in a way. Because obviously getting involved with Dare would be a very bad idea,' Kat continued.

'I would have thought so, yes.'

'But God. The temptation. It was driving me nuts. I started having these long conversations with myself. Would he ask me out again? Wouldn't he? And if he did—maybe it was just drinks. Maybe nothing more would come of it. Did I want anything more to come of it? Obviously, yes and no. You get the picture.'

'I do.'

'Then I started thinking, Why don't *I* ask *him* out? It's the twenty-first century. I'm a grown woman. I'm allowed. Could be a bit of fun. I haven't been on a date in years.' Kat took a breath. Wilson was looking at her oddly, a mix of stunned and sad. Or maybe he was just bored? 'Sorry,' she said. 'I'm banging on, aren't I?'

He shook his head. 'No, I... I'm interested. Keep going.'

'You sure?'

He smiled at her. 'I'm sure. So you asked him out?'

'No,' said Kat ruefully. 'I did not.'

'Thought better of it?'

'Sort of...' The temptation had been powerful. It had been so long since she'd had sex with anyone, clinging to common sense had been difficult in the extreme. The thing that had finally stopped her was imagining this moment, where she was right now. If she had asked Dare out for that drink, and they *had* had sex, could she have ever looked Wilson in the eye again? She'd been *almost* prepared to sacrifice her own self-respect, but to lose Wilson's good opinion—and how could she not, if she'd gone through with it?—was something she couldn't face.

Once that decision had been made, resistance had been easier. That was not, however, a part of the story she chose to share. Instead she just said, 'I chickened out.' Which was also true. 'Anyway, sorry, all that is just back story. I am getting to the point.'

'There's more?' asked Wilson, slightly alarmed.

'You *are* bored.'

'No, I am definitely not bored.'

Kat looked at him quizzically for a moment, then launched into the next chapter of her story.

While she'd been wrestling with her own unexpected O'Donnell fixation, Kat couldn't fail to be aware that ever since their first introduction, when Heidi had been literally struck dumb, the young woman had developed a fierce, silent obsession with the ex-footballer. Whenever he was around her brain seemed to just stop working. She'd stop speaking mid-sentence. She became deaf to anything said to her, oblivious to everything going on around her. Her eyes would follow the man's every move. The entire office had noticed, including O'Donnell, who sometimes met Kat's eyes behind Heidi's back in a pointed way.

It was funny, but Kat also felt a little embarrassed for the girl. Over the last few months she'd become quite protective of her: she didn't want her to make more of a fool of herself than was absolutely necessary. Or get her heart broken.

'I was thinking that maybe I should just try and have a word with her,' Kat said. 'Just, you know, gently encourage her to get a grip.'

'How old's Heidi again?'

'Eighteen? Nineteen?'

'So O'Donnell's twice her age.'

'Exactly.'

'Not that that's ever stopped anyone.'

'Well!' said Kat, leaning forward, reaching the climax of her story. 'So there's me, tortured by these ridiculous O'Donnell fantasies, at the same time thinking, as a responsible adult I really should, you know, warn Heidi off.'

'And then?'

'Then tonight I leave my phone in my office. I'm about five k's down the road when I realise, and there are numbers I need for some calls tonight. So I drive back here. Everything looks deserted. I run upstairs...'

And at this point Kat found words failed her. Along

with never having had a speeding ticket and never having asked a man out, another glaring omission in her journey into adulthood was that she had never actually watched two people having sex before. Her first, instinctive reaction had been: Dear God! Is *that* what it looks like?

As she sat with her face in her hands, the truth slowly dawned on Wilson.

'They weren't,' he gasped.

'They were.'

'In your office?'

'On my desk!' Kat wailed.

'Oh dear.'

And as all the horror and the absurdity and the exquisite embarrassment of that moment came rushing back, Kat felt her face grow hot.

'Oh Kat,' said Wilson, reaching out to squeeze her hand. 'Poor Kat.' He was trying manfully not to laugh, but the effort proved too much for him. 'On your desk?' he choked.

'I have to *work* there tomorrow!' And Kat, with shaking shoulders, gave herself over to the ridiculousness of it all.

When they had both managed to stop laughing, Wilson wiped his eyes and poured more whisky. Kat received hers gratefully, saying, 'I feel like such an idiot.'

'Don't,' he said kindly. 'You've behaved impeccably. You didn't sleep with him, which is a good thing, especially in the circumstances. Heidi may be young, but she's an adult. And anyway, she has parents. She's not your responsibility. As for the rest—well, that's private, isn't it? No one but you knows what goes on inside your own head. Except now me, obviously.' Then, as another thought occurred to him: 'Did they see you?'

'No. At least—God, I hope not.' Kat paused, flushing all over again. 'No, they can't have. They would have been downstairs by now.'

'Why aren't they downstairs by now?'

Kat peered towards the street but reflection from the lights inside made it impossible to see out.

'Go and check,' she hissed. 'Is the Jeep still there? Or the Prius?'

Wilson walked behind the counter and pressed his face to the glass.

'Yep. Both there.'

'Then what are they still doing up there?'

She met Wilson's eyes, first in puzzlement, then in realisation. They both said in unison: '*They're still at it!*' And started laughing all over again.

25

After lunch with Betsy and the family, Kat headed out for a walk. It was cold but dry, the sun was shining, and down at the dogtopia that was Merri Creek the wattle was in full bloom. 'Fairyland!' one small girl had exclaimed as Kat strolled through a feathery avenue of green and gold. *Sure. If you can ignore the trees strung with shredded plastic and the penetrating odour of composting duck poop.*

Bonnie would have liked it here, Kat thought, with the familiar dull ache. Its wildness. The swings up near the oval. The dogs, all in a state of extreme and sustained joy. You could, she knew, follow the creek all the way from North Fitzroy, but for some reason they'd never ventured here. Miles never understood the pleasure of a long, dirty, vigorous walk. He preferred a short stroll through Edinburgh Gardens that culminated in a lengthy brunch at Green Grocer. Kat and Bonnie had tended to stick with that same routine: an amble around the park (also, it must be said, generously populated with dogs) capped off with a babyccino.

Now Kat could walk as far, wide and wildly as she chose. And if there was something a little lonely about that, there was freedom in it too. Just the action of walking was soothing. The cold air felt good on her face, the sun warm on her back. There was nowhere particular she had to be, nothing especially she had to do, except walk. And breathe. And let some of the junk that was rattling around in her skull either drift away, or settle in to some kind of order.

Over lunch she had finally had the chance to share with Betsy her Dare-ing adventures of the last week. Jim had kept one ear on their conversation in his usual quietly amused fashion while engaging Leo in casual chat to keep the boy's attention elsewhere. Bets had been as concerned about the potential—admittedly averted—of Kat crashing and dying during her wild ride as amused by the hilarious humiliation of her non-encounter with the sex-symbol footballer. ('Kat! You must be more careful!') She was most intrigued, though, by the story's eventual postscript.

'You told Wilson?'

'Of course!' Kat had replied. But it wasn't until Bets posed the question that Kat had thought perhaps it *was* a slightly odd thing to do. In theory, at least. But in practice? No. There was no more natural thing in the world than to share an adventure with Wilson as soon as possible, knowing he would appreciate all its implications, but especially its comedic aspects.

She had certainly developed the habit of stopping by at

the end of the day for a last coffee and a debrief, relating the latest absurdities of the *Survivor* shoot or chewing over the pros and cons of a particular challenge or location. In return she received the latest gossip and dramas from the café and its clientele, or perhaps an old anecdote from the corridors of Big Pharma. Funny things were funnier once she'd told him, and even the most exasperating developments revealed their lighter side.

So yes, of course she'd told Wilson. If only to ensure she tipped from tears—or screaming hysterics—into laughter. And it had worked. It had been just what she needed.

Ahead of her a young woman was walking two dogs: a fat, bug-eyed Chihuahua, and a glossy black greyhound, the former spinning deliriously between the high-stepping legs of the latter. Now there was a household, Kat thought, where you'd never be miserable for long. Perhaps we should have given each of the *Survivor* teams a dog. You certainly saw plenty of homeless people with a furry friend in tow. It must be just about the only thing keeping them going, the only thing keeping them sane. And there was no doubt the Cohen Clarke team had radically underestimated the pressure and general nastiness of the adventure into which they'd tipped their hapless contestants.

But that in itself looked like making some interesting telly, Kat thought, stepping carefully around a pile of dog shit. It was certainly unlike anything she'd seen before. At least locally. One of the things she'd always enjoyed about homegrown reality TV was the indefatigable good nature of the contestants. Where other nations bitched and backstabbed and schemed and wept, Australians tended to give the merest lip service to the idea of competition.

They might insist that winning was what they wanted

most in the world; that it would be life-changing; that they'd sacrifice anything to achieve it. But when it came down to the wire they couldn't help themselves. They were not only incapable of delivering the killer blow; if a rival stumbled they helped them up. We are a nation of John Landys, Kat thought.

At least, we were. Until...*Survivor: CBD*. She grinned to herself. Michael and Nick might be railing at their teammates' refusal to get political, to go strategic, but over at Waa, where a succession of failures in the challenges had deprived them not just of bodies but of luxuries like hot food, bedding, and a chance to bathe, animal instincts were finally and ferociously revealing themselves. The remaining members of Team Waa were emerging as every bit as nasty, ruthless and underhand as the best—or worst—of their international counterparts.

Have we been too nice to them in the past? Never having worked on an international production, Kat had no idea what kind of rigours reality contestants were subjected to in other countries. Just from watching them, they seemed to have it pretty easy. The UK *Survivor* was laughable: they were provided with enough tinned food to last out the apocalypse, and they still complained.

Perhaps we were really made of sterner stuff. Those original *Australian Survivor* contestants, dropped into the wilds of Eyre Peninsula, had certainly been way too good at hunting, gathering and building shelter—something the producers had discovered, belatedly, to their cost. We are also, Kat thought, much more ambivalent about winning. I wonder why that is? Some weird mutation of the tall-poppy syndrome, perhaps. We're suspicious of success in other people. Or at least suspicious of anyone who seems to be enjoying success, and distrusting that impulse in ourselves just as much.

Only to a point, though. Because the horrible, hypnotic, hilarious reality of what was happening to Team Waa spoke of a deeper truth. Rachet up the pressure and we all turn nasty. Grind us down sufficiently, and we'll eat each other alive. Trent, for instance, bless, had probably never even raised his voice to a woman in his life. But Kat sensed he'd been only seconds away from throttling Amber during that last challenge. And as for that last Tribal Council...

'He likes you.'

'Sorry?' Kat started in alarm and discovered she had not only gradually come to a halt but had been absent-mindedly stroking the large, slavering head of someone else's dog.

'He likes you.' Standing with one hand on the dog's hips was a pleasant-faced woman with cropped hair, dressed sensibly for the terrain in jeans, parka and hiking boots. The dog, some kind of rottweiler-cross, continued to lean its head against her and gaze up adoringly, a long string of saliva hanging from its jaws.

'He dribbles a bit,' said its owner redundantly as Kat continued to pat the dog on the back of the neck.

'He seems very nice,' Kat said, smiling faintly. Then, as the dog lady prepared to extend the conversation, Kat raised one hand in mingled greeting and farewell, and stepped off again down the track, brushing surreptitiously at her jeans.

Dogs. Apparently they were a great way to meet people. *Should I get a dog? Do I need to meet people? Where was I? Oh yes.* Tribal Council. Man's innate nastiness.

Kat took a deep breath and decided to let that particular long and unproductive train of thought go. We all have limits, she thought. That's really the end of that story. All of us have it in us to be destructive, and self-destructive. It's just most of the time, for most of us, circumstances contrive to make it unnecessary.

Around her now was a grove of eucalypts, long strands of coarse bark falling away from their trunks to reveal a smooth, silvery inner sheath. Like an advertisement for a beauty treatment, she thought. Some sort of uber-exfoliant. She touched her own face, which still felt soft enough but was, she knew, increasingly advertising her years.

Was that why O'Donnell hadn't followed up on his offer? In the car, in the dark, in the middle of the night, she'd seemed a likely proposition. But in the harsh light of day... Not that she'd really wanted him to follow it up. For a couple of days there she had wanted it quite desperately, but was unequivocally glad he had not. That was a scenario that was only ever going to end in tears.

Still. Sex with Dare O'Donnell. Or anyone, Kat thought bleakly as she made her way back to the street. Maybe I should get a dog. Then I could walk it every day by the creek. And meet some nice chap walking his dog. Strike up a natural sort of conversation. Then have sex with him.

Or, more likely, strike up conversations with pleasant short-haired women in sensible footwear. Should I become a lesbian? Kat wondered. It seemed to be the thing single fortysomething women did. That, or dye their hair blonde and get a boob job and post an inappropriately saucy ad on the internet. No. I don't think I'd make a very good lesbian. Or even a very good dog owner. And I'd look ridiculous as a large-breasted blonde.

Instead she was forced to conclude that this was her lot: this look, this life. And was surprised to find the great heaviness that accompanied the thought. It had certainly been a struggle these last few days, not to face O'Donnell but to deal with Heidi. She did not actually care all that much about the two of them getting it on. She'd lusted after Dare, certainly, but that was as far as it went. It wasn't jealousy, nor even envy of sex. It was, she'd had to admit, envy of Heidi's luminous youth that had made it such a struggle to meet the girl's eyes and, on occasion, even speak to her civilly.

On the one hand, Kat did not want to be nineteen again. A ghastly age. As the makers of *Home and Away* and *Neighbours* knew all too well. It was something else she yearned for, something to do with Heidi's unlined skin and glossy hair and endless energy and unselfconscious artlessness.

As she approached her flat Kat passed a house that had been a peeling shell when she had last lived here. Now, like so much in the neighbourhood, it was spotlessly renovated. But not the usual extra-bathroom-parent's-retreat-open-plan-living-kitchen-with-bi-fold-doors-to-outdoor-deck renovation. Instead the modest Edwardian had simply been scraped and painted, re-blocked, re-roofed, every-thing neat and sound. The lawn was close-mowed. Down one side were a vegie patch and a tiny, three-twigged lemon tree. A pair of Labradors, one black, one gold, roamed the yard hopefully. Even they were neat and sprightly. And the man of the house, some kind of tradesman, was, Kat knew, home by 5pm, embracing his bride and newborn.

Today he was working in the yard, his wife emerging from the house with two steaming cups, the baby in a sling across her chest, all faces alight with happiness and health.

That is what I yearn for. Not the husband, or the baby, or the house. Or their youth and beauty—although all those things would be nice. Certainly not the Labradors. What I want is their innocence. And I will never, she thought sadly, be innocent again.

26

'Kat?'

'Harry?'

'I think I'm in trouble.'

Kat took a breath, her mind racing. 'What's up love?'

'It's Jake and Amber. They're about to be in the news.'

Another problem that had quickly emerged with their new, revised format was that, unlike a *Survivor* set on a remote island, their mob had ample opportunity to wander off, opt out, jump on a tram and go home. Making Harry's job as controller of people a nightmare.

Michael had already been apprehended on the #48 tram, on his way to Box Hill. Just to say hello to his wife. Various other parties had been retrieved from the shores of Port Phillip Bay, from assorted suburban locations, even from the airport. And now...

'What? Who's gone missing?' asked Kat.

'If only they had. They're here. In a divvy van.'

'Where? A divvy van? What's going on?'

'Amber and Jake. They've been arrested.'

'Have you talked with GC? With BC?'

'No, I haven't talked with anyone else. I'm not sure what to do next.'

'Tell me what's happened.'

There was some scraping and shuffling, then Harry launched into his sorry tale. Amber had been complaining about the rations for some time. Jake and Zane had actually developed a bit of a taste for dumpster diving and other freegan mutations, regularly hanging around Vic Market at closing time and charming quantities of perfectly good food from a range of stall holders. But not only were the boys reluctant to share their spoils with someone who hadn't contributed to their acquisition, Amber often rejected their haul as unclean too.

Still, she had somehow managed to persuade Jake— not the most stable young man Kat had ever met—into helping her acquire real food. By rolling a young woman as she left one of the city supermarkets that evening, relieving her of both her handbag and her groceries.

Unfortunately for the thieves, it was still peak hour. Plenty of people had seen them. Several had given chase; others called the police.

'Was she hurt?'

'The woman? No, thank Christ.'

'Okay. That's good.' Kat pinched the bridge of her nose and closed her eyes for a moment. 'Where was the crew?'

'With them, of course.'

'And they didn't think to…?'

'Well, you know the rules, Kat. Rule No. 1: Don't interfere.'

'And where are they now?'

'I sent them back to Unit.'

'Okay. Call Ted first, tell him what's happened. Make sure he secures that film and gets the boys to keep their lips zipped.'

'And what about Amber and Jake?'

'I don't think there's much you can do for them right now. Call GC. Give the cops your number and leave them to it. I don't imagine they're going to get life for this, and it might settle them down to spend an hour in a lockup.'

'You're a hard woman, Kat.'

'And they're idiots. Honestly darling, what did they think they were doing?'

'Being creative?'

After she'd ended the call, Kat glanced at her watch. This was way too good to save for tomorrow. She switched off her computer, gathered up her things, and made a quick exit before GC—or indeed anyone—could catch her and share the amazing news.

Downstairs Wilson had just flipped the sign to Closed but when he saw her he unlocked the door and ushered her in, locking it again behind her.

'Hello!' he said, looking pleased. 'Thought I'd missed you for the night.' He glanced at her face. 'More big developments?'

'Yes!' she murmured. 'Although not of a sexual nature this time.'

Wilson made a disappointed face.

'But strictly confidential,' she cautioned.

'Of course.'

'Although I don't suppose it's going to stay quiet for long.'

'Scandal?'

'Oh yes,' said Kat, with relish. 'I think so.'

He made them both a coffee—hers with an exclamation point carved into it—then took a seat and gave Kat his full attention as she related the evening's adventures. Since he was already well acquainted with the *Survivor* contestants by proxy, and Harry in person, his enjoyment of the story was everything Kat could have wished, especially when she was obliged to explain the strange conventions of reality TV that required the camera and sound crew to stand by, still filming, as two filthy and slightly unhinged twentysomethings wrestled a chicken and a bag of oranges from the hands of a bemused commuter.

'They can't really blame Harry for any of that, though, can they?' he said when she'd finished.

'We—ll...' She waggled her hand. 'Theoretically, moving to and from a shoot and during a shoot, people are his responsibility. But when your shoot runs round the clock it's tough. I'm sure he'll be all right.'

'Good,' said Wilson. 'He seems like a nice bloke.'

'He is.'

'Not your boyfriend? Your ex?'

'No! Why?'

'I actually thought he might have been your brother at first, then it seemed like—I don't know—something more. You just seem close.'

Kat was aware of him watching her. She said lightly, 'Well, we are. Close, that is. But brother was probably a better guess. I feel like a sister to Harry. Though I guess the official term would be more like protégé. I trained him up, then sent him out into the world.'

'So it's just randy ex-footballers who catch your eye then?'

'Don't remind me.'

He grinned at her, then said, more gently, 'You feeling okay after all that? I thought afterward... Maybe laughing in your face might not have been the right thing to do. I didn't even think till later you might have been upset.'

'Laughing was exactly the right response,' Kat said warmly. She reached out her hand to cover his then, feeling suddenly flustered, took it back again. 'It was just what I needed. I mean, it did sting a bit at the time. But it was also...just ridiculous.'

'Well, you know O'Donnell's mad. No one in their right mind would choose Heidi over you.'

Kat felt her face warm, unable to meet his eyes. 'Oh, I don't know. She does have enormous breasts.'

'Really? I hadn't noticed.'

Kat laughed, then, as silence fell between them, watched Wilson's smile fade and a distant, almost stern look come over his face.

'Everything okay?'

He glanced at her, smiled again. 'Sure.'

'But not really,' she persisted.

He rubbed the top of his head. 'I'm okay. I just got thinking today... Something reminded me...'

'About what?'

'It's a long story.'

'I don't mind.' When the silence extended, Kat flushed a little. 'You don't have to, of course.'

He stood, the chair scraping. 'No, I don't mind. I guess it's all ancient history now anyway. But do you mind if I...' He gestured at the coffee machine.

'Go for your life.'

Wilson stepped behind the counter and for a moment concentrated on dismantling the machine, filling the sink with water, putting some odds and ends away in the cupboards. Kat sat with her legs stretched out before her, watching him, thinking what a strangely dear sight he had become over the last few months, the height and breadth of him, how comforting it was to know he was nearby. Wilson the Coffee Guy. After some minutes had passed without a word from him, she said, 'You killed a man in Reno just to watch him die?'

He smiled across at her, shook his head. 'I used to be married.'

'That *is* bad.'

'It wasn't really working.'

'Why not?'

'It's...hard to explain. Honestly, I still don't really know.' He rubbed a cloth around the inside of the filter. Thoroughly. Then re-attached it to the machine. 'After a while my wife just didn't seem to *like* me very much.'

'But you loved her?'

'Oh yeah. At least, initially. I was always trying to, you know, have the *talk*. Trying to fix things. Doing all the things good husbands were supposed to do—bought her flowers, did the housework.' He sighed. 'One sec.' With a startling rush he ran clean water through the machine. Kat took that moment to try and imagine him as a devoted husband. Coming home from work in his white lab coat and glasses, Wilson-still-with-hair, awkwardly carrying a bunch of flowers. She pictured him and Mrs Wilson living in the house in her street, the neat little house of dreams. It was a stretch. She wondered how long ago this all was.

How much the intervening years had changed him.

The hissing subsided and he said, 'I'm sure there were things I did wrong. Or maybe, I don't know. Maybe we really just weren't suited to each other. Anyway, nothing seemed to work. Everything I did just seemed to annoy her even more.'

'So you walked out on her?'

'No,' he said bluntly.

'But you fell out of love with her.'

'Yes.'

Kat waited. Wilson was wiping down the counter with intense concentration.

'You had an affair.'

He nodded. 'Yep.'

Kat sighed. 'Well, people do, don't they? It's not... It's not a *great* thing to do. But it's not, you know, like you killed someone.'

Wilson gave a snort of laughter. 'Maybe I should have raised that with her? She found out, of course. Probably because I didn't care if she did or not. There was a huge fight.'

'She threw you out in the street in the middle of the night?' Kat now saw Wilson standing in her street in front of the house of dreams, still in his lab coat and glasses, the tattered bunch of flowers at his feet.

'She threw me out in the middle of the night. There was a lot of yelling.'

'She called you an arsehole.'

'She did. And, you know? She was right. Why didn't I just leave her?'

'Why didn't you?'

He rubbed his face, his head. 'I don't know. I still

don't know. Maybe I still somehow thought the marriage could work? Maybe I just wanted to make her feel as shitty as she was making me feel? Maybe I am just an arsehole.'

'You're not an arsehole. Trust me.'

'An idiot then?'

'Oh sure. You're an idiot.'

Wilson expelled a long breath, not quite a laugh. Came out from behind the counter and propped against it, arms folded across his chest. They regarded each other for a moment.

'How long ago was this?' Kat asked eventually.

'About eighteen months.'

'Oh.' She'd assumed it had been longer. 'So you've only been doing this—' She gestured around the café '—for a year or so?'

'No, this was all part of trying to get things back on track. I was working long hours, I was never home. So we thought we'd go into business together. I retrained. Took out a lease on a place in South Melbourne.'

'And had an affair.'

'And had an affair.'

'With...?'

'With a woman who used to come into the shop. A regular.'

'Like me, then.'

He shook his head. 'No. Nothing like you. She was nothing like you.'

Kat stepped forward and took both his hands between hers. 'We all do dumb things,' she said. 'All of us. We all do things we regret. We all hurt someone else, at some time or other. We all have our limits. None of us are saints. All we can ever do is try not to do the same dumb thing twice.'

He gazed down at her, in the dim light his eyes almost black. Then a shadow of mischief came back into his face and he said, 'I'm glad we've had this talk.'

Kat grinned. 'So am I.'

But as she was about to step back he turned his hands to clasp hers. Her head was tilted back to see his face, his face inclined ever so slightly towards hers. Her heart was beating hard, his large hands warm around hers. The smile in his eyes had been replaced by something graver but no less welcome. Yes, she thought. Yes please. And as if hearing that thought he bent, and kissed her.

For a long moment they stood there, his hands holding hers tightly, his lips pressed gently to hers. And for that moment Kat felt every thread, every atom of herself focused in that one, warm, sweet point, the point at which their lips met. At what seemed the perfect moment, he shifted to rest his forehead against hers, his nose against her nose. Beautiful, thought Kat. You are beautiful.

And then, a second later: *What have we done?*

Reading her thoughts again, Wilson stepped back guiltily.

'Sorry!' they both said in unison. Then stood looking at each other, aghast.

'I mean, that was *lovely*,' Kat said earnestly.

'I know, yes, but...' stammered Wilson. 'You've just broken up with your partner...'

'I just don't want to rush into another...'

'I'm not sure I can...'

'I don't trust myself...'

'I'm still so fucked up...'

They both fell silent, then Wilson said, 'Are we babbling?'

Kat gave a choke of laughter, but felt tears in her eyes. 'I think, yes, we're babbling.'

After another moment's silence, Wilson said gently, 'I don't want to hurt you.'

'I don't want to *be* hurt,' said Kat.

Wilson nodded, looked away.

'Well,' said Kat. 'I guess I'll get going.'

He nodded again. As she reached the door he said, 'Kat?'

She turned.

'Friends?'

She smiled. 'Of course. Friends.'

27

As Kat had suspected, the matter of the two contestants being arrested for a mugging was not something that could be kept under wraps. The poor PR girl from Five was rapidly losing her mind. Keeping an eye on O'Donnell was stressful enough, fielding enquiries and complaints about the city campsites was becoming a bigger and bigger part of every day, and now there was this. Not just how to respond but how, if possible, to turn these two unruly lemons into lemonade.

Harry, to Kat's surprise and relief, had not been held responsible for the incident although the sound and camera guys had been quietly moved on to another project. Meanwhile Kat had her own issues. It was a short twenty-four hours until the busking challenge and she needed to make sure some field producers had been found to help manage the shoot on the day. She had to coordinate with Bev to get the contestants what they needed. And then there was the small matter of the multiple speeding tickets that had arrived the previous day, the result of The Box's mad bid for freedom under the hands of Dare O'Donnell.

Steeling herself, she tapped on BC's door.

'What?'

'Have you got five minutes?'

'Of course I haven't got five fucken minutes. Jesus wept. The whole fucken universe is unravelling. What is it?'

Taking this as permission to speak, Kat shut the door and sat in the threadbare visitor's chair, an article in some contrast to the pneumatic leather throne on which BC perched.

'It's about O'Donnell.'

'Jesus. Don't tell me you've been fucking him too. I thought you had more sense.'

Kat grew a little more pink, said: 'Of course not!' *Who else?*

'What then?'

'I did let him drive me home a couple of weeks ago. Drive me back here again at least.'

'So?'

'In my car.'

'Crashed it?'

'No. These,' she said, pulling the sheaf of VicRoads documents from her bag.

'You expecting me to pay them?'

'It's not that,' she said, hearing her voice increase in pitch slightly. 'It's...it's the demerit points. If I cop to these...'

BC scanned the documents a little more closely. 'Fuck me. Is this right? Who would've thought that clapped out relic could go this fast?' He shuffled through them again.

'Lose your licence. Right. I see the problem.' He sighed, and rubbed at the stubble on his chin. 'Fuck knows what we can do about it. Don't need O'Donnell bringing the full force of the law down on himself again.' He gave her a measuring look. 'Don't suppose I could persuade you to take one for the team?'

'Barry, I can't! I can't *not* drive. It's my job!'

He sighed again. 'Suppose so. All right. When was the last time you got a ticket?'

'A speeding ticket? Never.'

'You've *never* had a speeding ticket?' He gave a snort of laughter. 'You're a weird one, aren't you? Well, that's good. That gives us something to work with. Want to leave it with me? You've got twenty-eight days. We'll sort something out. Once this shit—' He waved both hands vaguely '—has settled.'

'Thank you,' said Kat, gathering up her bags and getting to her feet.

'Don't mention it. Now fuck off, love. I've got a mountain of shit to shovel here.' As she reached the door he said, 'Kat?'

'Yes?'

'How's the girl going? One with the bazookas.'

'Heidi? Really well. Didn't know a lot when she came on board but she learns fast. She's been great these last few weeks.'

'Good,' said BC blandly, picked up the phone, and started dialling.

Wondering uneasily what—aside from possessing note-worthy bazookas—Heidi had done to bring herself to BC's attention, Kat glanced at her watch and hefted her bags more securely onto her shoulder. She was jonesing for a coffee, and keen to keep up her Wilson routine despite some lingering awkwardness, but Bev was waiting for her. All she could manage was a smile and a wave as she tossed her luggage into the back seat of The Box—a nicety Wilson returned unselfconsciously—before turning the key in the ignition, and reminding herself yet again to book the old girl in for some of Ange's TLC.

The next day was drizzly, but Kat was in high spirits. There'd been a moment to at least say hello to Wilson and collect a coffee that morning, departing with a promise to make time Monday for a proper debrief. Her ill ease with Heidi had passed—really, she thought, I wouldn't swap places with that girl for anything, or anyone, in the world—and she listened with more than her usual forbearance to her chatter as they made their way to Bourke Street.

By lunchtime the crowd was building nicely despite the weather as Kat oversaw the assembling of the choir. Harry was in fine form, chatting with passersby, masterfully defending the show's reputation and encouraging them to wait and hear the performance, and give generously. In due course, Kat introduced Heidi to the other producers (both pretty girls—BC knew what he was doing) and found a doorway, out of shot, that gave her a good view of the show.

The sound quality was appalling, the constant passage of trams promised a nightmare in post-production, and the vocals were decidedly rough, but Zane was an accomplished guitarist so at least it was possible to recognise what the group was singing. An energetic rendition of 'Singin' in the Rain' was followed by a rather less successful version of 'I Will Survive'. And if Harry, who had joined her, mimed hanging himself during the final performance of 'Hallelujah', the crowd was remarkably enthusiastic.

After a twenty-minute break they ran through the set one more time, and quite a large sum of money had been collected by the time First Unit was breaking for lunch.

A second crew remained to capture the contestants— all, in their own way, turning on the charm—chatting with interested bystanders and explaining the hardships of life on the streets, while Heidi and her new BFs made sure as many of them as possible agreed to having their faces on film. All of which put them well behind schedule as they headed over to the Arts Centre. It was raining steadily now and that, combined with Friday peak hour, made getting out of the city an agonising process. Kat was aware of how small and insignificant The Box was as she attempted to lead her caravan around the edge of town and onto City Road.

'You need one of those flashing lights you can stick on the roof,' Heidi said. 'Like an undercover detective.'

'That would be cool,' Kat agreed. Then they both laughed as, directly in front of them, a nondescript sedan suddenly whooped into life, lights flashing on the front and rear dashes and both bumpers, pulling away in as great a burst of speed as the sticky traffic allowed.

'I guess you don't put your hand out the window and stick it on the roof anymore,' Kat said.

'In this car you would.'

'True.'

'You wouldn't think anyone would be speeding in this,

would you?' said Heidi, indicating the near-stationary cars on either side of them.

'Are they chasing a speeder? Or do you think they just spotted a Wanted Man?'

Kat turned into a narrow access way, and prayed everyone was still behind her as she pulled up next to their reserved space and handed Heidi the key to the boom gate. As she wrestled with the padlock Heidi craned to see who was following. 'There's Harry, at least,' she said.

A moment later Harry jumped out of the mini-van. 'We seem to have lost the main crew and our director,' he said, turning up his collar against the rain.

Kat sighed and pulled her own coat closer. 'They know where they're supposed to be. Does someone need to wait here for them? Or should we just go on up and get set up?'

'Why don't we go up? If they haven't appeared in fifteen minutes I'll come back down and try and find them.'

Accordingly, the contestants, buoyed by their recent public acclaim, tumbled out of the van and made their way into the underpass beneath Princess Bridge. Kat and Heidi constituted the forward party and were first to encounter a handful of randomly parked police cars. Then the dark sedan that had sped away from them earlier. Then a long ribbon of police tape patrolled by several grim-faced constables to a soundtrack of urgent but indecipherable radio chatter.

'What are you doing here?' asked one of them as Kat approached.

'We're filming here.'

'No, you're not. No news crews.'

'We're not a news crew, we're a reality show,' Kat said,

belatedly realising that this information was unlikely to endear her.

'Madam, I'm sorry. You'll have to get back.'

At that moment Harry arrived with the chattering, dishevelled tribe, all of whom instinctively pressed as close to the tape as they could, craning to see what was being so thoroughly protected.

'Sir, Madam, I am ordering you to step away from the tape and return to your vehicles,' he said with some urgency.

Suddenly three booming cracks, hideously magnified by the underpass, made the police constables spin to face the action. Heidi and Peru screamed shrilly, and Kat staggered with surprise.

'Get! Back!' repeated the constable. This time, without hesitation, Kat and Harry—with outstretched arms—gathered their motley flock around them and ran, as fast as they could, back the way they'd come.

28

That night it was all over the news, of course. The crazed gunman in the Arts Centre underpass. The next morning Kat sat up in bed with her coffee, the papers spread out over her legs, poring over the multitude of stories. They all said more or less the same thing but she soaked it up anyway. It was the kind of yarn journalists lived for. Ex-biker. Custody issues. Illegal firearms. (Someone else who'd reached their limit, thought Kat.) Good Samaritans. Acts of foolhardy bravery. Two deaths—including Crazy Guy—and two injuries. The only thing it lacked was a footballer, someone famous, or a reality-TV show. Thank Christ they'd been running behind schedule.

Thinking about what might have transpired if they'd already been set up made Kat feel sick. As far as she could tell, the mayhem had occurred almost exactly where she'd planned for the contestants to perform.

Afterwards it had been chaotic, with the girls hysterical and the blokes buzzing. The main crew were missing for at least another fifteen minutes, finally phoning in from somewhere in South Melbourne, having been unable to find the right turn-off from City Road.

Nightmare, thought Kat, leaning back against the pillows. Although also, undeniably—especially now they were all home safely—kind of exciting. Beside her, her phone vibrated. Harry.

'Hello darling.'

'Morning. Seen the papers?'

'Of course I've seen the papers! Can you believe it?'

'Kat, is that *exactly* where we were going to set up?'

'Exactly. Unbelievable. Unbelievably lucky.'

'That we were late? Jesus yes. Did you get Heidi settled down?'

'Eventually. She sobbed all the way back to Unit. I said a few soothing words, called her mum, sent her home. Is poor GC going to have to organise *more* trauma counselling?'

'Mate, by the time we wrap I reckon the entire crew is going to need trauma counselling. Don't know what else is being organised for them, but I got our mob back to camp, got the fire going. Afraid I also got them all some hot food.'

'They'll edit that out.'

'I still felt a bit mean just leaving them all there...'

'But the show must go on.'

'I know. And, you know, they did seem to bond a bit over it, so hopefully they'll help each other out. But I think the girls are feeling a bit vulnerable.'

'Not surprised,' said Kat, immensely glad she'd been

able to spend her evening snug at home, and not huddling in a dark alley under a sodden piece of cardboard. 'They are safe there, aren't they?'

'Of course,' said Harry reassuringly. 'They're out of the way. There's always a crew there. And this kind of thing... How often does it happen?'

'Well, once.'

'Which means it's even less likely to happen again any time soon, doesn't it?'

Does it? wondered Kat. 'I don't think that's actually how the laws of probability work.'

'They'll be fine,' insisted Harry. 'They're halfway there. We're all halfway there.'

'Thank Christ for that. Am I just getting old? Or has this been a particularly tough one?'

'I think it's fair to say it's been challenging,' Harry laughed.

'I think BC's losing his mind.'

'How can you tell?'

'Fair point.' Kat clasped her hand around her coffee cup, which was disappointingly cold. 'Well my love, I'd better get my day underway. Fancy a coffee over the weekend? Or a beer?'

'Definitely, but not today. Can I give you a call tomorrow?'

'Sure thing.'

After they'd said their goodbyes Kat pulled the doona up to her chin, watching a fresh burst of rain pepper the bedroom window. Halfway there, she thought. So far a suicide, a mugging, and a shooting. It had certainly been an interesting one. But then, she hadn't taken on this job for the security, for the routine. *Life is never dull, is it?* Her mind drifted to her neighbours, Mr and Mrs Innocent. Bet you didn't get caught up in a shooting last night, she thought. And, smiling to herself, closed her eyes and went back to sleep.

When the phone rang the next morning just as she was finishing breakfast, it wasn't Harry but GC. What fresh disaster? Kat thought, picking up.

'Good morning.'

'Kat? Sorry to bother you on a Sunday.'

'No worries. What's up?'

'Darling, are you able to come in to the office some-time today?'

'Sure. Problem?'

There was a slight pause. 'We're making some changes. I need to talk to you about what'll be happening going forward.'

Oh dear, thought Kat. Please don't tell me I need to find another location for the campsite. But she said, 'Of course. I can come down now if you're there.'

'That'd be great. Half an hour?'

'See you then.'

Sighing, Kat hung up and ran a hand through her hair. Halfway there, she reminded herself. And she'd dealt with everything they'd thrown at her so far. After applying some mascara and twisting her hair up into a knot—her Sunday clothes would have to do—she grabbed her coat and bag and headed out to the car.

'Footscray, thanks Box,' she said, and set the two of them to autopilot.

CityLink was almost empty of traffic but she was more

surprised to see the parking bays outside the office also deserted apart from GC's little Merc. Not a production meeting then, she thought. Just me.

The building was equally deserted as Kat let herself in and trudged upstairs. GC was in her office, uncharacteristically doing nothing but gazing into the middle distance, a pen twirling between her fingers. When she saw Kat she smiled and got to her feet. Her face looked strained.

'Kat. Thanks for coming in. Have a seat.'

'This looks serious,' said Kat lightly, before thinking with a sudden clenching in her stomach: *Actually, it does. It does look serious.*

They both sat there in silence until GC sighed and said, 'Kat, I don't have to tell you this shoot hasn't been going smoothly.'

'No,' said Kat.

More silence.

'We expect a lot of you. I know that. In the past you've always delivered for us. That's why we got you on board for *Survivor.*'

Kat gazed at her blankly.

'It's an important project for us, and for Five. It's a risk, too. A risk we need to pay off. And that means everyone has to play their part. Everyone has to deliver.'

Yes, thought Kat. Like me. I play my part. I deliver.

'This time you've let us down. And I think you know that.'

Kat could feel the astonishment in her face, saw GC flinch. But her boss ploughed on regardless.

'First location of the shoot, the suicide.' GC ticked off Kat's crimes against her fingertips. 'Then the whole schedule was put on hold while you found the campsites.

That put us weeks behind, and I don't have to tell you what every day's delay costs us. The locations you did choose have turned out not to be secure. It's put the contestants at risk, it's created problems for the rest of the crew. Then this business on Friday night. Kat, it was the last straw.'

Kat sat, wordless, her hands clasped in her lap. She had a vague sense of the manifest injustice of the complaints but found herself unable to formulate a response. GC's words were bouncing off her forehead, impossible to absorb. Still, she knew what was coming next. What she hadn't anticipated was how much it would hurt.

'Kat, we're going to have to let you go.'

Kat drew a sharp breath, held it for a second. 'I see,' she said. Thinking: Right. There is no way in the world I'm paying those fucking speeding fines now.

29

She had been remarkably, freakishly calm, responding quietly as GC apologised in a bloodless sort of way ('Okay. No, that's okay. Of course') as if they were discussing some minor mishap, not the termination of her employment, perhaps the end of her career.

Afterwards, she'd methodically cleaned out her desk. There wasn't a lot that was personal there. In fact, a whole lot of work papers were still at home, in one of her many bags. If they wanted them, they were going to have to come and get them.

GC had made no mention of who would manage the locations for the rest of the shoot and Kat couldn't help mentally running through what was still left to be done, what might be coming up in the next few weeks, any looming nightmares. Well, not her problem now. As she had when she'd cleared out of Miles' place, she was struck again by how little there was to pack, what a meagre collection of odds and ends, what a tiny impression she'd made. As she glanced around the space one last time, it looked, she thought, exactly the same. A little tidier, perhaps. Whether she was here or not here seemed to make almost no difference.

She had always felt, if not important, then certainly central to things. The director was important. GC and BC were important. But it was Kat—and the dozens of people like her—who kept the machine running. Wasn't it? Or maybe they were all just widgets, small components that could be easily replaced. Maybe they were all kidding themselves. Or maybe it was just her. Maybe everyone else was crucial and she was…expendable.

The numb self-pity, the detached exploration of the implications of her sudden dismissal, continued as she walked slowly downstairs, unlocked The Box, stashed the bags on the back seat and slid behind the wheel. *Well, this is television.* People get sacked all the time. For no particular reason. Projects fall over. People fall out. It was probably just her turn. She started the car and sat there for a while longer, listening with more than usual irritation to the rattling cough of the idling engine, the rhythmically jumping tachometer like someone ceaselessly drumming their fingers or tapping their foot. She didn't have the heart to say 'Home'. The Box knew where to go, anyway.

Back in Coburg she left her things in the car—she wasn't sure what she was going to do with them. Maybe just put them straight in the bin. Sat down on the sofa and thought: Okay, what do I do now? Outside, in the rest of the world, it was still Sunday. A day of rest. The papers were still full of Friday's shooting. Was that only two days ago? Less. She stared at them, remembering the fear and panic and then the strange exhilaration of the night.

Have I really fucked up? she wondered. Is all this really my fault? Suicide guy. Should I have somehow known? Or checked? Emptied the buildings? Checked the rooftops? I suppose I could have. Maybe that's what other location managers do. Maybe I really haven't been thorough enough. Maybe all these years I've simply been getting away with it, cutting corners.

She had no real way of knowing how other people operated. For more than fifteen years she'd been working solo or been the boss. She tried to think back to her early days, doing all the humdrum things Heidi had been doing for her now. Kat couldn't recall ever clearing an entire street. But that was the late 1980s, early 1990s. Things were different then. As for the campsites. Jeez. No one had ever done anything like it before. Of course unexpected things were going to happen.

Kat sighed and pushed the newspapers away from her, leaned back and closed her eyes. Shit, she thought. I've been sacked. I've just been sacked. I'm unemployed. Her eyes popped open again. She stared at the ceiling. *What the fuck am I going to do now?*

She stood, paced around the tiny flat, put the kettle on, rinsed out the coffee jug. When in doubt... She picked up her phone, put it down again. Make a coffee first, she told herself.

With the cup in one hand she sat down on the sofa again and picked up her phone. She desperately wanted to talk to someone, to vent, to debrief. Equally desperately she wanted to avoid saying the words out loud. She took a sip of coffee. Dialled Wilson. Hung up before the call could connect.

She'd never actually called him before. Apart from the day he'd helped her move, they had never seen each other away from the café, and she'd never had reason to get in touch otherwise. It was weirdly anxious-making to think of just phoning him as she would any other friend, especially about such a weighty matter. Especially since, well, their close encounter. Friends, they'd both said. But were they? The nature of the relationship remained rather mysterious to her, and confusing. Just thinking about him was making her tense.

Instead she went to her fallback position, and dialled Betsy. Got her voicemail.

'Hi,' Kat said. 'It's me.' Words and phrases thrashed around in her mind. Eventually she just said: 'Can you give me a call? Cheers.'

After a moment's hesitation she called Harry. More voicemail. She hung up without leaving a message. Called back. Said: 'Hi, it's Kat. Can you give me a call?'

She took another sip of coffee, grimaced, put the cup down. She really didn't need more stimulation. After the bizarre calm of earlier that morning Kat could suddenly feel an internal storm brewing. She jerked to her feet again, hands clasped together, tingling with...with what? Some kind of evil energy. With panic. With fear. Sorrow. Loss. With *rage*, she thought. I. Am. *Enraged*.

The injustice of it, the unfairness, hit her physically, making her hands tremble. I have done nothing wrong, she thought. I have done everything right. I have fulfilled the most ridiculous briefs, on the most insane schedule.

Brilliantly. Her hands balled into fists and she had a powerful urge to overturn a piece of furniture, sweep her coffee cup off the table, throw herself through the window. Something, anything, to assuage the anger roiling inside her. She took a few hasty steps, turned, walked back. *Damn, I wish this flat was bigger.* She felt caged.

Maybe I'll go for a walk, she thought. Work some of this off. If only I was the kind of person who went to the gym. Or jogged. She imagined herself opening the front door and just running, fast, for miles, away from everything. Sadly, even in the heat of her fury, Kat knew that any attempt at running would end, ignominiously, within five hundred metres.

But a walk. A fast walk. That might help.

She was tugging off her boots, tying the laces on her walking shoes, muttering to herself, aware she was behaving like a crazy person but perversely enjoying herself, when the phone rang. Thank goodness, Kat thought, someone to talk to. Then flinched when she saw who was calling. For one ring, two, she thought about not answering. Then took a breath and picked it up.

'*Kat,*' Heidi sobbed.

'Hi Heidi.'

'Kat, it wasn't my fault!'

'I know it wasn't, sweetheart.'

'I had no idea! No one asked me! Genevieve just called me in and said I'd have to do it all myself for the rest of the shoot!'

So *that* was the new location manager? Kat rocked back in her chair, the shock making her stomach turn.

'It's not *fair!*'

Kat breathed deeply, exhaled slowly. 'No, it's not. But that's television, love.'

'I won't do it. I'll tell them I won't do it.'

'Don't be an idiot.'

'I can't take your job!'

'Of course you can.'

'I can't do it! I don't know what to do! How will I know what to do?'

'You know what to do. You're already doing most of it, and you've watched me do the rest. You'll be fine.'

'It's not fair. I feel awful.'

You feel awful? 'These things happen, Heidi,' Kat said. 'It's just part of the business. It's a great opportunity for you. Don't worry about me.'

There was wheezing on the other end of the line as Heidi fought back a fresh bout of tears. Kat waited patiently, revisited by the out-of-body calm that had possessed her earlier. There was something decidedly unreal about the whole situation, her emotions seemed on delay. Unlike those of her protégé.

Eventually Heidi said, with a reverence that made Kat smile in spite of herself, 'You are so cool. You are, like, *amazing.*' She hiccupped. 'I mean, everything you taught me. And now...this. If it was me, I'd just be like... *Oh my God!* But you're just, like, no drama. You are *awesome.*'

Kat rubbed her eyes tiredly. 'Thanks. You know, you've been great to work with, I know you'll do a great job.'

'I'm going to really, really miss you. Everyone will. I know Dare'll really miss you, he thinks you're awesome too.'

'Well, I'll miss you all. But you'll be fine. Look, I have to go now—but thanks for calling. Good luck!'

For a moment Kat sat with the phone in her hand, one shoe on, one shoe off, almost smiling. Then she wrapped her arms around her legs, laid her head against her knees, and wept.

30

'You've been *what*?'

'Sacked,' repeated Kat, gratified by her friend's outrage.

'But...*why*?'

Kat rattled off the list of offences against her, for a moment at least able to see the humour in the ludicrousness of the charges.

'But Kat...that's...that's ridiculous. You can't be serious.'

'Perfectly serious, I'm afraid. Apparently I've screwed up royally this time and have become a liability to the team and the viability of the project.'

'Rubbish,' said Betsy emphatically.

'In fairness, Bets, you have no idea how I do my job. I could, in fact, be completely incompetent for all you know.'

'But you're not.'

'No,' Kat sighed. 'I'm not.'

Betsy rocked back in her chair, then lowered her eyes

to her friend's face. 'You seem to be taking this pretty calmly.'

'I'm not.'

She then related her conversation with Heidi, and her own hair-tearing extravagance of grief that had followed. 'It's times like that I'm glad I live alone,' she concluded.

Betsy stretched out her hands then let them drop back to the table. 'Well, at least you didn't wait three weeks before telling me this time,' she said. She scooped the last of the milk froth from the bottom of her cup, then licked the spoon thoughtfully. 'It's not *right*, Kat. It's not fair.'

'But there's not much I can do about it.'

'Isn't this what unfair dismissal laws are all about? Can't you sue them or something?'

'Sue them?' Kat instinctively recoiled.

'Yes, sue them. Darling, this is outrageous. Surely you have some sort of contract.'

Kat did in fact have a contract, which she hadn't read particularly thoroughly. It had seemed a standard sort of document that, while no doubt peppered with get-out-of-jail-free clauses for her employer, must also give her some sort of protection against being summarily dismissed. Certainly there was plenty of allowance for the parameters of the project changing, or for it falling over altogether. Only the biggest stars got insurance against a series being axed, and no one was guaranteed the success of a pilot.

'I suppose I could look at it,' Kat said without much enthusiasm.

'There must be lawyers who could give you some advice pro bono.'

'I meant have another look at the contract.'

Betsy rolled her eyes.

'These things are standard,' Kat protested. 'Unless there's something especially unusual about the project, all those contracts are sort of pro forma. Nobody reads their contracts.'

'Until something like this happens,' said Betsy dryly, signalling for another round of coffees.

They were trying out a new place in Coburg, recently sprung up to cater to the suburb's burgeoning population of White People and Breeders. It was ostentatiously child-friendly, with an employment policy that clearly stipulated cheerful pierced and tattooed types only. The coffee machine was glossy and of the right brand, the muffins were organic and the furniture the correct side of 1976. But Kat rated the coffee 6.5, maybe 7 out of 10, and the pastries weren't nearly as delicious as they looked.

Still, they could walk here. It was a good thing to support local businesses. And there was comfort in looking out the big windows at the familiar sights of Sydney Road that—unlike further south in Brunswick—remained steadfastly eclectic and slightly down-at-heel. If you didn't count the cars (Coburgians loved their cars), any one of which looked like it cost about two-thirds of what Kat earned in a year.

Used to earn in a year.

She sighed and rubbed her face tiredly. At the moment she was still caught up in a tide of rage and humiliation. But gnawing away at the periphery of her thoughts was something rather more pressing than her hurt feelings. Between her weeks at the Footscray Hilton and freshening up the flat, her savings had taken a substantial hit. She'd been earning since then, of course, and living frugally, as was her habit. But she hadn't been game to check her bank balance, and was worried about what she might find when she did.

'Would you like me to do a bit of homework for you? Find out who you should speak to?' said Bets, spooning sugar into her coffee.

Kat stirred her own pensively, nibbling at her lip. 'The thing is...'

'The thing is what?' asked Bets after a prolonged silence.

Cohen Clarke was one of the biggest and most successful television production houses in the country. Kat had been working for them almost exclusively for the best part of a decade, and had been involved with them for most of her working life. In a pond as small as the one she swam in, you had to be very careful about who you crossed.

'It would be a mistake,' Kat said, 'to make an enemy of them.'

'There are other companies you could work for.'

'Yes,' said Kat, thinking: Precious few I actually *want* to work for. And fewer still who might employ me after being first sacked, then dragging The Big Cs into litigation. She sighed. 'It's not a simple thing. It's not just about who's right and who's wrong.' Her throat tightened, in either sorrow or panic, she couldn't tell. 'What I do next will have repercussions. Maybe for the rest of my career.'

Bets squeezed her hand. 'So you just let them get away with it?'

'I don't know, Bets. I really don't know. I need to think.'

The other aspect of it was, Kat thought anxiously, her age. Things did blow over. People fell out but—again, the mixed blessing of a small pond—enmities tended not to last. Everyone ended up working with everyone else again eventually. But that was more the case for some people than for others. Dare O'Donnell, for instance, could go on fucking up monstrously (probably right until the moment he actually killed someone) and still be employable after a respectable hiatus. BC was constantly offending people, but he was a senior, respected figure with a very public track record of success. Everyone knew what he was like. Everyone forgave him eventually.

For widgets, the case was more complicated. There were some trades in which you were allowed grow old. Camera crews, for instance. As long as you could still haul the gear around, you were all right. But locations? That was something you were supposed to pass through, like an adolescent phase. A starter job. A young person's job.

Kat had always liked to think that her experience was appreciated, was valued. She had also, though, become increasingly vague about her age over the last couple of years, sometimes joking about it in a self-deprecating way but more and more wary of actually naming a figure. On paper, she knew, she was an anachronism. She should be a producer, or at least a production manager by now, or—if she was to stay in her field—perhaps managing big film shoots. Not pissy local reality shows. And Heidi being appointed as her successor? Quite apart from the personal hurt, it was an ill omen for her future employment prospects. The idea of asking to be taken on as a location scout in her mid-forties was one that made her blanch.

'I need to talk to someone,' she said at last.

'Who?'

'I don't know. I need advice. Not,' she touched the back of Betsy's hand, 'that I don't value your advice.

But from someone in the industry. Someone who knows how it works.'

Betsy nodded. 'What does Harry say about all this?'

Kat took a breath and said, as lightly as she could, 'Don't know. Haven't heard back from him yet.'

'What do you mean?'

'I left a message for him on Sunday.' And Monday. And again on Monday. 'But I haven't heard back from him yet.'

There was a long silence during which Betsy stared hard at her friend. Eventually she simply said, 'How odd.'

31

Have I made a terrible mistake?

Kat slid the last knife into the draining rack, squeezed the dishcloth and began slowly wiping down the counter. *Has this, all this, my whole working life, been one terrible, endlessly compounded error of judgement?* From the idea of working in television—no job security, patchy pay cheques, fierce competition, temperamental colleagues and bosses—to the one that somehow doing work you enjoyed was more important than making loads of money? No job security was not so bad if you made a motza while you were employed. But she had somehow deliberately manoeuvred herself into a position where she made ordinary money in a low-level job with, it now became obvious, no assurance of ongoing employment and the dubious reward of having made herself redundant by training her own successor.

For twenty years, whatever else had happened, she'd

told herself that having fun and making enough to get by on was what really mattered. The politics, schmoozing, climbing the career ladder: she had no time for it. Do a good job, be pleasant and professional to deal with, be generous to the people around you, and everything else would take care of itself. Was all that in fact not the secret to a happy life but absurdly, dangerously naive?

Kat picked frowningly at a stubborn spot of melted cheese on the countertop with her thumbnail, her mouth set in an unhappy line. What I should have done, she thought, was be a completely different person. Someone who cared about being important. Someone who cared about being rich. Someone who cared about the way the world actually worked, rather than drifting along in some infantile *Teletubbies* niceness-will-win-out fantasy.

Would I have been different, more sensible, more ambitious if Dad hadn't died? she wondered. Probably not. Kat had only the haziest memories of him, but from discussions with her mother he didn't appear to have been a Master-of-the-Universe type. He certainly hadn't left behind much in the material way. And Kat supposed her parents wouldn't have married if one had wanted a quiet life and the other to rule the world.

Poor Mum, thought Kat. How on earth did she cope? She returned to the sink and let her hands rest in the soapy water. How hard it must have been to lose a beloved husband, in such a way. To be left to raise a daughter on a schoolteacher's salary, to keep it all together, to provide a normal life carrying that grief and loss, and then—then—just as you might be thinking of having another go at making some kind of independent life for yourself, you get cancer.

Tears pricked at Kat's eyes and she brushed at them with her wrist, for the first time in her life not crying for her own loss but her mother's. *How did she do it? How did she keep going?* For all their life together Kat had taken her cues from her mother: that it was Kat's loss, first of a father, then a mother. That it was she who needed to be protected and nurtured and provided for, emotionally and physically, and Nancy's job to do the protecting and nurturing and providing, right up until the end. And she had been about this age, about Kat's age, when she died, after a life of loss and sacrifice that she never once acknowledged or even mentioned. How did you do that? Kat wondered. *How did you keep going? What were your limits? How bad would things have had to get before you gave up or lay down?*

She pulled the plug and let the water drain away, slow tears puncturing the suds. 'Sorry,' she murmured. Sorry it's taken me all this time to realise what you must have gone through. Sorry for not understanding. Sorry for every time I made your life harder than it had to be. Sorry for not...*admiring* you more.

Kat sniffed noisily and reached for the tea towel. *Fuck. What a mess my life is. What a mess the inside of my head is.* She dried her hands, wiped her face with a tissue, blew her nose. Things were shit, no question about that. But at least she wasn't a widowed single mother. At least she wasn't dying of cancer. She had somewhere to live, food to eat, friends. A tiny bit of money in the bank. Which, while alarming, was better than nothing at all.

All I have to do, she thought, is decide what to do next. Once I've done that, I'll feel better.

But this was exactly the point at which she'd been stuck for days now. She didn't know what to do next. She knew she had to get work, somehow, from somewhere. She had to start making some money. But it had been years since she'd actually had to get out and spruik for work. For a decade she'd just moved from one project to another, sometimes with a break of weeks, at most a couple of months. But BC and GC had always had something on the go. And whatever it was, she'd been involved.

Now she'd have to start cold calling, and while she certainly knew who to call, she couldn't think of a Melbourne project not already fully crewed. It might be possible to get some locum work. Or there could be something in the pipeline that she could secure for later in the year. But all of that was predicated on making the call. On explaining that she was looking for work because she'd been let go. The thought of that made her sick with shame.

Still. It had to be done.

So with the freshly heroic image of her mother in her mind, Kat unearthed her battered contact book from the kitchen drawer, and was steeling herself to sacrifice her ego on the altar of pragmatism when the phone rang.

'Kat Kelly.'

'Kat. It's Ted. Time for a beer?'

Ted? 'Hi. Sure.' Nothing but time, thought Kat. Did he know? He must.

'You're in Coburg?'

'Yeah, near Sydney Road.'

'I'm going to be over that way about 6pm. Any good pubs in the area?'

There was, and Kat gave him directions to her favourite,

still too stunned to enquire why he was going to be in Coburg, why he wanted to have a beer with her, or indeed why he'd called at all. She and Ted had known each other for years, certainly, and worked together a number of times but she would not have called them friends and neither, she thought, would he. Still, it'd get her out of the house.

Ted arrived promptly at the pub, a few minutes after 6, gave her an awkward peck on the cheek and surveyed the room. 'Got a beer garden here?'

'Out the back,' said Kat.

'Right-oh. Want to head out there? I'll buy us a couple of pots. Got a favourite flavour?'

'Carlton's fine.'

'Good girl,' said Ted, and made his way to the bar.

Kat buttoned up her coat, pulled her gloves back on, picked up her bag and resettled at a table in the unsurprisingly deserted beer garden. Some outdoor gas heaters were ensuring ice wasn't forming on the tables but it wasn't exactly warm. Kat turned her collar up and shrank her hands into her sleeves.

'Fuck, sorry,' said Ted, putting the pots down on the table and slapping his hands together. 'Brutal, isn't it? But I can't have a beer without a ciggie. It's not natural.'

'Fair enough.' Kat grinned and took a sip of her beer. They may not be friends, but she did like Ted. There was something comforting about his presence. She'd felt her absence from the shoot keenly. Sitting here with him felt like she was suddenly back in touch with reality again, grounded.

'Cheers,' he said, drinking deeply then pulling a family-sized pack of cigarettes from his pocket and firing one up. In the icy air his smoky exhale seemed to go on forever. 'Heard about what happened, obviously,' he said through the haze. 'How are you feeling?'

'Shit!' said Kat cheerfully.

Ted nodded. 'Yeah. Well, they're arseholes. We miss you around the place.'

'Thank you,' said Kat, genuinely moved. Then couldn't help asking, 'How's Heidi going?'

Ted gave a snort of laughter. 'Look, she's fucking annoying. But she's doing all right. We're on the home straight now so we're all just, you know, counting the days.' He took another slug of beer, looking at her over the rim of the glass. 'You did a good job with her. Just like you did with Harry. Everyone knows that.'

'Do they?'

''Course. BC and GC can't say that. A few things they can't say, in the circumstances. That's why I'm here.'

'They sent you?'

'Christ no. I meant we've known each other a long time.'

'We have.'

'Everyone knows you've been stiffed. No one's going to do anything about it, though. BC and GC can't, obviously. Bev's had to let all her freelancers go, she's got her own worries...'

'Oh no!'

'Yeah, down to a one-man team now. Solo. All the challenges. Tribal Council every week.'

'Shit.'

'My crew help her out when they can. Multi-tasking. Brave new world.'

Kat shook her head, dismayed by Bev's misfortune but secretly comforted by the fact that she hadn't been the only one struck down.

'Had a feeling Harry hadn't been in touch, either,' Ted murmured.

Kat clasped her hands around her glass. It had soon become apparent to Kat that, for reasons of his own, Harry was deliberately avoiding her. In the middle of that first week he had finally responded to her messages with a text, arranging a catch-up. Then texted again the next day, cancelling. *Thinking of you.* What he was actually thinking remained unsaid but it clearly wasn't good. Kat hadn't heard from him again, and hadn't had the heart to keep calling. Now she just said, 'No, he hasn't.'

'Thought that might be bothering you.'

She nodded.

'Another beer?'

'Sure.'

She sat hunched against the cold until Ted came back.

'The thing is,' he said, sitting down and lighting another cigarette. 'Harry. He's just a kid. He's ambitious. And he's frightened.'

Kat stared at him.

'He's scared of the taint.'

'The loser taint?'

'Something like that.'

Kat sat back in her chair. 'Thanks,' she said. 'I feel so much better.'

'*Plus*,' said Ted, ignoring her, 'he feels guilty. Everyone knows that thing with Jake and Amber was his responsibility, even if everyone *also* knows in the circumstances 'no one could have done anything about it.'

'Is everyone talking about this?'

'Of course they are. It's like fucken Nicaragua. Turn up for work and half the crew's disappeared.'

'Who else has gone?'

'Basically anyone who wasn't on contract. And you.'

'I feel so special.'

'Well, you are. That's what I'm trying to tell you. You're not a troublemaker. You don't have a massive fucking ego. You're not political. You just want to be left alone to do your job, right?'

'But...Harry. I don't understand. Why should Harry be worried? Everyone loves Harry.'

'Everyone loves Harry. Everyone *trusts* you.'

'I'm still the one who got sacked.'

'Love, everyone gets sacked sooner or later. That's what Harry doesn't understand. He's scared, he's guilty, he's embarrassed, he doesn't know how to handle it. He knows he should stand up for you but he doesn't know how, and he's afraid if he does he'll be next for the chop.'

Kat drank some more beer. 'Is all this supposed to be making me feel better?'

Ted sighed impatiently. 'They sacked you because they're running out of money and they knew you wouldn't make a fuss. It's not personal. Harry is a coward, but he'll grow out of it. Everyone gets stiffed at some point in this business. The question is, do you get re-employed?'

'Will I get re-employed?'

'For fuck's sake, that's what I've been trying to tell you. Don't panic. The Big Cs will have something else sooner or later and when they do they'll want you on board. If Paragon or one of the other mobs don't snap you up first. In the meantime, don't know how you are financially, but I do know someone needing a location. Nothing flash, but it'll pay.'

'Oh Ted,' said Kat, her heart suddenly very full.

32

'Hi. Kat Kelly to see Marcus Wakefield?'

The razor-edged receptionist (looking a little like a young version of that snappy woman from *The Collectors*, thought Kat) glanced at her with a slight thinning of the lips that could be taken as a smile, and pushed a clipboard towards her.

'Sign in, please. I'll let him know you're here.'

As Kat neatly printed her name and business on the log sheet and received in return a visitor's ID, she surreptitiously scoped the reception area, thinking with a mixture of amusement and sadness that nothing could be more different from the office she'd just left. No wire-reinforced warehouse windows opaque with grime here. No sagging hard-rubbish-collection-day sofas, mismatched chairs and chipboard desks. Definitely no industrial-sized urn. There was a bowl of fruit just off-centre on the vast expanse of coffee table, but it seemed more in the nature of an *objet* than a source of nourishment.

'Take a seat. He'll be right down,' said the receptionist.

Kat was on the third floor of a rather unprepossessing building on Albert Road, and while it was certainly crisp and immaculate, things had changed since she'd last walked into an ad agency. The days of massive St Kilda Road edifices wholly given over to commercial dream factories, where every day was Casual Friday, beanbags were making their first comeback and indoor basketball half-courts for the inspiration and invigoration of the creative team were *de rigeur*.

This joint was strictly business. Sign of the times, thought Kat, reaching for a shiny, un-thumbed copy of *AdNews* just as a man loomed before her, hand extended.

Kat had been hoping for Jon Hamm but instead she seemed to have got Lachy Hulme, a towering black-haired gent in his mid thirties.

'Marcus Wakefield,' he said, shaking her hand. 'Nice to meet you in person. Thanks for coming in.'

'My pleasure,' said Kat, picking up her bag and following him—trying not to break into a trot—through a door, down a corridor, and into a room where three people were already sitting, well spaced, around a handsome conference table of reclaimed wood.

'Let me introduce you. This is the team from Sunshine Productions: Toby Wright, cinematographer. Audrey Shapiro, production designer. And have you met Sam King, our director?'

'I know his father. Hi Sam,' said Kat, after nodding and smiling to the other two.

'Kat,' said Sam, reaching over to shake her hand. 'I've heard good things about you.'

Kat bit her lip against a smile. Sam looked as if he'd only just shrugged off the uniform from some mid-level private school and—having known his father, also a director, for years—she had clear memories of Sam as a gangly kid, hanging round shoots on school holidays. But she just said, in a friendly way, 'Thank you. I'm looking forward to working with you,' and took a seat.

Marcus clasped his hands. 'Kat, I know you have the broad outline of what we're looking for here, and we'll run through the full brief once the client arrives, but I just wanted to say the location here is crucial, absolutely crucial.'

Kat nodded gravely and took a notepad and pen and a small sheaf of photographs from her bag.

'People like to talk about the kitchen as the heart of the home,' he continued. 'But you know what?'

Kat raised her eyebrows in polite enquiry.

'The laundry. That's the true heart of the home. And that's what we need to convey here.'

'Of course,' said Kat, not bothering to write that bit down.

'We need something modern, obviously, but with character,' said Audrey.

'It needs to feel warm but contemporary,' said Sam, with perhaps an excessive degree of urgency.

The intercom on the large complicated telephone in the centre of the table buzzed. 'Marcus? Russell Dwyer is here to see you.'

'Thanks,' said Marcus briskly, getting to his feet and leaving the room, returning minutes later with a couple Kat assumed constituted The Client. Everyone else around the table leapt to their feet respectfully and Kat did the same, suddenly aware that she had perhaps not assumed the right uniform for the occasion. As account manager, that Marcus was wearing a plain dark suit was to be expected. He was the businessman of the equation, the dealmaker. But both Toby and Sam were also dressed as if they were heading to a three-hat restaurant: no ties but also in suits and crisp shirts open slightly at the neck.

Even Audrey was wearing dark trousers, towering heels, a cardigan that could well have been cashmere and some sort of soft blouse with a slight sheen to it. Kat, meanwhile, had dressed in her most formal daywear (high-heeled boots, custom earrings made by a friend, and a printed paisley wrap dress she'd always considered flattering). The idea was 'creative professional', but she had a sneaking suspicion that the image she was projecting was more middle-aged hippie.

Well, she thought, too late now, extending a hand to The Client: an older man, also in a suit, who looked unnervingly like Michael Caton; and a slight, blonde woman in a classic navy business skirt and jacket. Livinia Nixon, thought Kat. Thirty years on.

Introductions completed (Russell Dwyer was the male half of The Client; the woman, Suzy, apparently did not possess a surname. Or was she Russell's wife?), they resumed their seats around the table. Marcus made a short speech, welcoming everyone to this auspicious event, then dimmed the lights, and began presenting his 'little gem': the television advertisement for a revolutionary soap powder that would reinstate the laundry to its rightful place as the heart of the home.

Kat tried to pay attention, but she'd already read the script, such as it was, the production notes, and the brief. With no actual information to claim her attention she found the closer she listened to Marcus' presentation, the harder it was not to snicker. She was also distracted by a soft gleam of light on the cinematographer's cleanly shaved head (his one badge of creativity, she assumed), which reminded her powerfully and painfully of Wilson.

Wish you were here, she thought. Wilson would have very much enjoyed Marcus' Ode to the Laundry. Failing that, her re-enactment of it over a coffee or a whisky later in the day. Had he noticed she wasn't around anymore? Of course he would have. Had anyone told him why? She had still not quite summoned the nerve to call him, and the longer she left it the harder it got. The fact that he hadn't called her either was not encouraging.

Ordinarily Kat would have counted on Harry to have filled him in. She supposed, if he asked, Ted or Bev would have. *If he asked.* Feeling that surge of loss rising up in her chest again—of her job, her friends, the daggy production office, her annoying bosses that she'd known for years, of Wilson, of her self-respect—she took a quiet breath, raised her eyes, and focused again on Marcus just as he concluded the final PowerPoint. It was the last frame of the storyboard featuring a mother embracing her children in what Kat considered a startlingly generic laundry—washing machine, window, blank wall—all delicately shaded a minty colour she privately christened *Asylum Green.*

Russell was nodding appreciatively. Everyone appeared to be awed anew. The concept would have been presented to The Client some time ago, and the production team had all received their briefs. But yes, that much had clearly not changed about advertising, Kat thought. Meetings. Meetings of truly epic quantity and duration. Meetings in which everything that had already been covered in the previous meeting had to be rehashed before any new business could be attended to. It must have something to do with billable hours, thought Kat. In television, meetings just ate into your budget. In advertising, they only added to it.

The Girl (not the receptionist; some other smart young bunny) had brought in refreshments and this time Kat said yes to a coffee. She was going to need it. And then almost choked on it when Russell said warmly, 'You get it. You really get it. This isn't about getting dirty clothes clean, it isn't about household chores. It's not even about the incredible science, the nanotechnology.' He paused, nodding to himself again. 'This is about love.'

'Exactly,' said Marcus.

Kat put her coffee cup down carefully.

'You're happy with the casting?' Marcus asked The Client. They both nodded.

'Delighted,' said Suzy, in a surprisingly husky voice. Choked by emotion, perhaps?

'So today we're talking about creating the right look, the right feel, the right vibe.'

Audrey sat up a little straighter and laid out some sketches and mood boards on the table. She did not, thank Christ, embark on a PowerPoint presentation; Kat had been experiencing a growing unease that her handful of Polaroids was suddenly looking not just meagre but amateurish. In her mind, this was to be a matter settled in thirty minutes: look at some options, choose three, arrange a reccie. She hadn't counted on the ritual. The ceremony. The bullshit.

But she held her peace and listened as Audrey talked

about the overall look she was after, a look in which the words 'character', 'modern', 'urban' and 'family' repeatedly clashed. She looked at the sketches and swatches, the latter resembling no laundry Kat had ever seen in her life: there were scraps of lamb's wool, a leaf (that green again), striped wallpaper, a strip of chrome, a single white tile. Perhaps she just wasn't creative enough to assimilate it.

Then it was her turn. Kat took a sip of water and shuffled the photos before spreading them out on the table.

'These aren't suggestions,' she said. 'These are just options. Here's a range of rooms—of types, if you like— for you to look at and think about.' *Jesus. I've already started talking like them.* 'I'm not making recommendations at this stage. I'd just like your input.'

Everyone leaned forward to crane over the pictures, all snaps Kat had taken from houses she'd scoped in the past. 'Too cold,' Sam said, flicking at one of the photos with his finger.

'Too cramped,' said Audrey of another, fingering it as if considering tearing it into pieces in disgust.

'Mmm, bit bland,' said Russell, poking at a couple.

'This one's a bit... *Rrrrr*,' said Suzy, making weird claws with her hands.

'They all look a bit...laundry-ish,' said Toby.

Everyone nodded sombrely. Everyone but Kat.

Sam tapped at one thoughtfully. 'This could work. If it was a different colour. Something a bit warmer. A bit fresher. Green, maybe?'

'We can't...we can't really paint someone else's laundry,' ventured Kat, thinking: What is it with the green? Who has a green laundry?

'We could paint it back when we're finished,' he said.

She tilted her head, as if acknowledging the point. 'Okay.'

'Can I have a look at that first one again?' asked Audrey, gesturing to the reject Sam had shot across the table. Kat passed it to her.

'We could paint this one,' she said, pushing it across to Suzy and Russell.

You can't paint other people's laundries! Kat wanted to shout. Instead she tapped softly at another photo, saying: 'I think this might be a possibility. It is a family home. Four young kids. They're a creative couple, in Brunswick, so it's urban, contemporary, but still warm and with a lot of character.'

'Brunswick?' said Audrey, leaning back slightly in her chair as if even naming the place contaminated her.

Sam patted Kat's hand where it rested on the photo. 'This is about *our* input, Kat,' he said kindly.

Kat sat back and folded her hands in her lap. 'Of course,' she said blandly.

33

'I mean, who has a green laundry?'

'Actually, I know someone who has a green laundry.'

'You're kidding.'

'Nope. Sort of minty-green.'

Kat paused, one hand on the cupboard door, the other resting on the wine bottle.

'Who has a *minty-green* laundry?'

'Chrissie and John. You met them last Christmas at Leo's concert. He's a manager or band booker or something. Never quite figured it out. She works for ACOSS. Amelia's parents.'

'Red head? Alison Whyte-ish?'

'That's the one. They bought a place in Carlton last Easter, just behind Drummond Street. The Green House. The living room's a kind of British Racing Green, then it slowly fades as you move towards the back of the house to a minty colour in the kitchen and laundry.'

'Would they have repainted?'

'Don't think so. They loved it. Unless they're sick of it by now.'

'Huh,' said Kat, opening the cupboard, lifting out two wine glasses and holding them up to the light.

'Dirty glass or filthy glass?'

'Dirty glass, thanks.'

Picking some sort of fossilised foodstuff off her own glass, Kat poured a good glug of red into the one that was merely smeared with fingerprints and passed it to her friend. 'All well at home?'

Bets waggled one hand indecisively, taking the wine with the other. 'Leo's started swearing,' she said.

'Oh dear.'

'He called Jim a "plump dog" the other day.'

Kat gave a shout of laughter. 'Bets, that isn't swearing! That's...*literature*!'

'Yes, well, he called *me* fuck-face.' Bets grinned ruefully.

Kat laughed again. 'Ah. Well, I'm sure he's just trying it on.'

'Let's hope so,' said Bets. 'Cheers.'

'Cheers,' said Kat, sinking onto the sofa beside her and taking an appreciative sip.

'Here's to earning again.' Bets tilted the rim of her glass towards Kat, who responded with a small grimace.

'I know. I should be grateful. I am grateful.'

'It's just an interim measure. Your mate was right. You'll be back where you belong before you know it.'

'I hope so.'

'And in the meantime, think of all the new friends you're making.'

If Betsy hadn't quite reacted with Wilson-esque

appreciation to Kat's recounting of her big meeting at Next Creative, she had at least appreciated both its humour and humiliation. It would be some time before either of them entered each other's laundries without murmuring reverentially, 'I feel love...'

It had certainly lifted a great load to begin calculating billable hours. After Kat had suggested that she go out and source some concrete 'suggestions' rather than conceptual 'options', Marcus had seen her out and managed to indicate, in an oblique manner, that he appreciated both her forbearance and the difficulty of her task.

And now this. A minty-green laundry!

The next morning, after setting up a rudimentary office on her dining table, Kat called Chrissie and arranged to inspect the laundry. She also went through her files and pulled up more laundries—thank goodness she never threw anything away—to present to her colleagues.

She called the owners, checked that they were still, in theory, open to the idea of having a film crew in their houses, and organised to re-acquaint herself with them. She had a rough idea of how much gear they'd need to get in and out, but still needed to have a proper look at the location: the parking, what the neighbours were like, how close the nearest freeways and tram lines and train tracks were, when the rubbish trucks would be around. If by some stroke of insane good fortune all the various parties actually approved of one of her suggestions, she wanted to be ready to go.

Kat couldn't wait to get back in The Box and start cruising the suburbs again. It felt good to be working, even on something as mundane, and inane, as this. It becomes who you are, she thought. Work. It fills so much of your day, so many of your thoughts, takes so much of your energy. The skills you acquire, the arcane knowledge, the jargon and the practical particulars. Being in command of all those things was as much a part of your personality as being a reader or a gardener or a sports nut. To have that taken away was to be diminished in some fundamental way. Its loss wasn't quite the loss of a loved one. It wasn't like losing Bonnie. But it was significant, and it felt good to be immersed again in its familiar routines.

The next afternoon she took her first trip, down to Carlton, to re-introduce herself to Betsy's friend and—with some trepidation—ask to see this legendary laundry. As Bets had said, the whole house really was very green.

'I know it's a bit over the top, but we just had to buy this place,' Chrissie said as she ushered her in. 'Green's my favourite colour.'

'You don't say,' said Kat, looking around. Not only the walls but dark green-and-bronze rugs in the living room, a green leather wing-backed chair, a rolltop desk with a green leather top. Pictures in the hallway had green-and-gilt frames. A quick glimpse through the open door of a bathroom revealed products in pale greeny-grey packaging—Endota, Kat thought—on the pale green marble vanity.

'And here it is,' said Chrissie cheerfully, opening the door.

Kat took a long breath and looked around carefully. It was, thank goodness, a decent-sized room. Big enough for a mother to hug her children in ecstatically, and still accommodate a camera, lights and boom. There was a neat washer-dryer pair, a white cane clothes basket with a green-striped cloth lining, a matching hamper, and a row of cupboards with acrylic handles in the shape of eucalypt leaves. No window, which was a mixed blessing. A window was generally a good thing, but a west-facing one, as this would have been, could have caused problems with the lighting. They could always hang a blind or curtain and pretend.

'It's beautiful,' said Kat, exhaling. 'It's perfect.'

'We think it's cute,' said Chrissie. 'No one likes doing the washing. This makes it a bit more bearable.'

Resisting the temptation to say something about love, Kat turned, smiled, and said, 'Want to talk about the details?'

Over a cup of tea (green tea, green mugs) she explained the likely payment, the time it would take, the access they'd need. If you had the *Neighbours* crew in here it'd take twenty minutes, Kat thought. With this lot she cautiously estimated between one and two days. Chrissie would meet them and let them in before she and the family cleared out for the day. They'd lock up as they left, leaving everything as they'd found it.

Chrissie squealed briefly when she heard the dollar figure. 'A holiday!'

'Well, five monstrous egos all have to agree that this is what they want first,' Kat said. 'As far as I can tell, it's exactly what they've asked for. But that doesn't necessarily mean anything.'

'That's fine. If it works out, it's free money. If it doesn't...' Chrissie shrugged happily.

'I'll take some photos. If they like them, I'll bring them

round for a look—I'll call you to arrange a time. If they like what they see, it's all systems go.'

'Deal,' said Chrissie, extending her hand.

At the following meeting at Next, Kat did not, thankfully, have to sit through another concept presentation. She did have to endure more lip curling from Sam and some very odd contributions from Suzy. But they did all agree that the Green Room could be a goer. Not wanting to give them the chance to change their minds, Kat called Chrissie on the spot and set up a time for the following afternoon for a reccie. Leaving the building, buoyed by mild praise from Toby and Marcus, she felt happier than she had in weeks.

'You know what, Box?' she asked as she started the car. 'I'm pretty good at this.'

The Box burped noisily.

That evening she cleared the rubbish out of the car, buffed up the leather seats, rubbed down the dash. 'Want to make a good impression, don't we?' she murmured.

The following morning she ran it through the car wash, and that afternoon, after only the mildest of double-takes, Toby, Audrey and Sam slid into the freshly gleaming auto, Toby even offering, 'Cool car,' as Kat pulled out onto Albert Road and headed north.

Audrey cooed appreciatively when Kat indicated their destination—a handsome bluestone terrace lavishly adorned with wrought iron—and all three smartened themselves up (straightening shoulders, brushing down jackets) as she rang the bell.

After some rather awkward introductions in the

cramped confines of the hallway, Chrissie led them through the house.

'Do you mind if I...?' Audrey asked, gesturing to the rooms off the hall.

'Not at all,' said Chrissie.

'Did you do the decorating?'

'Yes and no,' said Chrissie. 'All the furniture's ours, the rugs and paintings and so on. The colour scheme was already in place.'

'It's amazing,' said Audrey, gazing around. 'Where did you find the chair?'

'It's my grandfather's.'

'Really? How fabulous.' Audrey ran her hand over the leather.

Toby looked around the kitchen with a critical eye, taking in the soft green walls, bright Laminex benchtops, rows of mugs in every shade from sage to jade. Then they all trooped on to the laundry.

'Wow,' said Audrey when Chrissie opened the door. Sam stepped forward and into the room, looking left and right, up and down. Back in the hallway, he made a frame with his hands, peering through it. Seeing Chrissie's lips twitch, Kat held up a warning finger.

'Audrey? Come in here and stand... No, over there a bit. There.' Sam gestured her into position. 'Toby, you be the kid, the boy.' He waved the cameraman into the circle of Audrey's arm. 'Kat? Would you mind...?' Kat found herself also loosely embraced, taking the place of the daughter.

Sam peered through his hands. Stepped back. Peered again. Shook his head. 'The scale's all wrong. Can you two...?' He made a downward chopping motion with his hand, gesturing for Toby and Kat to reduce themselves to fit their roles more closely.

Toby dropped to his knees, and Kat found herself in a painful half squat, Audrey's hand resting lightly on her shoulder. Behind Sam, Chrissie had turned away, overcome by the sight. Kat dropped her head and pressed her lips together, wobbling slightly as her quads began to protest.

'Kat, could you look up? At the camera please? Thank you.' More peering. 'Can everyone smile?' Kat tried not to imagine what she looked like, crouched like a grinning monkey in a minty-green laundry, a strange woman's hand caressing her shoulder.

After an interminable moment Sam said briskly, 'Okay. Thanks.' Kat eased herself back to an upright position.

He was nodding to himself thoughtfully. Kat smoothed back her hair, avoiding Chrissie's eyes. Audrey laid a hand on her host's shoulder. 'It's great, really great.'

'Amazing house,' said Toby.

'Thank you,' said Sam.

'My pleasure,' said Chrissie brightly.

The three made their way back to the front door, murmuring further accolades to the general awesomeness of the house. Kat lingered for a moment. 'Thanks,' she said, shaking Chrissie's hand. 'On the day, we'll be in and gone before you know it.'

'No worries,' said Chrissie, and waved them off.

Back in the car Kat pulled on her seatbelt and put the key in the ignition.

'Well? What did you think?'

There was a brief silence, then Audrey said, 'It's a bit...*green*.'

'A *bit* green?' said Sam. 'Does that woman have some kind of problem?'

'The room itself could work,' said Toby, the voice of reason. 'If only it wasn't so...'

'Green,' said Sam.

'We could always paint it,' said Audrey.

Kat started the car.

34

When the alarm went off Kat groaned, rolled over, and pressed snooze. She'd had an early night, one glass of wine with dinner, made sure she'd drunk her two litres of water during the day—the Sunshine Productions crew were very keen on bottled water—and she still felt like she'd been on a massive bender. Her body was sore all over, her head was pounding, her stomach churning. I have an idiot hangover, she thought. A wanker hangover. I have been over-indulging in the company of fools and my body is finally starting to reject them.

She imagined herself over the next days, weeks— months? It certainly felt like this job would never end— developing more and more severe physical symptoms. Breaking out in hives. Losing her hair. Developing a series of tics and twitches until they had to cart her off, drooling and flailing, to some sort of secure facility for the terminally aggravated.

Even as she smiled at the idea, two miserable tears trickled down her temples. *I don't know how much more of this I can take.* Part of her really felt like she was losing her mind, trapped in a hideous *Groundhog Day* of door-knocking, polite enquiry (each time she made the spiel it sounded more ridiculous, felt more humiliating), laundry inspections and pointless reccies in which Sam, or Audrey, or Toby, or all three, would trot out the same objections over and over again. Too white. Too coloured. Too cold. Too cramped. Too boring. Too cluttered. Until she was ready to scream. Or slap them. Or both.

The Box was objecting, too. At first, being out on the road again had been a delight, even if it was searching for something as dull as the archetypal laundry. Choosing a suburb, cruising the avenues and groves and closes and ways, radar on alert for a freshly renovated street frontage that might conceal a tasteful, modern, relatively spacious washroom.

But after the first couple of hundred kilometres the Box's occasional throat clearing had become positively tubercular. The tacho ticked and jumped wildly even in third; in first the old girl had started stalling, much to Kat's embarrassment and the annoyance of her passengers. She still insisted on couriering the terrible trio to and from locations. To let that go would be to surrender control completely, and she couldn't bear the thought of it.

Meanwhile, even the most handsomely renovated homes didn't display a lot of creativity when it came to their laundries. Let alone love. They were, almost without exception, plain white rooms distinguished only by a greater or lesser degree of utility. And the ones that differed from the template generally only differed in a bad way, frequently through some twee decorating experiment that cast the Green House into the shade.

Today, Kat thought, was the last-chance saloon. If they didn't bite this time, she was really at a loss. She'd found a room in a house in South Melbourne that was certainly clean and white—Kat had realised that any kind of 'character' only sparked violent creative clashes between her colleagues—but it was extremely well proportioned, felt welcoming, and had a pretty window looking out at a lemon tree laden with fruit. In truth, it was neither especially different from nor better than half-a-dozen other rooms she'd sourced, but the owners were perfectly happy to take a couple of grand in return for handing over the keys for a day, as long as it didn't interfere too much with their schedule.

Which meant they all had to be there by 8.30 this morning. On the dot. Which in turn meant Kat really had to get out of bed. Now.

As the clock radio blared back into life she threw back the covers, shivering, and trotted into the bathroom, switching on the kettle on her way. She drank coffee while pulling on her boots, tying back her hair, throwing various essentials into her bag. Mascara, perfume, overcoat, scarf. Car keys, which she pressed to her lips and silently said a short prayer over, and she was out the door.

Rather than taking the chance on everyone making it to the office on time, she'd arranged to pick them up along the way. All three lived Southside; it seemed the most efficient way to get everyone on site, on schedule. After a quick refresher from the *Melways* Kat headed down Moreland Road, onto the freeway—not quite so free at this hour of the day—sliding off again at Montague

Street and down into Albert Park, one eye on the clock.

'Sure you don't want to take my car?' asked Toby when she pulled up. The Box was now shuddering in neutral, something Kat chose to ignore.

'No, we're fine. Jump in,' she said.

He climbed in beside her and pulled on his seat belt.

'So you think this is the one?'

'I hope so!' she said cheerfully, thinking: *If not, tomorrow's headlines could well be 'Shock South Melbourne Triple Stabbing'.*

Sam looked a little disgruntled that Toby had nabbed his front seat position but eventually squeezed in behind him. When she turned into Audrey's street, Kat felt a little tightening in her chest. This was the street they'd shot for *Survivor's* opening montage, before it was even *Survivor*. Then it had been autumn, the elm and plane trees lushly gold. Was that really only four or five months ago? Now the street trees were bare but in pocket front gardens magnolias and camellias were covered in blooms. And there was the bay, steely under a pale sky.

Kat remembered her last time here so clearly: the sun shining in a cloudless sky, the air with that mistiness Melbourne had in April, everything just a little bit soft focus. The excitement that always accompanied the beginning of a shoot, a kind of anxiety but also the sense of potential. How proud she'd been of the result. It had just been her and Ted and his crew: a straightforward sequence of shots they'd accomplished with elegant efficiency.

Kat sighed. It felt so close. It felt like another life. *How did I end up here, again?* Putting the thoughts aside, she checked the traffic, checked the clock—8.15, perfect—and pulled out from the curb.

On Saturday Kat woke early. It was still dark outside, but she could hear the dawn chorus of birdsong, the distant rattle of a tram, the occasional car. When she rolled over and looked at the clock it read 6.15. For a while she lay there in the gloom, hands behind her head, gazing at the shadowy outline of the ceiling fan.

Having had the sudden inspiration to lightly style up the South Melbourne laundry before she let the crew from Sunshine Productions see it (some green towels in a basket, a child's drawing on the wall), that last inspection had won them over. Never mind that it was virtually identical to the dozens of other laundries they'd inspected. Audrey had admired its character (perhaps that was the towels). Sam had confirmed it had the X-factor (that would have been the kid's drawing). Kat—thinking, *You idiots!*—had held her tongue, just relieved to finally have it over with.

But now the rush of having at last secured the Laundry of Love had faded, leaving her grumpy and anxious once more. They would shoot on Monday. On Tuesday she would again be unemployed.

Marcus O'Connell at Next had declared himself delighted with her work. She couldn't think why, unless he privately appreciated what a bunch of irrational prats she was working with and was astonished she'd managed to fulfil the brief. Sunshine made its living from advertising. Were they always this way, or was it just her? Still, he had hinted that there might be more work for her. She wasn't sure how she felt about that. Lavish as the pay was, the thought of another job like this one made her want to kill herself.

She pushed her hands into her hair, rubbing at her scalp with her fingertips, feeling the tension there. *Must wash my hair*. The house needed cleaning, she needed to go to the supermarket. Her life these days seemed a toxic combination of dreary chores and emptiness. It was hard to see where the joy lay any more.

Every time she thought of her ignominious dismissal from *Survivor*, which was often, she felt the hurt and anger all over again. The pain of Harry's betrayal—she couldn't think of it in any other terms—still felt raw. The bedrock ache of Bonnie continued to haunt her, while her future didn't bear thinking about at all.

It was a comfort to know Bets was nearby. And Jim. And Leo, of course. But having debriefed thoroughly over the last few weeks Kat didn't feel there was much left to say, or that Betsy could possibly have any interest in hearing it. She would listen. Of course she would. But there came a point—quite quickly, Kat thought—when grinding out the same old grievances again and again served no purpose except to depress everyone concerned. What would she say? I *still* feel like shit? I'm *still* worried I'll never work again? I *still* really hate Sam King and want to throttle him every time I see him? Bets would say: *Poor thing* and, *You'll get another job before you know it!* and, *Of course you do. Who wouldn't?* And the next morning Kat would still be lying in bed, dreading the start of another day.

She rolled onto her stomach, her face pressed into the gap between the pillows. *I need cheering up. I need to find the joy. Somewhere. I need a laugh.* She slid her hands under her cheek. *I need Wilson.*

This was her most private, deepest thought; her most private, deepest loss; the one she mentioned to no one and rarely acknowledged to herself. The job, and Harry;

Bonnie, and Miles. They were horrible disappointments, crushing blows. But with Bonnie and Miles there had always been an inevitability about her decision, as well as the comfort, bleak though it was, of knowing she'd made the right one. In her more rational, less self-indulgent, less self-pitying moments, she supposed she would, at some stage, get another job. That it was the nature of the business that her path would cross with Harry's again. And that they would sort things out, one way or another, in due course.

Wilson was something else entirely, something sitting awkwardly on the border of possibility, of potential, and outright fantasy. Unquestionably, his presence had been a highlight of her time on *Survivor*; an unlikely friendship but, she thought, a real one; a completely unexpected gift. Of all the things that had happened since Cohen Clarke set up shop in Footscray, her conversations with him were the most entertaining, memorable, enjoyable; and those conversations had made everything that much richer, that much more fun.

And now? Every other loss was real enough. But the loss of Wilson from her day-to-day life, and the idea that she might never see him again, was the one thing that made her feel sick with dread. She didn't know where he lived. She had only once seen him outside the café. About the only personal detail she knew of him was that he'd cheated on his wife. But, Kat thought—and letting the idea float to the front of her mind filled her with a mixture of acute embarrassment and wild exhilaration—I think I might be in love with Wilson the Coffee Guy.

She had certainly, from time to time, revisited their kiss in her imagination, and indulged in modest fantasies about resting against his substantial chest, or reaching up to stroke the smooth contours and fine stubble of his head. This was more than that, though. She'd fancied plenty of blokes before—Jesus, she'd even fancied Dare O'Donnell—and if in the past she'd often mistaken that for love, she was far less likely to do so these days. What excited her about Wilson, almost more than the buzz of being near him, was that they never ran out of things to say. She never tired of talking with him. She never tired of hearing what he had to say. She could say anything to him, uncensored and unmediated, and be understood, never be judged. She was pretty sure she had never felt that with a man before in her life and, to be honest, with precious few of her friends.

She thought of him constantly, regularly reaching for the phone, thinking, I'll just give him a call. But at the last moment her nerve would fail her. Dialling that number somehow felt so *loaded*, and the more she put off calling him, the harder it became to do it. He could have called her at any time, but he hadn't. *Why not?*

But I'm not ready to give up just yet, Kat thought, sitting up in bed. Today is Saturday. The office should be empty, so I won't run into anyone. I have nothing better to do. I can drive down to Footscray and say hello. I am not going to make a big deal of it. I am just going to say hello.

The idea was terrifying. But it had been a month now since she'd gone, and they had last parted as friends. There was nothing weird or stalkerish about dropping by. She repeated these calming thoughts to herself as she showered and washed her hair, had coffee and breakfast, brought in the papers and made a pretence of reading them for half an hour, then pulled on her coat and went out to the car. 'Box? I am just going to say hello,' she said, feeling sick with excitement. 'Footscray, please.'

There was only one car outside the office when she arrived. Everything looked reassuringly deserted. But no sooner had she locked the driver's door than someone called, 'Kat!' Emerging from the rear of the other vehicle where she'd been retrieving an unwieldy box was Bev.

Kat was surprised at the rush of joy she felt as she walked into Bev's open arms, clinging for a moment and feeling tears sting her eyes. Bev wasn't at all disconcerted; in fact, she looked a little teary herself.

'Kat, it is *so* good to see you. We've all missed you so much.'

'I've missed you too.'

'Have you been all right?'

'Of course! I'm fine.'

'We were all so shocked. And angry! It's disgraceful.'

'Ted tells me you didn't get off scot-free either.'

Bev grimaced and gestured to the box at her feet. 'Ridiculous. That's why I'm here today. And back tomorrow. Making props for those blasted challenges. Come upstairs and chat with me. Do you have time?'

It was the strangest feeling climbing those stairs again, at once familiar and discombobulating. Kat sniffed the stale air, a combination of decades-old cigarette smoke, photocopier toner, coffee dregs and pencil sharpenings. It smelt like home.

Following Bev to her workroom she sat with her for an hour, helping her wire together bits of rough pine that would eventually form hinged octagons—why octagons, she didn't know—that concealed something or other, clues or coloured ping-pong balls or some other object essential to the progression of the game. Bev had long ago lost interest in the details. Her attention was focused on finding or making whatever was needed for the next day's shoot, then moving on to the next job.

'I won't say you're better off out of it, because no one's better off out of work and God knows we need you, but it's not much fun around here any more,' she said.

'I'm sorry to hear that,' said Kat, not quite truthfully. She wanted to ask how Heidi was going but couldn't bring herself to. To hear Bev say she was missed was both safest, and sufficient. Instead she said, 'I've also been really missing Wilson's coffee—thought I'd come over for one, say hello. Do you have time to come downstairs for ten minutes?'

'Haven't you heard?'

'Heard what?'

'Wilson's gone. Not long after you went.'

'*Gone?*' said Kat, accidentally stabbing herself with the wire. 'Is he all right?'

'Oh yes,' said Bev, gingerly testing the fit of one of her creations. 'At least, I think so.'

'But why? Gone where?'

'Up north, on family business I think he said. To Shelby, I do remember that bit, because my parents retired there. But there was something or other else. I can't remember.' Bev looked up from her work and smiled briefly. 'Nice bloke. We miss him.'

Tears were streaming down Kat's face, dangerously obscuring her view of the road. I am cursed, she thought. *Someone, somewhere, has a lock of my hair and a drop of my blood and is calling down every possible sort of evil on my head.* Anger and confusion and sorrow surged through her in a torrid stream. Just being back in the office had been deeply unsettling: the rush of memory, the familiarity of it, the reminder she no longer had a place there, the cruelty of that. And then—gone? How could Wilson be *gone*? After all the hurt and loss of the past year, it felt like the last straw, the cruellest blow of all.

Everything else—even Bonnie, even Harry—felt like the end of something, something she'd lived with and worked on or towards for years. That was hard, but everything ended. Everything ran its course. That didn't necessarily make it any easier when the time came, but she'd been around the block enough times to know that was just how life worked. Things began, and changed, and ended or evolved into something else entirely. But Wilson: that had been a beginning. That had been a little flickering spark, the promise of something new and better, her chance to do things differently. And now it was gone too.

35

Monday began badly, when Kat's alarm failed to go off. Some kind of power surge or outage overnight had reset her ancient clock radio in the early hours. It was only daylight through the blinds that alerted her to the fact that it was clearly after seven. Kat came to the realisation dully, muttering 'Cursed' as she hauled herself out of bed and into the shower.

'Just get through the day,' she told herself, grabbing an apple in lieu of breakfast, or even coffee, on her way to the car.

It was unexpectedly cold outside, The Box's windows covered in frost. Pouring cold water over them from a container in the boot only seemed to create a thicker layer of ice, forcing Kat back into the house to fill a bucket in the bath and try again, liberally wetting herself down in the process.

With numb hands and soaked feet she turned the key

in the ignition, and listened to the motor catch, then die; catch, then die. She had promised herself that with the shoot over and money on the way, she'd have The Box over to Ange before the end of the week. The poor thing was on her last legs. 'Please Box,' she moaned. 'One more day.' Resisting the temptation to pump the accelerator and flood the engine, she gently teased it into life and lurched, hiccupping, away from curb.

The boom gates at Moreland Station were stuck down, forcing her to divert south into Brunswick, then north again on to the freeway, The Box protesting every step of the way. At least the old girl seemed to have stopped stalling, the temperature looked good, and if the revs were all over the place they only had another thirty or forty kilometres to cover before she had her well-earned rest. Coming down the on-ramp Kat shifted up into fourth, taking a deep breath. Almost there.

She was late, fifteen minutes late, but she'd picked up the keys yesterday, and if Sam and the crew had to wait, well, let them. Normally fastidious to the point of paranoia about both punctuality and preparedness when it came to a shoot, Kat was finding it hard to care. She had the parking permits in her bag; if anyone was pinged before she got there (and suburban parking inspectors could be diabolical, especially in that neighbourhood) she'd deal with it later.

She'd issued idiot-proof instructions about where everyone needed to be, and when. This was a simple job with, she suspected, a monstrous budget. A small delay could be easily absorbed. It would annoy Sam, but that, she thought with clenched teeth, was a bonus.

In her rear-view mirror she could see a big white ute,

its grill filling her field of vision. 'Bloody four-wheel drives,' Kat grumbled, accelerating cautiously. Beside her was a truck, a real truck, the logo of a supermarket chain emblazoned on its side, creating an awkward slipstream; in front of her, one of those big American SUVs, like a shipping container on wheels. Normally Kat enjoyed The Box's modest proportions, but today she felt buffeted and unsteady.

Suddenly, there was a soft, percussive *whump*. For a moment Kat thought she'd run over something, a cardboard crate perhaps. Then she realised there was no sound at all from the engine; she was steadily decelerating, the car in front pulling away, the one behind looming closer. Kat resisted the urge to slam on the brakes and pull on the steering wheel. With a squeak of fear she managed to steer into the emergency lane, the ute tapping its horn as it surged past.

Kat's heart pounded as she waited for a wave of nausea to rise and recede, trembling hands resting on the wheel. She closed her eyes. Took a breath. Took another breath. There were strange sounds coming from under the hood, and belatedly she turned off the ignition.

It was then Kat noticed thick, bitter smoke rising from the front of the car. 'Oh God,' she moaned, popping the hood and clambering out. With the hem of her coat wrapped around her hand she eased the bonnet up then leapt back as the sudden influx of oxygen brought the smouldering fire there to life. 'No! No! No! No! No!' she cried, dancing, distraught, on the spot.

The smell was appalling, the heat intensifying. Kat knew she should do something to put out the fire but had no idea what. She didn't have a fire extinguisher.

Could she smother it with a blanket? She didn't have a blanket either. Her coat. Fumblingly, she stripped it off and flung it onto the flames, where it promptly ignited. 'No,' she moaned again.

Suddenly, a young bloke in a hi-vis vest over a fleecy jacket appeared beside her, a small extinguisher in his hands. 'Out of the way, miss,' he said, and proceeded to cover the engine, and her coat, in white foam. Kat realised the ute she'd been cursing had pulled over and its occupant had now come to her aid. 'Noticed the smoke when you pulled over,' he said. 'Gives you a bit of a fright, doesn't it?' As if exploding cars were something he dealt with every day.

'*Thank you*,' said Kat, turning to face him. 'So much.' He barely looked old enough to have a driver's licence, smooth-skinned and with a soft-looking beard clinging uncertainly to his chin. The odour from the car was still positively toxic, but the fire seemed to be out and cooling rapidly, the engine ticking and clunking in the still-icy air.

'You need to call the CityLink rescue mob now,' he said. 'They'll give you a tow.'

Kat nodded numbly.

'Like me to do it for you?'

Was there no end to this chap's resourcefulness? Kat nodded again. 'Could you?'

'Used to drive an old shit heap myself,' he said as he dialled. 'Know what it's like. These things happen.' Connecting with the appropriate authority, he read out Kat's licence plates and gave them her location.

'On their way,' he said cheerfully. 'You be okay?'

'Yes. Thanks again.'

'No worries. Shame about your coat. Bit nippy, isn't

it? But they shouldn't be long.' He paused. 'I wouldn't get back in the car, though. Just to be safe.'

'Okay,' said Kat, her throat tight. 'Sure.'

'Well, better get to work!'

Kat watched him trot back to the ute, climb in, and ease himself back into the flow of traffic. She was shivering, with cold and shock, and hugged herself hard. When the ute was no longer even a speck in the distance she turned to face her own car again, its mouth agape, the engine a stinking, lava-like mess. She dropped to her knees and laid her hands on the bumper. 'Oh Box,' she sobbed. 'What have I done to you?'

36

It was a slow drive off the freeway and into Brunswick. Kat called ahead to Ange, asked him to cover the tow, then hopped out of the truck on Moreland Road, called a cab, and texted Sam to let him know she was finally on her way. Her stomach lurched when she saw the time: almost 10.30am. The Sunshine crew had been waiting outside the South Melbourne house, ready to shoot the Laundry of Dreams, for more than two hours. Fifteen minutes late was one thing, a discreet Up Yours. This was something else entirely. A sackable offence, Kat thought with a sinking heart.

When she arrived the street was crammed with trucks. That was no surprise. The catering tables, she noticed, were a shambles of leftovers. Obviously everyone had been killing time by eating and drinking. Too bad if they wanted to eat or drink later in the day. The adult actor was sitting on the steps of the make-up truck, flicking through a magazine. One of the child actors was in tears. Then there was Sam, striding towards her, his face set with rage.

'Where the *fuck* have you been?'

'I'm so sorry. My car broke down...'

'And it took you two hours to get a fucking taxi?'

'I broke down on the freeway, I had to get a tow...'

'Two hours! Two hours we've been waiting here, this whole show costing God knows how much every fucking minute you don't show up.'

'I know, I know. I'm so sorry. The car...'

'That pile of junk!' he exclaimed.

Kat winced. 'I'm sorry... The car caught fire... I got here as quickly as I could.'

Sam made a strangled sound of disgust. 'Give me the fucking keys. Get out of here.'

With shaking hands Kat fished the keys out of her bag and handed them to him, unable to speak, let alone argue. Who knew what would happen in the house without her there. Today, though... Not only did she not feel able to press the point, she could not wait to get out of there. 'I'll be back before five,' she murmured.

The taxi she'd arrived in had long gone. Hitching her bag more firmly onto her shoulder, Kat turned and started trudging back to the main road.

'I've killed her!' sobbed Kat.

'You haven't killed her,' said Ange, patting her back awkwardly. 'Although I wish you hadn't melted your coat all over the carburettor.'

'I was trying to put the fire out!'

278

The Box sat forlornly at the entrance to his cramped workshop, hood yawning again over the charred mess of the motor.

'The good thing is,' said the mechanic, returning to the comfort of the vehicle after his alarming stint as emotional prop, 'these old engines have proper blocks. Not that aluminium rubbish you get these days. A new car? The whole thing would've melted. I reckon we can salvage this.'

Kat hugged herself and rubbed her upper arms, coming to stand beside him. It was an awful sight, but Ange's pragmatism was having a soothing effect. Traditionally she took care of The Box by making sure Ange took care of it. Unlike her mother, Kat had no interest in anything mechanical, took no pride in being able to change a spark plug (could not, in fact, identify the spark plugs) and considered an afternoon spent tinkering under the hood a shocking waste of time, even if she had known what she doing.

The technical stuff she left to Ange. Except this time she hadn't. She'd been criminally neglectful and felt it now as an unforgivable moral failing. How long had the old girl been making that funny noise? Just after she'd started on *Survivor*. Before it was *Survivor*. She was still living with Miles—God, that felt like another lifetime, although Kat supposed it was only a few months ago. Still, months of relentless driving with an ominous rattle under the hood, not to mention hooning through the city at ridiculous speeds with Dare at the wheel. Should she mention that to Ange? Would it make a difference?

No. The engine was fucked. Didn't really matter how it happened. She watched Ange pick at it first with a filthy fingernail, then with a tool he produced from his pocket, trying to excavate through the melted plastic and wire and wool-blend coat and hardened fire retardant, feeling another wave of guilt.

She'd known the old girl was sick and she'd kept on forcing her on—one more day, then another—too consumed by her own problems to pay proper attention to The Box's needs. And now she'd killed her, or at least mortally wounded her. The Box was in a coma, one from which she may never wake, and it was entirely Kat's fault. Like the lacklustre pet you never quite get round to taking to the vet, or the whiny kid complaining of headaches who suddenly drops from a massive aneurism, Kat had wilfully ignored the symptoms of a loved one in her care. The thought made her weak with shame.

'Come and sit down,' said Ange, wiping his hands on a filthy cloth and gesturing to his office. 'Like a cuppa?'

Kat nodded. She knew it would be cheap instant coffee in a filthy mug, but she hadn't had anything since an apple at 7.30am and just holding a warm cup in her freezing hands seemed like a good idea at the moment.

Ange's office was as dirty and chaotic as always, papers, manuals and car magazines in teetering piles held down by miscellaneous auto parts, everything smeared black with oil and covered in dust, the room reeking of cigarette smoke and fried food. She sank into one of the sagging green visitors chairs and gratefully received a milky coffee.

'Well,' said Ange, sitting down behind his desk. 'You definitely haven't killed her. Although I hate to think what your mum would say, God rest her.'

Kat just looked at him over the rim of her mug. He then launched into a detailed account of his investigations, which parts were salvageable, which cactus. It was all gibberish to Kat, but she did her best to look attentive.

'There's a little bit of bodywork, too. Just the bonnet,' he concluded. 'All up, I reckon you'll get away with eight to ten grand.'

'Ten grand!' Kat slopped coffee over her fingers.

'Six to eight,' amended Ange, seeing the panic in her face.

'Ange... I *can't*!'

'What do you mean?'

'I just lost my job. I lost my last job and then I got another one and then today...' Her voice trailed off and she put the mug down unsteadily. 'Ange, I don't have that kind of money.'

Her thoughts had been so consumed with saving her beloved car, the cost of doing so hadn't crossed her mind. When she had The Box serviced, it was a few hundred. If something needed repairing, it was a few hundred more. But thousands? Of course this was going to cost thousands. The reality of it, the implications, gradually took hold. She had let the insurance lapse last month. A 'saving', she had told herself.

Ange scratched his head. 'You don't have to pay it all at once. We can work something out.'

'I can't.'

'Kat, you'll get another job. Before you know it. In the meantime, I can get to work. Don't worry about it now. You're upset.'

'Ange, you can't afford to do the work for nothing. And I can't afford to pay you.'

They stared at each other for a moment.

'You're upset,' he said again.

Kat nodded. 'I am upset.' She swallowed hard. 'But that doesn't change anything. I can't afford to get her fixed.'

'Kat, no.'

'You'll have to... You'll have to send her to the wreckers. Or sell her for parts. Can you do that? Is she still... Is she worth anything?'

'Kat, *please*...'

'I need you to sell her for parts,' said Kat, standing and picking up her bags.

Ange stood too, distressed. 'Kat, just think about it for a bit. I don't mind keeping her here for a few days, a few weeks, whatever you need.'

'Thank you,' said Kat. 'But a few days or weeks won't make any difference. I can't afford to keep her anymore, Ange. I need you to get rid of her for me. Can you do that?'

After a long pause he dug his hands into his pockets and said, 'Sure. Okay.'

'Thank you,' Kat said again.

They both stood there in silence for a moment.

'Do you need a lift home?' he finally said.

'No thanks,' said Kat. 'I'll walk.'

She was almost home when the phone rang. Fishing in her bag she checked the caller ID and paused a moment. At any other time she would have been shocked. Right now, in a stupor of loss, all she felt was bemusement.

'Hi Miles,' she said listlessly.

'I hope you don't mind me calling.'

'Of course not.'

There was a pause, then Miles said, 'I only just heard. About *Survivor*. I'm sorry.'

'Yeah. It was a bit of a...' Kat couldn't think of quite the right descriptor.

'Outrageous, Kat. But you know what this business is like.'

'I do.'

'And I did warn you about getting involved. It was never a good idea, that show. It was always going to be trouble, one way or the other.'

Kat said nothing, thinking, *Fuck off, Miles.*

'Anyway, I just wanted to say, you'll be fine. You'll be back in work in no time. And if I can put in a word for you... Or if—I don't know—is there anything you need?'

Kat felt her throat tighten and tilted her head back for a moment. Eight to ten grand, she thought. That's what I need. But just said, a little hoarsely, 'Thank you. I'm okay.'

'Well, anything you need.'

'Thank you,' she said again.

'Okay, well...'

'How's Bonnie?' Kat blurted.

Miles paused. 'She's good.'

'Could I... Can I see her, do you think?'

Another pause. 'Kat, I know how much you love Bonnie, but...she's only five. It's confusing for her. She was so upset, about everything. Now Victoria's about to get married, so there's going to be another dad in the picture. And—' He cleared his throat uncomfortably '—I've started seeing someone...'

Kat said nothing, holding the phone to her ear with one hand, the other hand pressed hard against her chest.

'It's confusing for her,' he repeated. 'And Kat, I'm not saying this to hurt you, but she's started to forget about you. She doesn't mention you anymore. It wouldn't be

283

good for her to see you again right now. You understand that, don't you?'

'Yes,' Kat whispered.

'I'm sorry,' he said. 'I know she means a lot to you, but I have to put her first.'

Kat fought for breath. The gentleness of his tone as much as what he was saying was undoing her. 'That's okay,' she eventually murmured. 'I understand. And thanks for calling. It was...kind of you.'

'Well, as I said, anything you need...'

'Thank you,' said Kat. 'Goodbye.'

37

The days were definitely getting longer. By 6am, the birds were in full chorus and a grey light was coming through the blinds. When was daylight saving? October? Kat couldn't remember, wasn't even sure what day of the week it was, although they'd passed into September recently, she did know that. Footy finals all over the front page, the Grand Final the only thing anyone was talking about.

She sighed and rolled over, the view changing from the dim ceiling to the closed blinds. She closed her eyes but knew there was no chance of sleep. Once again the nights that seemed endless had resolved themselves into another day, a reality that filled her with dread.

She lay there looking at the light seeping through the wooden slats. I could open them and look at the garden, she thought. But she didn't. She could hear the clock in the kitchen ticking, the trams on Nicholson Street, a steady hum of early traffic. In another hour or so the bell at the primary school on the corner would sound and that would be her cue to get out of bed. I could open the blinds, she thought. I could switch on the radio. But she did neither, as had become the pattern these days.

Betsy had been sympathetic about the call from Miles, she understood Kat's pain, but also the truth in what he'd said. How many mummies should a little girl go through before she reached primary school? It was one of those occasions when Bets had nothing to offer but a hug, and a few tears of her own.

The whole family had been horrified at the loss of The Box. Jim instantly offered her the money to salvage it, but she couldn't take it from them, any more than she could accept the work from Ange. They couldn't afford it, and in the circumstances it was a massive debt she had no hope of paying back.

Nor could she explain, even to her dearest friend, how deep a loss it was. She couldn't quite figure out herself if the numb misery she'd sunk in since was simply due to that single event, or the cumulative sorrows of the year.

Certainly with The Box gone Kat felt she'd lost her mother, finally and irrevocably. That she had no one to blame but herself made it even more bitter. The guilt was still something that haunted her every day. Before Nancy died the two of them had sorted through her possessions. There hadn't been much there that Kat had wanted to keep. How could I have been so heartless? she thought, remembering those days. *How could I have been so unsentimental about my own mother?* But she'd never been very interested in things, in possessions. They weren't her mother. Things weren't people. Kat had felt quite sure The Box was the only reminder of Nancy that she'd ever need.

The car was also the last in a succession of losses that Kat found herself calculating, over and over again, a sort of mental self-flagellation, every loss made heavier and deeper by her age, her time of life. In your teens and twenties things hurt, they were agonising. But life was also infinite. Some part of you just knew you had endless chances to do-over. You'd get another job. You'd find another bloke. You'd buy a better car. And kids were something for the distant future.

Now, life was palpably finite, Kat thought with an ache. Second chances were unlikely and in some cases impossible. The Box was irreplaceable. And the loss of Bonnie, of course, contained deeper levels of loss, of family, of children of her own. The pain of Miles' words continued to haunt her, but Kat had reached some kind of peace with letting Bonnie go. Bonnie was never hers to keep. That deeper emptiness, though, was hers all right. She would never have children of her own. Time had simply run out.

Work. Sometimes when she thought of it her breath still caught, the emotions so vivid and confused. The wild careening through self-doubt, anger, frustration and shame continued. Ted and Bev had assured her of the great injustice of her sacking, but that didn't deliver much comfort. She had certainly done nothing wrong. She had, however, been singled out—as Ted had so pithily explained—as the one who wouldn't complain. The runt, the weakling who took her beating then thanked you for it. The realisation made her cringe.

Her inglorious association with Next and Sunshine was even more painful. She had not, she thought, done a good job. She had blamed her colleagues—Sam especially—for their intransigence and petty squabbling, but she could have solved that particular problem weeks earlier if she hadn't been so blinded by her own ego and contempt. As for leaving them stranded for half a day... Her rage was at least partly directed at herself, for being an idiot.

Harry. Kat rolled over again to resume her surveillance of the ceiling. That was a different kind of hurt. It was a kind of betrayal and yet she found she was unable to muster much anger about it. Despite their long friendship, she and Harry had never shared their deepest secrets. It wasn't the kind of relationship where they ever discussed life outside work very much. It was, she thought, light-hearted, and she had enjoyed that about it. What left her discombobulated now, though, was realising that she never really knew him at all.

Then there was Wilson, thought Kat, curling into a ball. Why had he gone? Why hadn't he contacted her? Those questions nagged at her. Every time she contemplated it some part of her brain just refused to accept it as true. *You can't be gone. I'm not ready. I'm not finished. I've hardly even started.* Again, she'd thought they had time. That kiss—it was too soon. Yet, in her mind at least, it had also been a beginning, a hint of the future. *Only now it turns out there is no future.*

In the distance, the school bell rang, accompanied by the faint sound of small children shrieking. A while ago she might have gone for a walk by the creek (she'd read somewhere that such things were good for your mental health), but these days it seemed like too much trouble. Earlier on, she'd spent afternoons watching old DVDs of shows she'd worked on. The idea was that it might cheer her up, remind her of everything she'd achieved. But Kat discovered it merely reminded her of everything she'd lost.

Sundays she got up, made herself presentable, and walked the block to Betsy's house for lunch with the family, during which she found it easy enough to fake a calm, cheerful ordinariness. There were even moments when she thought she was enjoying herself. But as soon as it was over she was straight back home, more often than not undressing and getting back into bed, sinking back into the familiar loop of self-pitying regret and self-recrimination.

Today, even the thought of collecting the mail defeated her. On the kitchen counter was a pile of unopened envelopes, mostly unpaid bills, and a letter from the bank, no doubt in reference to the mortgage payment she'd missed.

Which would be the next thing, Kat thought. The next loss. She was going to have to sell the flat, and she was going to have to do it sooner rather than later, before things got any worse. She could lease it out, as she had before. The market rental neatly covered the mortgage repayments. But then she'd have nowhere to live. If she sold it, she could at least pay rent of her own for a while, clear the bills. Until that money ran out too. And then she really would have nothing.

A few months ago, in the middle of the supermarket, she had thought of Suicide Guy. Things get better, she had silently said to him. Now she felt like he was answering her: *See? Sometimes they don't. Sometimes, they get worse.*

Sometimes they get so much worse all you can do is

step off the top of an office building. At the time, it had seemed to Kat a bizarre thing to do. Now she saw the sense of it. The idea of just leaving everything behind. There seemed a wonderful peace in it. I would not, of course, jump off a building, thought Kat. Too gruesome. Too public.

She ran the palm of her hand across the pillow next to her, dispassionately considering her options. The idea of a drug overdose, of just falling asleep and not waking up, was a very pleasant one. But was that really what happened? She thought vaguely of people choking on their own vomit. Not good.

The gassing-yourself-in-the-car thing also seemed like a peaceful solution. She didn't have a car, of course. But she supposed she could hire one. Nor, she realised, did she have a garage. She sighed and shifted on to her other side. *My life is so pathetic I don't even have off-street parking.*

On telly people often shot themselves. She quite liked that idea. It'd be fast, and it was simple, requiring almost no preparation. One problem, of course. Unless you were part of Melbourne's notorious underworld, where on earth did you get a gun?

She had no idea how to tie a noose, so hanging was out.

Maybe I could throw myself under a train? She assumed it would be relatively painless, although the wait for the train would be a bit scary. But how easy to just walk to the pedestrian crossing behind Sydney Road and step out. No materials or equipment required and no preparation beyond checking a timetable. It'd be quick. Simple. I could do it tonight, if I wanted to. What a relief, she thought. What a blessed relief it would be to be dead.

She pondered that for a while longer.

Someone would have to identify the body. Kat imagined Betsy in a morgue, the sheet being pulled back, having to look at her corpse. *What a terrible thing to do to a friend.* Strangely, the thought that Betsy loved her wasn't comforting at all. Being loved didn't solve a single problem, or restore one jot of what she'd lost. It didn't even make her feel less alone. Grief, thought Kat, was by its nature a kind of solitary confinement that no amount of affection or goodwill could breach.

But knowing that Betsy loved her, and imagining her distress at that call from the police, made Kat's heart ache. It was just too awful, it was beyond what you could ask of anyone.

As the sun continued to climb, Kat continued to consider her options. Having settled on the notion of suicide, she was reluctant to let it go. The promise of nothingness, of release from everything, was powerfully attractive and she railed against giving it up. But no matter how she came at it—the neatness or peacefulness or painless of the method, what planning or safeguards she put in place—there was no escaping the fact that someone would have to find the body, someone would have to identify the body, and the people who cared about her would spend the rest of their lives haunted by it. What a terrible, *terrible* thing to do to someone.

I guess, she thought drearily, I'll just have to keep on living after all.

38

On the morning of the first day of the rest of her life, Kat was not especially filled with *joie de vivre*. On the contrary, she felt almost precisely as shithouse as she had for the previous however many days. She couldn't remember the last time she'd felt happy. The dullness that blanketed her now cast a long shadow back over all the times she supposed she'd been happy but now seemed like fantasy.

She glanced at the clock—8am, a perfectly respectable time to get up—pushed back the covers, swung her feet to the floor, and shrugged into her dressing gown. Pinching the sleep from her eyes, a cheering thought occurred to her: *Hey! I've actually been asleep!*

'Good,' Kat said to herself firmly, sliding her feet into her slippers.

In the kitchen she put the kettle on, spooned coffee into the plunger, opened the blinds. The sun was shining.

She took a deep breath. Maybe this living thing will work out after all.

Then, to her astonishment, the phone rang. There was nothing particularly astonishing, of course, about a telephone ringing. Except that she couldn't remember the last time someone had called her.

'How odd,' Kat said, pouring boiling water over the coffee grounds, not quite astonished enough to actually answer it. Then the phone rang again. Followed by the little Tinker Bell tingle indicating she had a message. And then, God, someone knocking on the door. Quite loudly and insistently, using the knocker rather than their knuckles.

Reflexively Kat crouched down in the kitchen, afraid her shadowy self might be glimpsed through the front windows. She didn't want to be seen fresh out of bed, in a manky dressing gown and with her hair awry. She certainly didn't want to talk to anyone.

Then the phone went again, another text.

For a moment Kat wondered if she was, in fact, still asleep and dreaming. It was a bizarre amount of activity for this hour of the morning, especially as her days had passed uninterrupted for weeks now. *What could possibly be going on?* Eventually the knocking stopped and she listened to heavy footsteps treading back down the path; a car door opening and closing; the engine starting; the car driving away. Cautiously, she stood.

It was all so odd she actually pinched herself. It was mildly painful but not especially reassuring. Was there any reason a pinch wouldn't also be mildly painful in a dream? she thought. And was still puzzling over whether it was the pain of the pinch or the act of pinching that was supposed to reassert reality when the phone tinkled again.

Straightening, Kat went to the back windows and peered out, looking for leaping flames, aeroplanes falling from the sky or perhaps a mushroom cloud over Merri Creek indicating something she really should be paying attention to. All she could see was the lawn and the lemon tree, the fence, the sky. Unpolluted, as far as she could tell, by evidence of Armageddon. Okay, she thought. No emergency. She poured herself a cup of coffee. But still...

It took some minutes to find the phone, buried under a pile of unopened mail (the sight of which almost drove her back to bed again). Coffee in hand, she sat down to solve the mystery. The first text, as she suspected, was to let her know she had voicemail. The second simply read:

Call me. Barry.

BC? Curiouser and curiouser. Taking a sip of her coffee, Kat dialled voicemail, and heard not BC's but Betsy's voice, sounding slightly strangled.

'Darling, it's me. Have you seen the paper this morning? Isn't that your guy?'

No, I have not, thought Kat, blessing the fact that her newspaper subscription, prepaid, still chugged along under its own steam. Tugging her dressing gown a little more tightly around her, Kat opened the front door. Scouting for passersby, she made the short bolt to the mailbox and back again, two fat, plastic-wrapped rolls of newsprint under her arm. There was nothing above the masthead to indicate World War Three had been declared. Picking at the plastic with clumsy fingers, she managed to shake the first paper flat. The front page was all politics and football. It was only when she wrestled the other free of its wrappings that she understood—with a gasp—why Bets had called.

'Oh. My. God,' whispered Kat, her chest tightening. 'My God,' she said again, smoothing the paper flat on the kitchen counter and trying to absorb the details. As Bets intimated, it was indeed her guy. Their guy, at least. *Survivor*'s guy. Dare O'Donnell had made the front page again, it looked like for the last time. Light-headed, Kat sat down to read the story.

It must have been a hold-the-press kind of situation to make the morning's edition as there wasn't much there. Simply that football legend and TV personality Dare O'Donnell had been struck and killed by a car in Queen Street in the early hours of the morning. Police and paramedics had attended, called by the driver, a woman in her twenties, but he'd been pronounced dead at the scene. There was the famous picture of a much younger O'Donnell, bare-chested and brandishing the Premiership Cup above his head.

That was it. But Kat read and re-read it, then combed the second paper, finding a short paragraph that just reiterated the same information. 'My God,' she murmured again. Fumbling for the remote control she turned on the television and worked her way through the news channels and morning chat shows until she struck a grave pair ensconced in an inappropriately cheery set, providing a cobbled-together obituary. Kat sat, dazed, in front of a succession of clips from O'Donnell's playing days. After so many weeks of feeling nothing at all, she was now paralysed by emotional overload.

For all his flaws (the chat show host was now enumerating some of them), Dare had been the most vivid person she had ever met. Kat thought about the first time she'd encountered him in the flesh, the magnetic field that surrounded him that she never became completely immune to, the visceral power of his charisma. Their wild ride through the sleeping city. *I should have had sex with him. What harm would it have done? I should have had sex with him when I had the chance.*

She let the papers slide to the floor and returned her attention to the television. Apparently the young woman who had run Dare down, a nurse on the way home from late shift, had gone into hiding, was refusing to comment to the media. Dare left behind no family but his partner— *His partner?*—was devastated, and of course his legion of fans and the club for which he'd played were stunned and mourning. Suddenly GC was on screen, shockingly familiar in the midst of so much weirdness and looking genuinely upset, explaining how much they'd all loved Dare, how sorely he'd be missed, and that no decision had been made on the future of the series, which was due to wrap that day.

When another montage of Dare's career highlights led into an ad break, Kat turned off the telly and sank back on the sofa. What a waste, she thought. What a shocking waste. Fat tears—the tears she'd been longing to shed for weeks—began rolling silently down her cheeks, dripping off her chin and running down her neck. She didn't move to brush them away, didn't move at all. Let them pool in her collarbone, let her nose run. She didn't want them to stop. It was such a relief to be properly, thoroughly sad.

It was not that she had cared so very much about Dare.

She'd rarely given him a thought since she'd left *Survivor*. And while he was certainly charming, and capable of being kind, he was not someone you could trust. He was not someone you could ever have a real relationship with. But... 'What a waste,' she said out loud. What squandered potential. What a short, brutish thing life really was, and so insanely unpredictable.

It seemed impossible that such a person could be dead, but he was. It was a thought Kat found both frightening and strangely energising. She reached for the tissues and blew her nose luxuriously, her thoughts churning. The phone tinkled again, and this time she snatched it up.

Keys under doormat.

Kat stared at the message for a full minute, but unable to glean any further meaning from it she stood, slipped her phone into the pocket of her dressing gown, opened the front door, and lifted the mat. Under it was a plain envelope. Inside was a pair of keys that made her heart suddenly palpitate with dizzy excitement, along with a scrawled note that simply said: *Pay me when you can.*

Leaving the front door wide open and not caring now who might witness her dishabille, Kat sprinted down the path and out into the street, casting herself upon what she found there.

'Box!' she said, her throat tight, laying her cheek against the roof, breathing oil and duco and freshly minted metal. 'Box.'

Having hugged the car as much as possible, she unlocked the door and slid behind the wheel. The leather seats and the wooden dash had been recently waxed. Her bare toes gripped the familiar planes and ridges of the accelerator, the clutch. The bonnet, she could see, was a slightly different shade to the rest of the car and certainly shinier, but straight and clean. She slid the key into the ignition and turned it, listening to the engine growl into life. 'Oh Box,' she breathed. She sat there for a long time, her hands caressing the steering wheel and her eyes closed, tears again streaming down her cheeks, inhaling the dear scent of it and listening to the smooth purr of the motor.

And was still sitting there, entranced, when the phone in her pocket rang yet again. Pinching her nose and wiping her eyes, she glanced at the number, hesitated, then answered it, switching off the engine as she did so.

'Kat Kelly,' she said a little huskily.

'Don't hang up,' BC said without preamble.

'Okay.' Kat held the phone away for a moment while she cleared her throat, re-ordered her thoughts.

'Suppose you heard about O'Donnell.'

'Yes. In the papers.'

'Pissed as a newt, of course.'

'Was he?'

'Strictly between you and me. Staggered out of some club and straight into that poor bird's car. Fuckwit.'

'Off the wagon again?'

'A bit. Not too bad. Turned up most days.'

'Until today.'

BC sighed extravagantly. 'Bad luck shoot. You get 'em sometimes. Remember that guy in Lonsdale Street? The jumper?'

'I don't think any of us will ever forget.'

'No. Suppose not. Should have called the whole thing off then.'

Kat waited, unsure where this was all heading. BC didn't do chitchat, or friendly calls. He wanted something, and it wasn't to debrief about Dare. The silence stretched a little longer, then BC said, 'Look, Kat. I just wanted to say. You know, that other business. It wasn't personal.'

'What, sacking me?'

'Yeah, that. You know we love you. You're fucking brilliant at your job, you know that.'

Kat said nothing.

'Not going to make this easy for me?'

'I don't know what you expect me to say.'

'No. Fair enough. Well, we had to shed some costs. Budget blown to pieces. Network breathing down our fucking necks. You know what they're like. Gen didn't want to, but I got her to do the dirty. Didn't think I'd say it right. She's better at that sort of thing.'

Another pause.

'This is strictly between you and me.'

'You mean, don't tell Kat in case she sues you for wrongful dismissal?' asked Kat.

BC laughed his dirty-old-man chuckle. 'Yeah. Something like that.'

'Look, if you're trying to get me to come back on to *Survivor*, you're dreaming.'

'What? Fuck, no. They're wrapping today. Anyway, I didn't call you to talk about any of that. Ancient history. Been working on another project. Want to ask you something, and I don't want you to just say no straight off.'

'What is it?'

'Promise you won't just say no.'

Kat took a breath, expelled it. 'Okay. I promise.'

'Pitched this new drama series to the ABC a while

ago. Finally got them to yes. Thirteen eps, with another thirteen if it takes. Miriam Smart wrote it.'

Kat sat up a little straighter.

'It's already cast, it's fully crewed.'

'So what do you want me for?'

'Well, I know you keep saying you're happy doing locations, you only want to do locations, yada yada. But we both know you're better than that.'

Kat narrowed her eyes in suspicion. Where was this going?

'Are you doing that squinty-eyed thing?' BC asked.

'Yes,' said Kat.

'Thought you might be. But just listen. This is an out-of-town job and I need someone with their head screwed on to keep an eye on it. Had you in mind for it since day one. Right up your alley. Gen and I want you to produce. Line producer, production manager, producer, whatever you want to call it. We'll be here, if you need us. But you won't.'

Kat's head was spinning. This was a hell of a day to decide to get out of bed. She gripped the steering wheel with her free hand.

'What's the catch?'

'Fuck me, don't mind looking a gift horse, do you? There is no catch. Offering you a promotion and a pay rise, and not on some half-arsed reality gig either. The real thing.'

'Guilty conscience?'

'Nah. Don't have a conscience, you know that. Know you're the person for the job. Wouldn't offer it to you otherwise. Think you'll enjoy it too. You like Smart, don't you?'

'Yes,' said Kat. 'I do.'

'Right then. Sorted.'

'I haven't said yes yet.'

'You will. You're not a complete fucking idiot.'

Kat let this pass.

'There is one thing.'

'Yes?'

'It's quite a way out of town.'

Here it comes, thought Kat. 'How far out of town?'

'Well, depends which town you're talking about. If you're talking Byron Bay, you'll be about ten minutes out of town. Melbourne? About three days.'

'The shoot's in New South Wales?'

'North coast. Can't remember the name of the town we're setting up in. Do know it's not Byron. Have you seen the rents there? Fuck me. Might as well film the fucking thing in Paris. Don't know how those ferals afford it. Anyway, I'll get you in, give you all the details. Buy you lunch. Be good to see you again. We've missed you.'

Kat released her grip on the steering wheel and leant back in her seat, thoroughly overwhelmed. A pay rise. A promotion. A job. And BC was right. She had insisted, for years, that all she wanted to do was locations. But production manager? She could do that. It might be interesting. It might even be fun. She didn't know Miriam Smart well but she loved her work. God knows she was ready for a change, ready for a fresh start. All things considered, thought Kat, as a plan for the future it had a number of advantages over lying down in front of the last train to Upfield.

'You still there?'

'Yes. I'm here.'

'Just waiting for you to say yes now, mate. Don't have all fucking day.'

'Yes,' said Kat. 'Of course. Thank you.'

'Good girl. Call you next week once this shit storm's cleared,' said BC, and hung up.

Almost immediately, the phone started ringing again. This time when she saw the caller ID she squealed—quite loudly—and leapt in her seat, her heart banging. 'Hello?' she shouted, her voice an octave too high. Then realised she hadn't accepted the call, and stabbed at the screen with a shaking finger. 'Hello?' she squeaked again.

'Kat? It's Wilson.'

Breathe, Kat told herself. Breathe. 'Hi,' she said.

After a brief pause Wilson asked awkwardly, 'How are you?', sounding every bit as unsettled as she felt.

'I'm good. I'm...happy to hear from you.'

'Good, thanks,' said Wilson. 'I mean, I'm glad...you're good.' Then: 'Shit. Sorry. I'm really nervous.'

'I'm really glad you called,' said Kat gently.

'I'm sorry I haven't called sooner. Everything happened so quickly, there was everything to sort out with the café. I was hoping I'd see you before I left, but I didn't. And then it all seemed...' His voice trailed off.

'What did happen?' asked Kat. 'Is everything okay?'

There was a long exhale on the other end of the line. 'I'm fine. It's all fine. It's just...*complicated*.'

'Believe me, I'm good with complicated,' Kat said, her heart now settled into a joyous staccato.

'It's just... God, there are other people involved. And I feel like such an idiot. I really want to tell you all about it—you wouldn't *believe* how much I've been wanting to talk with you about all this, everything that's happened.

302

I just…' He paused. 'Kat, this is going to sound crazy, but I don't suppose you could take some time off, could you? Just a week? Or even a couple of days? I'm up in northern New South Wales, I can't get away, but I'd really like to see you, and explain everything in person.'

Kat pressed one shaking hand to her forehead. 'Well, it's funny you should mention that,' she said. 'Quite a few things have been happening here, too.' And proceeded to give him the bare bones of her dismissal, and subsequent rehiring.

'You're joking!' He laughed. 'They're sending you to Byron?'

'Some town outside Byron, anyway.'

'Well, I'm about fifteen minutes outside Byron. Place called Shelby. It's beautiful. You'd really like it here.'

'Looks like I'll get the chance to see for myself,' Kat said, trying to keep the trembling from her voice.

'When would you get here?'

'Not sure. I'll have a meeting next week, sort out the details. But… Soon, I hope.'

Wilson gave another short laugh. 'That's unbelievable. I'm… I'm *really* happy to hear that.'

They both fell silent for a moment.

'Kat, I'm really sorry I haven't been in touch sooner.'

'I haven't called you either. I wanted to, but I didn't.'

'It's all been kind of weird, hasn't it?'

'It has.'

'But we'll see each other soon?'

Kat felt her chest tighten. 'We will,' she said happily.

There was silence for a moment, then he said softly, 'I've *missed* you.'

'I've missed you too.'

'Talk soon?'

'Yes. Talk soon.'

Kat listened to the dial tone for a moment after he hung up, then slipped the phone back into her pocket, becoming aware that she was still in her dressing gown. Early spring sunshine was streaming into the car, warming it luxuriously. Her throat felt constricted, her breath short. Am I happy? she asked herself. Terrified, yes. Exhausted, weirdly. But feeling something, and that was so much better than feeling nothing at all. Dare. Work. Wilson. The Box. And she hadn't had breakfast yet. Choose life! Kat thought, and for the first time in a long, long time felt her lips twitch in a smile, not a grimace; felt a bubble of laughter in her chest. Kat ran both hands over the dash, let one drop to its familiar position on the gearstick. Her whole body was humming as she leaned forward and pressed her lips, then her cheek, to the steering wheel.

'Well Box?' she murmured. 'Fancy a bit of a road trip?'